Hearts Return

It takes a father

A Relational Adventure

Cheryl Hug

Hearts Return

Cover and layout design by Donna Miller.
Cover photography by Eric Valentine, PraisePhotography.com.

All Scripture quotations, unless otherwise indicated, are taken from the *Holy Bible: New International Version*, NIV, Copyright © 1973, 1978, 1984 by International Bible Society. Used by permission of Zondervan Publishing House. All rights reserved.

Scripture quotations marked NLT are taken from the Holy Bible, New Living Translation, copyright 1996, 2004. Used by permission of Tyndale House Publishers, Inc., Wheaton, Illinois 60189. All rights reserved.

This novel is a work of fiction. Names, characters, places and incidents either are the product of the author's imagination or are used fictitiously. Any resemblance to actual events, locales, organizations, or persons living or dead is entirely coincidental and beyond the intent of either the author or publisher.

- - -

HopeUnitingGenerations@Live.com

HUG Publishing
La Grande, Oregon

✦✽✦ ✦

Dedicated to the New Hope community, in memory of my father, David Agnor, who loved me well and taught me of Jesus. I miss you still, Daddy. And love you.

And a special thank you to my stepfather, Norman Pratt, who took in nine children besides his own on a ranch in Northeastern Oregon. Thank you Dad, for being an awesome father to many children, step children, adopted children and their families.

And thank you Kent Hug, for your love, patience and pursuit of God. You are a great lover, counselor, teacher and father to our children. As we grow in relationship with Jesus and each other, you show me his love and bring me healing like no one else can.

CONTENTS

*He will turn the hearts of
the fathers
to their children,
and the hearts of the children
to their fathers . . .
Malachi 4:6*

A GOOD SON?

My peace I give you. . . . Do not let your hearts be troubled and do not be afraid.   John 14:27

"Don't tell me you have no money!"

Jeff Carson stopped.

Not again.

He glanced along the breeze-way.

Empty. At least this time there was no one around to witness the scene. He opened the door and left it.

Open, it promised air. Fresh air. And space.

"Come on, I know you got some!" His father emerged from the kitchen in pursuit of his mother. Angry eyes found Jeff. "Shut the damned door!"

The words cut like a dagger.

Jeff closed it.

His father grabbed his mother's arm. "I get a check next week. We'll be okay. . . . It's just twenty bucks. Come on Molly, gimme twenty bucks!"

She pulled away. "No, John, I can't! It's the rent. And it's overdue!"

A vein bulged beneath his rumpled collar. "Dammit! I shouldn't have to beg from my own wife!" His clenched fist loomed. "Hand it over!"

Jeff jumped between them. "Dad, stop!"

A calloused hand clenched his upper arm and threw him against the wall. "Get the hell out of my way, you wimp!" A table lamp tipped, teetering on the edge of disaster and his mother scrambled to right it.

Sharp laughter lashed out. "What you gonna do, fight me? You'll never be a man if you keep hiding behind your mama." He shoved him again. "Come on boy, show me what you got!"

"John, don't hurt him!"

Cursing, his father lunged at her. Surprising himself, Jeff sprung from the wall, returning to his mother's side.

A fist slammed into his shoulder and pain shot down his arm. Jeff swung around to defend himself, but—

The look in his father's eyes . . .

It was *hate*.

Foul breath blew in his face. He was stinking drunk!

Again.

Jeff wilted.

⁂

Four days later, in P.E. class, Jeff's three point shot swished through the net.

"Yes!" he shouted, fist in the air. Billy Watson's attempted block had failed. Loping backwards, Jeff encouraged his teammates. "Only three points to go! We can do it!"

A shrill whistle pierced the air.

Puzzled, he stopped and turned.

There's no foul.

Coach Bower motioned him toward the bench and Jeff trotted to the side, grabbed a towel and caught his breath.

"Carson, your mother wants to talk to you. She's waiting in the hall."

Mom? . . . Now what?

The whistle blew and the basketball game resumed. Billy dribbled down the court. When Fred Johnson stumbled, Billy went around him for an easy lay-up.

Jeff jogged to the gym door. Maybe he could take care of this quickly. If he didn't hurry, Billy Watson and Brandon Spears would take over the game.

In the hallway, his mother leaned against the wall, face hidden behind dark hair.

"Mom?"

Swollen eyes, filled with tears, found him. Her lower lip quivered.

Jeff's stomach dropped.

He must have hurt her again.

"What happened?" he said, still breathing hard.

"Your dad was in an accident, Jeff. It was horrible." She swallowed and looked away. "The other driver was killed."

He stared.

"I know," she said. "I just found out too. The police came by and woke me up."

"So where is he?"

"In the hospital. Would you come with me?"

"Now?"

Eyes brimming, she pleaded, "He's asking for both of us, Jeff. The nurse told me he's hurt real bad."

Too thin for her tall frame, her shoulders drooped. Once Jeff had taken pride in her beauty, but today she was just old and sad. With a sigh of resignation, he yielded. "Should I go change?"

She nodded. "I'm parked out back. I'll wait in the car."

After a quick shower, he left the gym. Still pulling on his sweatshirt, he tripped over a garbage can and sprawled on the pavement.

Between buildings, he was at the back of the school.

Alone.

Jumping up, he let loose on the senseless can. The lid sailed into the wall and the can spun, rolled and buckled under the onslaught of his kicks.

"It was bad enough being the son of a drunk. Now he's *killed* somebody."

Few knew his struggle. Fewer knew his anger. And no one knew how hard he worked to keep it together.

Now everyone would know.

Now he would be shunned.

Or worse . . . *pitied*.

He stopped.

Mom's waiting!

Looking around, he righted the can and headed toward the parking lot.

Ominous silence filled the car as they drove through the small town of Fishtrap and turned south toward Wallua Crossing.

Finally, he asked the question.

"Was he drunk?" He could always hope.

She shrugged and looked away. "I suppose."

Jeff set his jaw, folded his arms and slumped in the seat. Staring out the side window, he fixed his eyes on the fields of dry grass.

How did she stand it? And she kept making excuses for him. He, for one, was sick of it. His father didn't give a damn about them. All he cared about was his stinking bottle. Was he supposed to feel *sorry* for him? He didn't even want to see him. His father reeked when he drank. He hated it.

But she said he was bad.

He turned and looked at his mother. Tear-stained eyes were fixed on the highway, the lines of her face worn and weary.

In Wallua Crossing, his mother stopped at a red light and laid a hand on his knee. "Honey, I'm sorry about all this."

"I know, Mom. It's not your fault."

They parked the car, entered the hospital and headed for the trauma unit. Jeff halted when a tall man, followed by a nurse, stepped into the hallway.

Ben Watson.

What was *he* doing here?

Face grim and deep in conversation, Ben turned back toward the nurse. Jeff and his mother hesitated while Ben and the nurse continued in low tones.

Jeff knew Ben from high school sports events. Billy, his son was a friend and teammate. But why was his father here now?

When the nurse dismissed herself, Ben recognized them. Eyes moist with emotion, relief spread across his face.

"Jeff and Molly. You're here! Thank God!" he said, placing a hand on her shoulder. "He's been asking for you."

A nurse led Jeff and his mother down the hall and opened a door. The smell of disinfectant fought a stench.

Cigarettes, sweat and . . . alcohol.

He had been drinking.

At the doorway, he hesitated. Tubes and lines extended in every direction from his father's bed. Monitors blinked and beeped. Nurses scurried in and out. One leg and one arm bound, his father lay on his back, his large body extending the full length of the bed. It seemed every inch of exposed flesh was either cut or scraped. His shaggy dark hair was full of dried blood and his breath came in short, distressed gasps.

At the bedside, his mother reached for his father's hand. Reluctantly, Jeff advanced into the room.

Through bloodshot eyes, his father looked past his mother and focused on Jeff. A tear rolled down his cheek.

"I'm sorry." He gasped. "Please forgive me."

His eyes turned to Jeff's mother and he cleared his throat. "None of this had . . . anything to do with you, Molly . . . It's all been my fault. . . . You've been good to me . . . and I love you . . . And you, Jeff . . . are a good son—"

Violent coughing seized him, followed by a string of screeching alarms. His whiskered face turned ashen. Frozen, Jeff watched his father's desperate struggle to breathe. The room filled with people.

Heart beating wildly, Jeff continued to stare, until a male nurse ushered them out, shutting the door behind them.

Then it hit him.

He could die!

Wasn't it just a few days ago he told him he *wished* he were dead? This couldn't be happening.

Jeff sunk into the waiting room chair, closed his eyes and leaned forward. A small boy again, his father smiled down at him, reached for him and lifted him onto his shoulders. A mixture of warmth and sadness filled him.

He's still my dad.

⁂

Two weeks later, Jeff stood over a casket, wishing he could bury the anxiety and pain with his father. The short ceremony completed, he left the small group at the grave side and wandered alone to the edge of the cemetery. Down the hillside and over the wide expanse of Haywacah Valley, he gazed. The valley of his birth. The October wind was cold, but he didn't notice, his heart already frozen and numb with pain.

Dark clouds rolled in from the north. Ominous shadows threatened rain. Jeff stared blankly over the landscape.

"The Indians called this The Valley of Peace," he muttered, "but not for me—"

A warm hand on his shoulder interrupted his despair.

Ben Watson.

"Jeff, I want you to know your father made his peace with God. He wanted me to tell you he loves you."

Turning, Jeff pulled away.

"If there's anything I can do, let me know," Ben said from behind.

"We'll be okay . . . He was never there for us anyway."

⁂

Trudging up the apartment steps, Jeff's backpack full of books was heavy on his shoulders, but the weight in his heart was heavier. A month had passed since his father's funeral. Life was not easy before, but now tidal waves of depression and loneliness swept over him.

Before he died, his father had called him a "good son." Good son? That was a first. After everything else he'd called him, how could he believe it?

Emptiness and darkness greeted him when he unlocked the door. He hesitated to close it, but a gust of cold wind caught it, whipped it out of his hand and slammed it against the wall. Shivering, he pulled it back, forcing it shut. He switched on a lamp.

It failed to dispel the lingering darkness.

His father had asked for forgiveness. What good would that do? Was that supposed to make it all better? Were all the bad memories supposed to just go away?

When he needed to cry most, he just couldn't. Caught in a storm of anger and grief, Jeff was stuck.

Ben said his father had made his peace with God. Big deal. What good was that for him? Or his mother? Or, for that matter, anybody?

He killed somebody. And himself.

Now he was dead. Dead and gone.

The pastor said he was with Jesus.

Jesus? . . . So what?

Practice for basketball had started and Jeff was glad for the diversion. He played hard, but Coach Bower was concerned.

"Jeff, you're one in a thousand," he had said. "And a great player. I know you're hurting, but you have to remember you're part of a *team*. You can't treat your teammates like this. Take your anger out on the court, not the team."

One in a thousand? His mouth twisted. Yeah, sure. But he liked Coach.

Okay, maybe he had been rude. But he didn't care. No one understood. If Brandon Spears or one of those other losers said one more thing about his father, he was going to make them pay. Somebody was going to be sorry. People should mind their own business and keep their mouths shut.

But everyone knew. They were all talking about him. He knew it. It was just too quiet when he showed up. Everybody avoided him. The teachers and those he thought were friends. Even Billy. No one dared really talk to him.

But then, he didn't want to talk.

Coach Bower offered to take him out to lunch. But he didn't want to go. He didn't want to be somebody's project.

Coach wanted him to get counseling. Face his feelings.

He didn't want to feel. Why should he? It was his dad's fault.

The dark cloud was bad at school, but at home, in the cold, lonely apartment it was worse. A framed wedding picture of his parents stood before him, on the coffee table. His mother must've fished it out of the drawer. He picked it up.

They looked so happy.

She was smiling.

It had been a long time since he'd seen her smile.

He laid the picture down and turned away. Was she going crazy? She was always crying. Last night he heard her again. Those tears had to be for more than just missing Dad. But he didn't know and didn't have the courage to ask.

He knew she worried about him. He wished she wouldn't. There was enough stress without that. Overworked and depressed, she was often in pain from what the doctors called fibromyalgia. They had always struggled financially, but now without his father, it was overwhelming.

He threw the backpack on the kitchen counter. "My life sucks," he said. "I can't help Mom . . . and it's so depressing around here."

Lingering in front of the refrigerator, he searched for something to eat.

"Isn't there any food? I'm hungry. No milk?" He slammed it shut.

In the breadbox, a few dry slices lay in a crumpled bag with heels. He found the jar of peanut butter, made a couple of sandwiches and choked them down with two glasses of water.

Heavy backpack in hand, he made his way to the corner of the front room and turned on his computer. "I can't wait to get out of this dead end, hick town. There's nothing happening here. I'm gonna leave this place in the dust and go somewhere I can make some money. Maybe Mr. Thomas is right. Maybe I can get a scholarship."

After grinding out an essay on the earth's depleting energy resources and the dangers of global warming, Jeff twisted his lips. "That helped. Now I can feel guilty about being alive, using up valuable resources and ruining the environment."

While surfing the internet for a game to play, a pop-up caught his eye. Scantily clad, a young woman beckoned, glancing sideways through half-closed eyes.

Aroused and curious, he froze.

Normally he stayed away from this stuff. His father wouldn't have cared, but strong opinions from his mother had kept him away.

But what did she know about being a man?

"Oh, what the hell."

Every night that week, he returned to that and other related internet sites. Jeff looked forward to the excitement and comfort it gave him during the lonely evenings at home. At least he received a little gratification in this imaginary world. It was one of the few things he could enjoy in his dismal, depressing life. The niggling sense of guilt grew heavy, but he carefully kept his secret.

His mother would consider him some sort of pervert.

The first week of December, while Jeff rummaged through his locker, someone bumped him. He fumbled for a falling book.

"What the—?"

It was Kelsey Langford.

"Oh, sorry," she said.

Jeff bent to retrieve the book. When he straightened, she stood there, peering at him, with a penciled and knowing eye, straight black hair covering the other.

A large silver ring protruded from a scabbed red sore in her lower lip. Wasn't she standing a bit close? His gaze fell to an overflowing black tank top and his stomach quivered. The green scorpion on her shoulder whipped a stinging tail.

He stepped back and almost fell into his locker. Regaining his balance, his face went hot. It was just a tattoo.

Shrill laughter pierced the air. "Hey, Jeff." She clicked the lip ring on her teeth. "Do you know Brooke Donner?"

"Sort of."

She nodded down the hallway. "She's over there. She thinks you're hot."

Brooke smiled at him from the other end of the hall and his heart hammered.

"She wants to know if you'll come to her house tonight for a party. She was afraid to ask."

"I have basketball practice."

"Don't worry. Come afterwards. About seven or eight. Her brother's my boyfriend and he bought a keg." She smiled, lip ring gliding and red sore cracking. "We had lots of fun last weekend."

"Uh . . ."

The smooth blond girl leaned against a locker and tilted her head. Throwing long shining hair over one shoulder, she made an inviting picture in her tight fitting, low-slung jeans. A knit shirt clung to her slim waist and enticing curves.

Brooke Donner. New in town, she was already known for her many boyfriends and parties.

She was pretty.

A surge of satisfaction pulsed through him.

She thinks I'm hot.

Straightening his shoulders, he brightened.

After basketball practice, he started down the street, then hesitated. He didn't usually hang with this crowd. But who did he belong with now, anyway? He didn't fit anywhere.

Oh, what the hell. She likes me.

Jeff got wasted. But for the first time in over two months, he laughed. Brooke hung on his arm the whole night. She even kissed him. Right on the mouth. It felt good. Made him feel wanted. Needed. Like a real man.

Late that night, his mother still at work, he drug himself home and to bed. Nausea and a pounding headache greeted him in the morning, but he forced himself to get up and out the door to school.

Brooke was there to greet him. She hurried toward him and grabbed his arm. "Hi Jeff. It was fun last night, wasn't it?"

A snort came from behind. With a huff, Billy Watson rolled his eyes and disappeared down the hall.

Watson thought she was screw-loose, but he just didn't understand. The attention of a girl felt good. It was amazing.

For the next few weeks, he looked forward to seeing Brooke at school. She clung to him and said they were dating now. He often found himself at her house. And her brother's parties.

Sometimes he argued with himself, but lost. Besides, he only did a little. Just enough to fit in.

Uncle Ryan had invited Jeff to visit during winter break, but Jeff made excuses. Unpleasant experiences with his father's brothers kept him away. They were always drinking, smoking pot, teasing, cussing and fighting. If they weren't fighting with each other, they fought with the women in their lives. And there were different women every time he saw them. Exchanged like sets of old clothes.

Now Uncle Ryan had another woman that Jeff didn't know.

Besides, he would miss out on seeing Brooke.

Jeff and his mother made a feeble attempt to decorate a small, fake tree in their drab apartment. They exchanged a few gifts the morning before Christmas. For extra bonus money, his mother planned to work a double shift at the care center on Christmas Day. She told Jeff it would help pay off their debt. He agreed. Since Brooke was busy, it was just another lonely, depressing day.

He returned to Brooke's house the next weekend, only to find her clinging to the arm of a burly senior. Acutely aware of his long, boney frame, Jeff's heart dropped.

She glared at him. "You didn't come."

"Come when?"

"To the party last night. Remember? I told you to come the day after Christmas."

"Oh, that. I told you Mom was off work that night. I stayed home with her."

She lifted her chin and nestled her head against her new-found trophy. "Well then, I guess you made your choice, didn't you?" Taking his hand, she pulled him down the hallway to the bedroom.

Jeff helped himself to a beer. In fact, he helped himself to several.

She'd never taken *him* to the bedroom. Did she have to flaunt it in his face?

Rejection and betrayal hit him, surprising in its intensity.

Sam Wallace, another senior, nudged him with a laugh. "Don't take it so hard, Dawg. She does that to everybody. I know someplace else you can party. But you just as well get used to it." He returned to the keg and refilled his cup.

Late the next morning, Jeff's mother noticed him sitting on the couch brooding. "Jeff, are you okay?"

Head throbbing, he glared at her. "Of course I'm okay."

"I just wondered." Eyes sad and head tilted, she looked at him. "You don't seem like yourself lately."

"And just what is 'myself,' anyway? I'm the son of a dead, murdering drunk!" Storming out of the apartment, he slammed the door, leaving her in tears.

A cold wind slapped him in the face. Shivering in his sweatshirt and shorts, he wandered around the block, filled with self-loathing. He kicked a rock with the worn toe of his shoe and groaned.

"I promised Mom I would never do this. It destroyed Dad . . . She's suffered enough."

His mother needed him. He wanted to be strong for her. But he wasn't. He was weak. Like his father. Depression and despair swallowed him like a snake, pulling him into a dark pit.

Trapped, he succumbed.

It would kill his mother to know the truth. She thought he was so *good*. But he was a miserable excuse for a son.

"I'm just a mama's boy. Hiding behind her," he said. "She'd be better off without me."

So why try?

His dad's rifle was still under their bed.

On Billy's sixteenth birthday, several guys from the basketball team came to the Watson ranch for a Sunday afternoon sledding party.

Billy and Jeff, in search of a greater thrill, had moved further up the steep slope to begin their run. They built a small jump in the road and planned to hit it with more speed and intensity. Careening down the hill, they lost control, flew over the bump and landed in a roadside ditch piled with powdery snow.

Jeff couldn't breathe.

His arms and legs groped for anything to free himself from the cold, powdery prison. His two feet flailed until he felt Billy grab and pull. Covered with snow, he sputtered. Springing up, he slipped and landed on top of his friend.

Billy laughed. "Whoa, Dude, that was intense! Are you okay?"

Sliding on the slippery road, they helped each other back to their feet. Jeff spat snow from his mouth, removed his stocking cap and beat it on the side of his leg.

"That freaked me out!"

He stomped his feet and brushed the cold powdery crystals from his borrowed snowsuit.

Jeff looked for witnesses to their exhilarating run and snowy crash, but the others had already left.

"Hey, everybody's gone! Let's head back to the house. I'm cold," Billy said. He slogged through the deep snow, retrieved the large runaway sled and dragged it toward the house.

Jeff followed.

Long shadows darkened the white landscape. It was cold and getting colder. The promise of warmth beckoned from the house with its bright windows and smoking chimney.

Around the living room fireplace the boys relived their snowy adventures with great bravado.

"Dude, you should've seen our last run. We really bit it!" Billy said to Fred Johnson. "After I finally climbed out of that ditch, all I could see of Jeff were his boots sticking out of the snow."

"I thought I would suffocate in that snowdrift," Jeff said. "I couldn't move. I was sure glad when you grabbed my feet and pulled me out. But it was awesome! We must've been airborne for thirty seconds!"

"Thirty seconds?" Fred scoffed, "Yeah, right, Carson."

Raucous laughter filled the room and Jeff joined in. It had been fun. He reached for a cup of hot cocoa offered by a young girl with a wide, friendly smile. Bold brown eyes met his and she giggled. This had to be Billy's younger sister. Something about this place warmed him all over. More than just a fire and hot cocoa on a cold January afternoon.

Ben Watson relaxed on the couch, casually resting his arm on its back and his wife, Linda, snuggled close. Two young children sat on the carpet at his feet. He and Linda observed the celebration, laughing along with the group. Their eyes met and they exchanged smiles. Pleasure and enjoyment radiated from their faces.

"Cass, bring us some popcorn, will you?" Billy asked the brown-eyed girl.

"Okay big brother, since it *is* your birthday." She grinned and disappeared into the kitchen. Bowls of hot, buttered popcorn filled a serving tray when she reappeared and she passed them around the room.

Billy had invited Jeff to spend the night and ride to school with him in the morning. The other boys soon departed and Jeff joined the Watson family for dinner. Home-cooked food filled the table. A large pot of chili, corn bread, carrot salad and apple raisin cake. Drawn into the lively conversation, he listened attentively, amused and intrigued.

Laughter rang out, warming his frosty heart. Little Joey and Hannah Watson glanced up at their parents with wide, eager eyes, shining with the joy of life.

Was he ever so innocent? Or happy?

A pain of loss and regret stabbed him. He shifted in his chair.

After dinner, Billy took the little ones into the living room and Jeff followed.

Three-year-old Hannah danced circles around her brother. "Horsey rides! Billy, horsey rides!" Eager brown eyes begged persistently.

Billy lowered himself to his hands and knees. "All right. Mount up."

Both children squealed and climbed on their older brother's back. Five-year-old Joey took charge, his blue eyes sparkling with glee.

"Giddy-up!"

Jeff watched in interest from the couch, laughing with them. Billy bucked and snorted, throwing them off repeatedly. Finally weary of playing bronco, Billy pinned Joey to the floor, tickling him until he pled for mercy with howls of joy.

"You give horsey rides?"

Startled, Jeff turned to see Hannah staring up at him, brown eyes pleading. Tousled blond curls protruded in all directions from the playful carousing. His heart melted.

"Sure." He lowered himself to the carpet. Romping with both small children, he found himself laughing from deep in his belly.

"Be careful," a voice said from the kitchen doorway. "Mom won't be too happy if you break something."

Jeff looked up to see Billy smiling at him. His arm rested on his younger sister's shoulders. He looked again. Billy's arm was around his sister like it was the most natural thing in the world! He'd never seen a family like this. They were different.

The next morning as the two boys left to catch the bus, Billy's sister remained where she was, sitting on the couch reading to the little ones. Jeff was curious. "Isn't your sister going to school?"

"No. Mom teaches Cass at home." Billy smiled and stomped his boots in the snow when they reached the bus stop. "Until last year, Mom taught me too."

"So that's why I never saw you at school when we were younger," Jeff said.

 za ❧ ❧ za

Jeff stared at his darkened bedroom ceiling. The image of Billy smiling and standing with his arm slung over his sister's shoulders returned. Again. It had been three days and he still couldn't get it out of his mind. He'd never seen anyone treat a *sister* like that.

And Billy's parents. They laughed and smiled at each other.

That was different.

The Watson's. Something about them drew him in and scared him off at the same time. They were happy. They loved and honored each other. If he ever had a family, he wanted that.

But could it happen?

For him? All he knew of marriage and family was pain and dysfunction.

Billy had invited him back to visit and had even hinted about working for his father this spring.

He had refused.

He turned over and heaved a sigh.

Finally he drifted into a trouble sleep. At the Watson table again, he couldn't get the food to his mouth before it disappeared. The warm family circle had turned to chanting monsters.

"Not enough! . . . Not for you! . . . Not enough! . . . Not for you!"

He awoke in a cold sweat, tangled in blankets and pulled the pillow over his head.

"God help me."

CAN YOU TRUST A FATHER?

*I will be a Father to you, and you will be my sons and
daughters, says the Lord Almighty.*   *2 Cor. 6:18*

eighteen months later . . .

"Cassie! Get out of there!"

"I can do it, Daddy. I read the book!"

"Cassie!"

"He won't hurt me, Daddy. He likes me!"

"Get out of there! Now!"

The high-pitched voice again pierced the air. "You never let me
do anything fun!"

"Not again," Jeff said to himself. He peered through the half
open barn door, careful to stay out of sight.

Cassie dug in her heels and tugged against her father as he
pulled her out of the barn lot.

"You're hurting my arm, Daddy. Let me go!"

"Your arm isn't the only thing that's going to hurt if you don't
stop fighting me. I told you to stay away from that horse!"

"I forgot, Daddy. I'm sorry!"

Those big brown eyes got to him every time, but had no effect on Ben. Mouth set in a firm line, he strode forward with his daughter in tow, pulled her through the back door and slammed it. Raised voices rang through the house, fading into the upstairs and ending in a mysterious silence.

It had been over a year since Jeff started working for the Watsons. A rainstorm the day before had interrupted the cutting, baling and stacking of alfalfa hay. The boys were doing odd jobs before returning to the fields. The drama between Cassie and her father had distracted Jeff from his barn-cleaning assignment.

Almost every day, he found an excuse to be here. Ben and Billy had taught him to do physical labor, operate farm equipment, work cattle, and do mechanic and general farm work. His body was growing hard and strong, along with his confidence. A new world had opened for him, learning to work and be independent.

But this family sure didn't try to look good for him. Sometimes he wished they would. Ben was sometimes rough. And wonder of wonders, Cassie was seldom intimidated. These loud and expressive people didn't fit with his fantasies about a functional and intact family.

Weren't they Christians? And wasn't Ben supposed to be a good father? Everyone spoke well of him.

Jeff gazed over the green expanse before him. Perched on the side of a mountain, the Watson ranch was a beautiful place. Lush green grass, sprinkled by a purple haze of wild flowers, covered the valley below. However, for Jeff, the many conflicts seemed to mock the peaceful beauty. He admired them, but every day someone got into trouble. Usually Cassie.

He didn't like it. When Ben raised his voice, Jeff's stomach knotted.

Valley of Peace? Right. Every time he came here, there was war.

He really appreciated them, but he'd just about had it. He just didn't connect with Ben. When he yelled, he wanted to run.

Jeff left the barn door partially open and returned to his work.

She was in trouble again. What would he do this time? Would he hurt her?

A week ago, a similar scene disturbed a warm, quiet afternoon. It was followed by Cassie and Ben arguing from an open upstairs window. Then . . . smacking.

It must have been a leather belt.

Later, she sat alone on the back steps of the house with a tear-stained face. Bitter disappointment and defiant anger fought for control in her dark eyes.

Cassie was determined to train the young stallion her father had recently purchased. Ben repeatedly told her to stay away from him, but she remained headstrong and overconfident, ignoring her father's wishes. It was like that with Cassie. Although almost thirteen, she had not outgrown her stubbornness.

In fact, it seemed to be getting worse. Ever since he had arrived on the scene. Ever since he had been offered this job.

She had expressed displeasure at his presence from the start. And once she decided something, there was no turning back.

It was over a year ago now, that Billy had invited him to church, then to dinner at his family's ranch. He had finally accepted.

They lingered around the table after eating that day, reflecting on the events of the morning. Then the attention turned to him.

"You know," Ben said, "spring's coming on fast and we could sure use some help around here. Jeff, would you by any chance be interested in a job?"

Billy had mentioned the possibility this was coming.

"I don't have any way of getting here."

"How old are you, anyway?"

"Sixteen."

"Why don't you get your driver's license? I'll let you use that extra rig out there." Ben pointed out the window to an old, beat-up pickup, parked by the barn. "It isn't much to look at, but it runs good. I'll give it to you for five hundred dollars. It won't take long for you to work it off. Until you get your license, Billy here can give you a ride after school and we'll see that you get home."

His own truck? That sure ignited a spark of hope.

The whole family beamed at him. Little Joey and Hannah cheered. Billy's mother smiled warmly. Billy grinned triumphantly. It was probably his idea. But one face was not smiling. Eleven-year-old Cassie's.

Billy and Cassie were inseparable before he started working for Ben. Billy was his best friend now. They did everything together and Cassie wasn't happy about it. He was not one of her favorite people. But that didn't stop him from being fascinated and amused by her. She didn't know it, but he was partial to Cassie's side in her frequent run-ins with her father.

There was just something about Cassie. Something innocent, yet fearless and wild. She was a pretty girl, slender and strong, totally unaware of her promise of beauty. Usually dressed in a T-shirt, jeans and cowboy boots, she loved life and all its adventures. Adventure was something she craved and often created. Her vivaciousness brought joy to her parents, but also great challenge.

Passionate about horses and other animals, with little care for the outside world, she was happy here on the family's ranch. Summertime meant more time outdoors with the animals and unfortunately, more conflicts with her father.

Jeff continued mucking out the horse stalls. "He's too hard on her," he said to himself. "She can't help who she is. Does he have to spank her? It's so degrading. There's got to be a better way.

"And he yells too much. You can't force someone to respect and obey you. A person has to *earn* respect. Billy and Cassie don't seem to have a problem with him, and Joey and Hannah are too young to know any better, but I sure don't feel comfortable around him. He scares me."

꿈 ❦ ❧ 꿈

Inside the house, Ben Watson came down the stairs two at a time. At forty, he was fit and energetic, his body hardened by hard work and play. He fell into his favorite chair in the living room, leaned forward, elbows on knees, and groaned. Humming drifted toward him from the kitchen. Linda's attempt to diffuse the tension. Of course she had heard the whole loud and dramatic confrontation.

"Linda, she won't listen to me," he said, staring at the floor. "What should I do?"

"What *did* you do up there?" Linda asked, emerging from the kitchen.

"Nothing yet. She was in with that horse again. She scared me. I was hopping mad and didn't trust myself to do anything. I left her in her room and came down here to calm down."

"That sounds wise."

"I thought about spanking her, but I tried that last week, remember? It just about killed me and it didn't work. Besides, she's almost thirteen years old! We should be past this kind of stuff!"

"Yeah, I remember. We need another strategy. Fear of punishment isn't working anymore. Somehow we've got to make the shift. Responsibility for her safety needs to be hers, not ours."

"That's all well and good, but in the meantime, I'm afraid she's going to get herself killed! I've got to do something. The girl isn't safe out there with her present attitude!"

"She's so much like you, Ben. She's bold and adventurous. In our efforts to teach her, we haven't ruined that quality and we don't want to." Her hand ran through his hair. "She has the same wild streak that made me fall in love with *you*. And she loves you."

Gently, she pushed his head up and settled herself in his lap. Her arm went around his neck and she leaned her head against his ear. "Have you prayed about this? Worrying isn't going to help."

That evening the atmosphere at the Watson table was tense. Jeff was there, as usual. Billy, oblivious to the situation, chattered about his planned fishing trip the next day. The younger ones conversed in low tones across the middle of the table, but Ben, Linda and Cassie remained silent.

Finally, Billy spoke up. "What's going on around here? It's like somebody died or something. Cass, are you in trouble again?"

Having only picked at her food, Cassie suddenly choked back

tears. She fled the table.

Billy's eyes grew wide. "What was that all about? I was just curious."

"Cassie's upset," Ben said. "I don't want her near the horses for two weeks. If either of you boys see her within ten feet of one during that time, I want your word that you'll tell me."

Soberly, the two older boys nodded.

"Linda," Ben said, nodding toward the porch, "We need to talk."

He turned to the rest of the family. "Joey and Hannah, clear the table after dessert. Then go upstairs, wash up and get ready for bed." He rose, ruffled Joey's sandy brown hair and kissed Hannah on the forehead. "Choose a book and I'll read you a story."

Joey gave him a gap-toothed grin and Hannah glowed. Winking at the two, he took Linda's hand.

"Can we read the princess book, Daddy?" Hannah asked, eyes shining.

Joey groaned. "I want the pirate book!"

Smiling, Ben turned back. Reaching over with a large, rough hand, he smoothed Hannah's silky curls. "I figure we've got time for both."

Joey bounced up, blue eyes eager. "We'll be ready!"

"Billy and Jeff. After dessert, you two pitch in and do the dishes," Ben said over his shoulder. "Cassie isn't up to it tonight."

The two boys looked at each other. Billy made a face and let out a soft moan, but quickly resigned himself to his fate. Jeff took it in stride. He didn't mind.

Billy rose and brought the apple crisp to the table. After serving the younger ones, he and Jeff dug in.

Jeff opened the screen door to leave for the evening and heard voices. He turned. Two heads bowed together at the far end of the porch. Hands clasped together, Ben and Linda sat praying.

The sun was just starting to set as Jeff walked to his pickup and opened the door. He sat in the driver's seat and took a moment to reflect.

It hit him. Ben seemed harsh at times, but there was no doubt about his love and devotion to his family. Cassie, though dramatic and headstrong, had complete security in the knowledge of that love. She was her father's pride and joy. Daring and sometimes rebellious, Cassie knew no matter what, her father would be there and love her.

He never had that kind of confidence in *his* father's love. But then, as far as he knew, his father never *prayed* for him.

On his drive home, memories of his father flooded his thoughts. Emotionally distant and self-absorbed, his father had rarely expressed affection. He may have loved him, but Jeff didn't feel it. His mother loved him, but it would've been nice to know what his father really felt about him.

Why did he just check out?

Jeff pulled off the gravel road and onto the highway toward town. A quiet voice interrupted his thoughts, ringing clearly in his spirit.

It's time to forgive your father.

"I do forgive him. I know he didn't have what I needed, but who *am* I? How can I know what a real father's like?"

Get close to Ben. He'll teach you.

He'd invited him on a fishing trip. That would be a chance.

But just Ben and me?

"I'm not his son," Jeff said. "He scares me. Especially when he gets angry. Does he have to yell?"

My blessings come through imperfect people.

Recalling a series of events from the year before, Jeff rehearsed them again . . .

It was an early summer afternoon. He and Billy had snuck a couple of twenty-two rifles into the pickup. They fooled around shooting squirrels instead of fixing fence. When they returned home, Ben asked what they'd done and Billy lied. Jeff went along with it.

They were washing up in the utility room with Joey the following day, when Ben's pickup pulled up. The front door slammed.

"Billy and Jeff!"

The two boys froze. Faces sober, they looked at each other.

The utility room door opened and Ben entered, closing it firmly behind him. Feet planted and arms folded across his broad chest, he stood in front of the door, face grim.

"Tell me again. What were you two doing out there in the pasture yesterday afternoon?"

Jeff knew this time they'd better confess. He looked at Billy, whose tanned face had gone pale.

After removing his boots and hanging up his sweatshirt, Joey stood stock-still, wide eyes darting from his father to Billy and then to Jeff.

"Joey, this has nothing to do with you. You may leave."

With a relieved glance over his shoulder, Joey scampered past Ben and out of the room.

Billy winced and lowered his eyes.

"Uh . . . We were shooting squirrels."

"I thought so! When squirrel carcasses are all over the ground and nothing has changed with the fence, it's quite obvious. What were you thinking?"

Billy developed a sudden interest in the dirty linoleum.

More than angry, Ben looked disappointed, especially in Billy. Jeff was afraid for Billy, but mostly for himself. He was probably going to get fired.

Heavy silence followed. Arms across his chest and face stern, Ben studied his son.

"Billy . . . Look at me."

With great difficulty, Billy met his father's eyes.

"Go to your room. I'll be up later to settle this with you."

Temporarily reprieved, Billy escaped the room and hurried up the stairs.

Alone with Ben, Jeff tried unsuccessfully to meet his interrogating gaze.

"I'm disappointed in you, too, Jeff. I thought better of you. Since you fooled around most of the day, you won't be getting paid for yesterday. And another thing," he said, "I can't have someone working for me who lies to me. Don't let it happen again."

Jeff backed toward the door. "I'm sorry, Sir. Uh . . . it won't happen again." He grabbed his sweatshirt and fled the house.

The following day, Jeff came back to work. Assuming Ben would still be upset, he watched Ben and Billy out of the corner of his eye.

Though more subdued than usual, Billy was relaxed and comfortable around his father. They even joked. Jeff wondered what had happened between them, but it wasn't until a few weeks later, when he and Billy were out working in a hay field, he had the courage to ask.

They settled to eat lunch in the shade of a nearby tree. After finishing his sandwich, Jeff approached the subject.

"Billy?"

"Yeah."

"Can I ask you a question?"

Billy shrugged. "Sure, Carson. What's up?"

"That day when your father sent you to your room, a few weeks ago, uh . . . you know, when uh . . . when he was so mad. What happened?"

"Oh . . . that." Billy's face went red and he looked away. "Uh, I knew better than to lie to him. I guess I justified it by telling myself we never get time just to mess around and have fun. It seems like all we ever do around here is work."

"So, what happened? Did he yell at you?"

"Not really," Billy said. "He was calm by the time he got to my room. Dad didn't say anything at first. He just sat there."

Billy leaned back on his elbows and scanned the hay field, his long legs stretched out before him. A stem of grass protruded from his teeth and bounced as he chewed.

"It'd been a while since I'd done something like that and I could tell he was pretty upset. I would've got the belt when I was younger. God knows I deserved it. And for a minute there, I wondered. But he just sat there, waiting.

"What hurt him the most was I lied to him. My excuses were pretty weak. I felt like Judas the betrayer." Billy turned to Jeff, a self-deprecating smile on his face. "It was bad."

"He told me I didn't have to work for him if I didn't want to. I could find a job elsewhere and he could hire someone else. I refused. It made me feel worse. I ended up crying. Like a baby.

"I asked him to forgive me, which he did. I won't do that again. My dad's pretty rough sometimes, but I know he loves me."

That incident had returned to Jeff several times in the last year. It intrigued him. Although it made him uncomfortable, there was something between Billy and his father he envied.

This time a lump grew in his throat. He swallowed.

"Is it possible I could have that too?"

It's possible.

"What's wrong with me? Why can't I trust Ben?" A few minutes passed in silence.

A father's love comes with discipline. Don't be afraid.

Jeff stared at the road. Tears filled his eyes. "God, please change me."

He turned down the street where he lived and a warm feeling of peace settled on him. He heard the voice again.

You're my son. . . . I love you . . . I'm pleased with you.

"You're pleased with me?" Eyes wide, Jeff choked. "Really?"

A stab of guilt interrupted him. Internet images from the night before flashed across his mind and shame-sickness invaded.

"That can't be true. I'm dirty. You know what I'm doing."

He was trapped. He had confessed the habit to God and asked forgiveness. But it repeatedly seduced him and drug him back. He didn't have the will to resist. Keeping busy had helped, but it had not gone away. It was a cancer. Rotting his soul.

His father had done this sort of thing. An occasional movie. A girly magazine. His mother had protested and argued. But even at a young age, Jeff had secretly been intrigued. It seemed he was always trying to regain that original rush of excitement he had from the magazine he retrieved out of the trash at twelve years old.

Maybe he just had a huge sex drive.

He was obsessed.

Surely Ben would never understand a problem like this.

Why don't you trust me?

"I do trust you."

A scene from the week before came to him. Ben had told him to take the swather and start cutting a hay field, but it was unclear to him which field to cut. Rather than walk to the field next to him, where Ben was baling, he drove over to the far field where Billy was raking and asked him to explain what Ben wanted. Billy didn't know, so Jeff had to go back and ask Ben. Ben had noticed, but didn't say anything.

Jeff was so embarrassed.

It bothered him that he was afraid to talk to Ben, especially when he disagreed. If he had an opinion, he would tell Billy, who would then tell his father. Billy didn't understand Jeff's fear and Jeff couldn't explain it.

"You act like that wild kitten we found under the barn. You'll only eat food when no one's watching. Then you run and hide," Billy had said, wagging his head.

It doesn't have to be like this. Ben wants to be close to you.

"He doesn't understand."

How would you know?

Jeff took a deep breath and let it out.

"Okay, I give. I'll do it."

With new resolve, Jeff got out of his pickup and quickly climbed the steps to his apartment. On the refrigerator, clipped with a magnet, was a note from his mother and a grocery list:

> *Jeff,*
>
> *I didn't feel well today. There isn't much food in the house. Could you do a little shopping for me? Here's a list.*
>
> *Thanks. I love you.*
>
> *Mom*

P. S. Have you decided whether you're going fishing with Ben on Friday? It's fine with me.

He knew she would be at the care center, working her normal afternoon shift, but he hadn't known she was feeling sick again. It was probably her fibromyalgia. She seemed so sad lately and he hardly ever saw her.

"Father, give her strength tonight."

He grabbed a piece of paper and wrote:

Mom,
*   In case I miss you in the morning, yes, I'm going with Ben. We'll be back Saturday.*
*   Would you come to church with me on Sunday? I would like that.*
Jeff

List in hand, he went back out the door.

ᏻ Ꭷ Ꭷ ᏻ

Early the next morning, Jeff drove to the ranch with renewed hope and determination. When he arrived, Ben sat on the front porch with Cassie in his lap. He parked near the barn, jumped out of his pickup and headed for the back door.

Voices came from the front porch. Curious, he stopped to listen.

"I know you're disappointed, but that's the way it has to be for now. Honey, you're my beautiful daughter and I love you. I don't want you to get hurt. Can you trust me?"

Jeff peeked around the corner. Still in her pajamas and slippers, Cassie leaned against Ben's chest, feet dangling over the arm of the chair. She sniffled and occasionally wiped away a tear, but her face held an expression of contentment and peace. Ben's arm encircled her, snuggling her close. Stroking her rumpled hair with his other hand, he kissed the top of her head. "I'd feel terrible if something happened to you, Pumpkin."

Jeff smiled. "This is going to be a better day."

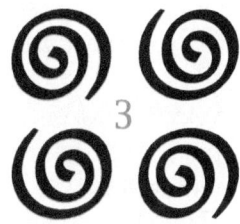

3

GROWING PAINS

. . . the LORD your God carried you, as a father carries
his son, all the way you went .   Deut. 1:31

Five years later . . .

Behind the wheel of the large grain truck, Ben Watson gazed at the
painted sky. Red beams emanated from a burning orb and crowned
the mountains on the west side of Haywacah Valley.

"It's beautiful. You're so good to me, Father. What a privilege
to live here."

The truck rumbled down the gravel road, leaving a cloud of
dust while Ben considered the next day's schedule.

"Cassie's turning eighteen tomorrow. I can't believe my baby's
that old." He smiled. "She's certainly kept life exciting."

Cassie was the first girl in a long line of Watson men. Named
after his mother, she had the same coloring and bold nature.
Remembering his daughter as a small child, he felt again a tug at
his heart. He loved his son, but this was a girl—a beautiful, fiery
angel whose world revolved around him.

Their relationship changed when Cassie was two and a half years old. She was so cute with those big brown eyes and dark curls. He loved her spunk and wanted to be her best friend.

One day he took note of her aggressive behavior toward her older brother. He and Billy had previously laughed about this, but it was no longer cute.

He picked her up and stood her firmly in front of his chair.

"Young lady, you will treat your brother with respect."

He could see her standing there still, eyes flashing and small hands resting on her hips. Her cleft chin lifted.

"I no yady!"

Then, with all the fierce defiance of a twenty-five-pound two-year-old tyrant, she kicked him squarely in the shin.

In a flash, he took her over his knee and swatted her little bottom. She screamed in surprise, indignation and pain.

He would never forget the look on her face when he set her back on her feet. She was shocked. Big brown eyes lifted to his, betrayed and hurt. No longer in control, her reign as queen of the household was over.

"You *are* a young lady," he said calmly. "You will do what Daddy says. And you will respect your brother."

Wailing loudly, she fell in a heap. After a moment, he lifted her to his lap and consoled her.

Ben chuckled. She never did that again. Too bad he hadn't done something sooner. That was before Joey and Hannah. Before he had much of a clue. He didn't have any trouble spanking Billy, he knew he had to teach him to become a man. But Cassie was different. She was his little *girl*. He had been stubborn and should've listened to Linda. She knew what was going on.

From that point on, the days of being a passive father were over. He became involved in his little daughter's life not only as playmate and provider, but as protector and authority.

But he had never seen Cassie very contrite. Outbursts of emotion were usually due to other's failure to follow her agenda. And she certainly had an agenda. She was full of plans. Plans that assumed everyone else's submission.

She could change her attitude. She had many times while growing up. But never while he watched, and usually after dire consequences.

He chuckled. "Thank God all she got out of the run-ins with that hair-brained stallion was a broken arm."

They both had learned something that summer. He, to let her suffer consequences and take responsibility for her own safety. She, to listen to caution. Thanks to what she considered overprotection, she was still learning that one. At eighteen.

"Thank you, Lord," he said, "for your grace and mercy. I haven't done it perfectly, but out of the struggle, she and I are close. I love her dearly. She's a warrior."

He and Linda had repeatedly given her to God. But he couldn't bring himself to totally release her.

Ben turned his truck into the long driveway. Scruffy, the family's border collie, appeared, running alongside the truck, barking a happy greeting.

"Father, I can't imagine life without Cassie. Help me let go. She's a woman now. Some young buck's going to come along, sweep her off her feet and I'll have to live with it." A smile teased his lips. "It's not going to be easy for the poor guy."

He parked his truck in front of the house, turned off the ignition, leaned back in the seat and sighed. Several young men had been trying to get Cassie's attention lately. Although flattered by their pursuit, her heart was not moved. Bold and opinionated, she was like him, he supposed. But also a bit naive.

"It'll take a special guy to give her what she needs," he said. "She needs someone strong. A man of faith. Send her someone who can give her freedom, but also has the confidence to stand up to her. Father, prepare the man and help her recognize him when the time comes."

A red sports car pulled into the driveway. Ben stayed in the truck and observed as young Allen Brewster got out. Shoulders slumped, he shuffled up the steps to the front porch.

Ben cringed. "I don't think so, Lord."

"Is Cassie ready?" Allen said toward the screen door, hands in his pockets.

Soon she bounced past him and down the porch steps in her jeans and "fashionable" T-shirt. It seemed a bit tight, but Linda said it was modest enough. Long, dark curls flew in the breeze as she jogged eagerly toward the fancy car, Allen at her heels.

He looked at his watch.

It was already eight-thirty.

Cassie saw him and hurried over to the large truck. Hesitating, Allen followed.

"Daddy, you're home! You've met Allen, haven't you?"

Ben nodded as he slid out of the truck. He reached for his lunch-pail. "You introduced us last week, remember?"

He turned and looked straight into Allen's shifting eyes. "Where are you planning on taking her this late?"

The poor guy's face turned pink. Looking down, he cleared his throat.

Cassie broke the awkward silence. "Mom said it was okay, Daddy. We're just going for a drive. We'll be back in an hour. I promise."

Ben focused on Allen. "Where are you headed?"

Allen described his planned route, avoiding Ben's interrogating gaze. His voice croaked a bit, but Ben gave him credit for the effort. He did want to please. He was probably harmless enough.

"Okay, I'll be watching for you about nine-thirty. Don't drive too fast on these gravel roads, or the paved ones for that matter."

Cassie rolled her eyes and flipped her hair over her shoulder.

"Don't worry, Daddy, we'll be good and be back soon. Come on Allen, we'd better get going." She turned to leave and Allen followed.

"Father, protect her," Ben prayed as he stood watching them drive off.

Scruffy at his heels, he headed for the back door and hung his dusty hat inside. In the mirror over the utility room sink, the whites of his eyes peered out of a dark and grimy face. A sweaty white forehead crowned him in gritty splendor. He turned on the water and grabbed the soap, chuckling.

"What's so funny?" Linda said from the kitchen doorway.

"No wonder I scared the poor kid out of his wits. I'd forgotten what I look like just off the combine."

She laughed. "What did you do? Give him the third degree?"

Billy spoke from behind. "Dad, to tell you the truth, it's not *Cassie* I'm worried about. When the poor guy called last night, I answered the phone. He was so nervous he could hardly talk."

"Yeah, she's probably not the one who's going to get hurt this time," Linda said as she returned to the kitchen.

Billy snorted. "Mom, she's never the one who gets hurt. She's a heartbreaker! The guy worships the ground she walks on and she laughs about it."

"Same song, second verse, a little bit louder and a whole lot worse," Linda chanted with a laugh.

"Mom." Billy's eyes grew intense. "This is serious! Talk to her. The front yard will be piled with the dead bodies of the poor guys she's dumped, if you don't do something."

Ben watched Linda's playful expression turn defensive. Blue eyes blazing, she pursed her lips. "Billy, it's late and we're all hungry. Dinner's ready. Can we talk about this another time?" Her eyes traveled to her younger daughter and back again. "In private?"

At the table, Linda spooned a few mashed potatoes on her plate and passed them to Billy. "I called Jeff this afternoon," she said.

Joey and Hannah both looked up from their food, suddenly at attention.

"Jeff?" Joey said.

"Is he coming for Christmas?" Hannah asked.

Jeff was one of Joey and Hannah's favorite people. They were now ten and twelve and kept their fond memories of him alive by reviewing the family picture album. It hadn't been below his dignity to play and romp with them, which wasn't common with other friends of their older brother.

"No, he won't make it. He doesn't want to leave his mother for Christmas," Linda said.

"Tell him to bring her along," Ben said.

"You know she won't do that, Ben. She always refuses. Jeff says she feels like she's imposing."

"It's been too long since we've seen him." Ben said.

"It sounds like he's doing well there in Seattle," Linda said. "After his mother finishes nurse's training, he says he would like to come back here to settle. He misses us."

"Ever since he moved, he hasn't visited at all," Joey said, lower lip protruding in a mock pout.

"He's busy and working hard," Billy said, helping himself to another piece of venison roast.

"Too bad he can't come," Ben said, "It would be good to reconnect."

Billy buttered a slice of freshly baked whole-wheat bread. "He's always admired you, Dad," he said. "He wouldn't trade the time he spent here for anything in the world."

Ben smiled and served himself another helping of potatoes. "I was surprised the first time he shared an opinion with me. After that he started to trust me. It was a good thing."

"I never did tell you how scared he was to cross you," Billy said. "He thought for sure you'd fire him."

"Really? I guess I forget how wounded he was. He sure was different when he left."

The younger ones settled in bed, Linda joined Ben and Billy in the living room and curled up on the couch to read a magazine. A car door slammed, followed by screeching tires. Cassie stormed through the screen door and raced up the stairs.

"I'm never going out with anyone ever again! They're all perverts!"

Her bedroom door slammed and the house quivered in the wake.

Linda sighed.

Oh, the peaks and troughs in a day of the life of a passionate teenage girl!

"It seems that outing didn't go too well," Billy said, "You might be able to help us out, Mom. Could you please talk to her?"

Linda put her magazine down and glanced at Ben.

He nodded.

She exhaled. "Yes, I suppose it's time." Rising, she climbed the stairs.

Cautiously, Linda opened the bedroom door and flinched when a shoe flew in her direction. She stepped into the room, picked up the shoe and quietly shut the door, standing with her back to it.

Angry steam condensed to frustrated tears. Cassie yanked on her pajamas and paced the floor, swiping at the betraying deluge with the back of her hand.

Linda crossed over and sat on the edge of the bed.

"Sweetie, this isn't working. You can't play with a man's heart."

"I told him I only wanted to be friends." Cassie's lips quivered, but she set her jaw. "He agreed! Besides, what business does he have falling in love with me or wanting to *kiss* me? Neither one of us is ready to get *married*." She threw a ruffled pillow across the room. "He's just a boy!"

A smile tugged at the corners of Linda's mouth.

Throw pillows they are.

"Cassie, he's nineteen years old. You should see the puppy-dog look of adoration on his face when you're not watching. Your brother saw this coming. He wanted me to warn you. They all start by agreeing to be friends, but it doesn't last. Haven't you recognized a pattern? Why do you think he wanted to take you for a drive?

"And that silly sports car. You must've guessed he borrowed it from his uncle just to impress you. You can't just listen to what a man says. You have to consider his actions."

"Now he's mad at me and says I led him on. I was just having *fun* with him. Why can't we just be friends? This is so stupid!"

Cassie flopped backward on the bed, staring at the ceiling.

A soft knock sounded on the door. "You two got it all figured out?"

It was Ben.

"Come in," Cassie said.

Ben entered.

She jumped up and flew into his arms. "Oh, Daddy, I'm so confused!" Clinging to him, she buried her face in his shirt.

"Boys are so dumb!" she said, through a barrage of tears.

Baffled, Ben shot a questioning look toward Linda, shrugged his shoulders and held his daughter close.

❧ ❦ ❧

Hand in hand, Jeff and a petite brunette walked through the fragrant pines at Camp Whitehorse. It was the last evening of camp and they had just finished eating dinner together. The sweet mountain air enveloped them as they shared counseling experiences from the week.

"You what?"

She dropped his hand.

"I let it go."

Her eyes flashed. "You let it go? What's that supposed to mean?"

"I prayed with the kid and destroyed the stuff."

"After he showed the whole cabin pictures of naked girls?"

"Yup."

"How can you be so calm? Something filthy and offensive invaded your cabin and all you did is *pray* with him? What's going to keep him from doing it again? There's got to be consequences! You've got to report him. Come down hard on him. He knew it was wrong. Now he's corrupted all the boys in your cabin."

"We had a talk about it. They're okay."

"I doubt it."

"Look, Marianne, they're teenage boys. The stuff is everywhere. They need to know how to deal with it. And the kid is having a rough time. I remember when I was that age."

"What's his name?"

"Uh . . . Sorry I brought it up. I thought you might understand. But you don't have a clue what that kid's been through. Forget it, okay?"

"So you're *protecting* him?"

"Yeah. I am. I struggled with this kind of stuff when I was a teen—"

"What?" Eyes widening, her face froze. It was a look of horror. *"Pornography?"*

"Well . . . yeah."

She pulled away. "No wonder you're so soft on it. I've got to get back to the girls."

He went after her. "Marianne, wait."

She kept going. "I don't think so. If you're into pornography, we're through."

"I'm not *into* it. I just think—"

Her hands waved dramatically. "There should be no punishment. No consequences. Sounds like 'The secret power of lawlessness is already at work.' Don't you have any *standards?*"

"Of course I—"

She stopped and turned. "Look, Jeff, you told me a bit about your past. I don't think you and I are meant for each other. I need someone strong. Someone pure. Solid in the principles of the Word . . . You have issues."

"What about grace?"

"Grace? Grace is the power to do what's right. Not a license for sin."

"I'm not—"

"Good night, Jeff."

"Can we talk about this on the way home?"

"No. I'll ride home with Gayle," she said over her shoulder, before disappearing inside the cabin.

⁂

The next morning Jeff watched Marianne load her baggage into Gayle's car. He had tried to say goodbye, but she wouldn't even look at him.

"Bye, Jeff." It was Kevin, the kid he had told her about.

"Hey, dude. Stay in touch, okay? I'm there for you."

"Thanks for everything. I had a great time." After a long embrace, Kevin hurried off to the bus.

Jeff glanced toward Gayle's car, only to see it leaving the parking lot. He threw his gear in the back of his pickup and climbed in, then turned on some worship music and made his way down the mountain. When he pulled onto the freeway towards Seattle, the warm wind played with his shirt sleeve and ruffled the ends of his hair. The late summer air soothed his aching heart.

Marianne Lawson. She was strong. Principled. Passionate. Everyone admired her. A bold campaigner against sexual immorality, abstinence was her favorite subject. That had to be good.

But their budding romance hadn't lasted long. Last night's argument was not the first. Grace was the power to do right? He was confused. Maybe it was mercy he had experienced. Whatever. Marianne wasn't impressed. She wanted someone strong.

And he had *issues*.

He snorted. That's for sure. She didn't know the half of it. If the porn bothered her that much, what would she say about his family? His father? Past addictions? Inner struggles? It was probably all for the best.

Right now he could sure use a talk with Billy. Or his father. But he'd refused Linda's invitation to come for a visit during winter break. And his mother wasn't the only reason.

"What's wrong with me, Lord? I should be excited to see them. Billy's the best friend I ever had. Ben and Linda were good to me. Joey and Hannah worshiped the ground I walked on. And Cassie—" He chuckled. "I wasn't her favorite person, but she tolerated me. I just don't want to go back yet."

But he missed Billy.

A smile lit his face when he remembered their first encounter. Billy was new at school and the other basketball players were teasing him on the bus. After snatching Billy's lunch, they divided it between them, taunting him about the tasty food.

Jeff joined the teasing. He had known most of these guys since first grade, but still wanted to prove he belonged.

They arrived at school and the torment continued. Determined to impress Fred Johnson, who tagged along at his side, Jeff approached Billy from behind and gave a sharp shove. Billy stumbled and fell.

"*Excuse* me," Jeff said, snickering to Fred.

But Billy surprised him. Springing from the ground, he landed a right hook on his jaw and the fight was on.

Coach Bower soon appeared and separated them, gripping the back of their sweatshirts.

"All right, who started this?"

Faces red and noses bleeding, they faced each other.

Silence hung in the circle.

"It was my fault," Billy said, swiping at dripping blood with his sleeve. "I lost my temper . . . I'm sorry."

At the time, Jeff didn't understand. He assumed Billy was afraid, but now he knew different. Billy wasn't afraid of anything.

"Okay, shake hands," Coach Bower said. "I don't want any more of this from you two, ya hear?"

Sometimes a fight can change things and this was one of those times. They nodded and their friendship began.

Even though he had thought Billy a religious geek, Jeff wasn't able to resist his friendly and straightforward manner. They hung out at school and had a great time together on the basketball court, eventually becoming best friends. It was Billy who had been there for him. Had opened the door for him.

He remembered the day hope dawned.

Six months after his father's death things were at their worst. Basketball was over and Brooke Donner had dumped him. One by one he had plodded through long empty days in boredom and loneliness. A cyberspace fantasy world had captured him, fed by drinking and drugs. It left him not only guilty and irritable, but bereft and suicidal. He had no hope.

After school one day, Billy gave him a ride home.

"Dude. Last night I had a dream about you," Billy said. "You were all alone and looking for your dad's gun."

Eyes wide, Jeff stared at him. How did he know about the gun?

"Your mom stopped you." A puzzled look crossed Billy's face. "You were somehow relieved," he said. "Then the dream changed. You were shackled and gagged in a dungeon. A humongous iron door was shut tight, locked with a giant padlock. Inside, you were bloody and in pain, but you couldn't yell for help."

"The door was *locked*?"

"Yeah, man. And there were snakes and scorpions everywhere."

"Snakes and scorpions?"

"Yeah, but here's the good part. A bright light shone into that dungeon." Billy finally looked at him. "The light got brighter and the snakes and scorpions scattered. The chains on your hands and feet, like, fell off and the gag on your mouth, it like, disappeared. The door opened. You stood up and walked out. You were healed. You were free!"

"A light? What's that mean?"

Billy chuckled, eyes shining. "That's easy. The light is Jesus. He's the Light of the World. You hear me? Jesus came to save you from this crap!"

And save him, he had. Billy led him to the Truth. The person of Jesus Christ.

But it was hard with Billy's father. Jeff had learned to trust him some, but he felt like a charity case. He always felt so . . . insecure. How could he be so uptight around Ben while yearning so much for his approval?

Once at a high school basketball game. Jeff had taken the final shot. An easy lay-up to win. It rimmed out. The other team exploded in celebration.

They had lost because of him!

The team left for the locker room, but he remained at the far end of the bench. Alone. Someone sat beside him, put an arm around his sweaty shoulders and embraced him.

It was Ben.

That embrace . . . He had almost lost it. He pulled away, darting to the locker room. Ben was just trying to be nice. Sorry for him. Probably because he knew his father.

It seemed he had always fought these feelings.

On the freeway, Jeff pulled up behind a combine loaded on a semi.

The last of his major mishaps at the Watson ranch was on a combine. He was done for the day and had forgotten to pull in the grain auger. It snagged on a power pole and the combine jerked so hard it almost threw him out of his seat. Off to his left, the auger dangled in the air.

Fear clenched his stomach.

What would Ben say?

When told the bad news, Ben just shook his head and bit back a comment. Jeff knew Ben wanted to yell at him, but had restrained himself.

He was relieved, yet disturbed.

Was it *pity*? Is that why Ben hired him? How could he yell at Billy and make such a big deal over a scratch on a dinged up car and then be so patient with him when it took over two days and a thousand dollars in parts to fix that blasted combine?

He must have been some kind of project.

His job at the Watson ranch had lasted four years and almost five full summers. He was grateful for the experience. But memories haunted him, feeding the self-doubt that had been his companion as long as he could remember. Rarely had he disclosed his feelings, let alone his troubled past. Unsatisfying and disturbing responses from church people discouraged it.

Some claimed he was doing well, considering his background, but would always suffer from the wounds of his childhood. This prophesy of doom fed a disquiet lying dormant in the mystery that was his soul.

Others said he would get over it.

Whatever. He was determined to conquer it.

God had asked him to press in for relationship with Ben and

he had tried. He made himself do it. Out of obedience. He even confessed his problem with pornography to Ben and Billy.

And God was right, of course. Free of pornography for almost four years now, he gave credit to Ben's love, acceptance and counsel.

But it was still easier to talk to Linda. He didn't feel inferior around her. He had always been more at ease around women. He assumed it was because he was closer to his mother than his father.

It was his older brother Jake that his father loved. When Jake was killed on a four-wheeler at eight years old, his father had never recovered. He grew more and more distant, escaping into drink.

"I've got to beat this!" he said aloud, pounding a fist on the steering wheel. "I want a better relationship with Ben."

Ben was wise, strong and blessed with a good family. He was the closest thing to a father he had. At times he was a little rough, but he had a good marriage and his children were happy, positive and well adjusted. Ben had good relationships. Jeff wanted that. From what he'd seen, it was rare. The thought of returning made him uncomfortable, but he had to go back.

A proverb came to mind. "Wisdom is supreme; therefore get wisdom. Though it cost all you have, get understanding." Then another. "Know also that wisdom is sweet to your soul; if you find it, there is a future hope for you, and your hope will not be cut off."

It sounded good, but was easier said than done.

He needed the wisdom and guidance of a father.

As long as Jeff could remember, his mother protected him from his father. He never had the chance to fight anything out with him or solve the conflicts between them. He could still hear her whining and begging his father not to hurt him, even when he had done something that deserved discipline. Granted, his father was often abusive and angry, but as far as he remembered, she had never trusted him. Even before he checked out. Before he started drinking.

Back then his mother was a mess, but never wavered in her love and devotion to him. She was suffering pain from fibromyalgia, but kept working to keep a home for them. He was grateful. And the truth was, she was probably the only thing that had kept him from doing himself in. He had not wanted to hurt her any more than she'd already been hurt.

But did his mother's fear and lack of trust contribute to his father's anger? His drinking? Jeff was glad for the protection at the time, but it hadn't helped the relationship between him and his father.

Did he miss something he could've had with his father?

This whole thing was confusing and troubling. It wasn't just his father who made him feel like a wimp.

He loved his mother, but he didn't want to marry someone wounded and fearful. He needed a strong woman. One who was bold and confident. A woman who would stand by him. Trust him to be a father and provider. Trust him to make decisions for his family. A woman with confidence in him and confidence in God.

But he hadn't met many like that. And the ones he had, like Marianne Lawson, weren't interested in the likes of him.

It seemed it was always the weak and manipulative ones that wanted him. They were clinging vines. Desperate for male attention.

Ashley Crampton had been like that.

He rolled his eyes. She wasn't bad looking, but hanging with her in high school wasn't much fun. Needy, clingy and threatened, she had made him feel like a pet she owned. He had resisted others that reminded him of her.

Another image flashed into his mind. Mounted on her horse, a young girl lifted her cleft chin in the air, tossed a dark braid over her shoulder and rode in the opposite direction. He smiled.

Cassie.

Little Cassie could never be a weak-willed woman. How old was she now? Whatever. She was Billy's kid sister and too young for him.

He chuckled. "Sassy Cassie," he said. "I wonder if she's still so stubborn and feisty."

HE'S BACK!

*He said to me, "You are my Son; today I have become
your Father."*   *Ps. 2:7b*

Two years later . . .

Cassie Watson galloped her horse to the top of her favorite knoll.
Shielding her eyes from the bright sun, she scanned the lush, green
field and the meadow exploding with flowers. The heads of two
does popped up above the tall grass. Ears standing alert, their large
eyes searched hers. Silently, she studied them, searching for signs of
little fawns hidden nearby.

Heads jerking away, they took off in the other direction,
bouncing above the tall grass.

She laughed.

Fresh, fragrant air filled her lungs. The school year was over and
it felt good. Summer was here! Animal science was interesting, but
school was sometimes unbearable. She hated being inside so much.

Her thoughts drifted to her social life, or lack thereof. She
hadn't dated anyone this past year. After many unfortunate

experiences, she had given it up. However, there was a growing discontent inside her.

"Lord, what am I doing with my life?" she said. "Will I ever get married? What do you have in mind for me?"

For you there is hope and a future.

She smiled. "I believe it. It's written in your word. But I don't have a plan for when I get out of school. What am I going to do?"

Trust me.

"I trust you. But, could you clue me in? I want a husband and children."

In all her dating, there was no one who had sparked her interest. In August, she would be twenty. Should she move? There weren't many options around here.

After returning to the barn, she started mucking out the stalls. Dripping with perspiration, she strained at the task of shoveling and filling the wheelbarrow. A commotion in the front yard caught her attention and she stopped. Excited voices drifted through the early summer air.

Joey burst through the barn door. "Cassie, come quick! Guess who just pulled in. Jeff!" Without waiting for a response, he turned and fled.

"I'll be there in a minute," Cassie called after him.

Jeff. What do you know? He had finally returned from the big city to see them. Well, she was not going to run out there and make a fool of herself. She had work to do.

She leaned on the fork and scowled at a blister forming on her right hand. Shifting her hands, she resumed her task. She had heard Jeff might show up today. It was always Jeff this and Jeff that. Why did everyone beg for him to come around?

Her chin lifted. She didn't believe in begging for someone's attention. It was disgusting. If he wanted to see them, couldn't he have come to visit of his own volition at least once in the last four years?

Methodically, she finished her chore, then went to bring in her horse. After settling her in the barn, she started for the back door.

A blue Chevy pickup was parked by the front porch, but silence told her everyone had gone in.

Gingerly, she opened the back door, removed her boots and washed her hands. Raised and excited voices came from the living room. She stepped into the kitchen.

Hannah marched up, hands perched on her hips. "Cassie! What took you so long? It's Jeff!"

"Come and get reacquainted, Cassie," her mother said. "Jeff says he's accepted a position at the university. He'll be working in the business department and will be moving back soon."

A tall, well-built man with short dark hair and intense blue eyes turned to greet her. He rose from the chair, smiled and held out his hand.

Cassie froze.

This is Jeff?

The good-looking and confident man was not the Jeff she remembered.

"Cassie?" Intense blue eyes twinkled and white teeth flashed in a broad, amiable smile. "Remember me?"

His eyes captured hers and pierced through her defenses. To her very soul. Something swept over her. She'd never—

It was strange.

She shook it off. Although well dressed and friendly, he was a bit too sophisticated for her taste.

But . . . sophisticated? Jeff?

She shook his warm hand. Suddenly she was aware of the dirty blister on her palm and her streaked, smelly jeans. She glanced down and wrinkled her nose. "Uh . . . I just came in from the barn. Would you excuse me while I wash up?"

Cassie hurried to the upstairs bathroom. In the mirror, she noted the smudge of dirt on her nose and blushed. What a picture she must have made! Little Cassie, playing in the dirt.

She giggled. He was better looking than she remembered. It was probably the haircut. Or the way he was dressed.

After a quick shower, she hurried to her room to dress, then returned to the bathroom to run a brush through her hair and apply some lip-gloss.

Over dinner, the story unfolded. Jeff's job at the university would start the end of July. The financial-aid officer was quitting and he would be taking over that position. He wanted to find an apartment in Wallua Crossing and would move the first of July, if everything went well. Ever the gracious hostess, her mother offered Jeff the guest room until he found a place to live. Everyone seemed excited to have him stay, especially Joey and Hannah.

"How's your mom?" Cassie's mother asked as she refilled Jeff's glass.

"Mom's doing great." Jeff looked up from his plate and smiled. "When I get settled I want to find her an apartment and look into job opportunities. She'd like to move back here.

"Remember when she received prayer for healing before we moved? It never ceases to amaze me what God did. She has some pain at times, but it's nothing like what it was. She's like a different person! Pain and depression were so much a part of her life. Now she's full of hope and faith."

A satisfied smile spread across her mother's face. "God is so good."

"Her faith has really grown," Jeff said. "She's my greatest encourager and prays for me all the time."

"That's wonderful, Jeff," her mother said. "I'm so glad to hear it."

Cassie remained silent through most of the meal, feeling a little uneasy. Out of the corner of her eye, she studied him. He had a strong and pleasant face, which shone with enthusiasm and animation. Yes, he was good-looking in a city sort of way. He was a bit too pale and she wondered if he'd done any real work in the last four years, but he seemed fit enough.

She quickly finished her meal and asked to be excused. "I'll be down in a bit to help clean up, Mom."

Billy watched as Cassie rose to leave the table. He couldn't help noticing Jeff's eyes follow her out of the room.

Oh God, not him too.

After looking at his father, who was absorbed in a second helping of his favorite green bean casserole, he glanced at his mother. She was studying him. They exchanged a look and she raised an eyebrow.

She knew. Why then, did she offer to let him stay for a while? This could be disastrous.

Later, on the porch, Billy and Jeff sat next to each other with their feet propped on a wooden box. They watched the sun slowly set over the mountain. Billy strummed his guitar and Jeff gazed at the sunset, lost in thought. Noticing his preoccupation, Billy fell silent. Neither spoke, enjoying the sounds of crickets chirping and soft wind blowing through the tall firs.

"How old is Cass now?" Jeff asked.

"She's nineteen. She'll be twenty this August."

His eyes lit up. "She sure surprised me. She was pretty when I left, but now? My eyes popped out of my head when I turned to see her standing there in the living room."

Billy strummed the guitar. "I noticed."

Jeff looked away. "She probably has all kinds of guys asking her out."

"That she does, but not as many as she used to. She scares them off. And on purpose."

Jeff's brow lifted, turning back. "Why's that?"

"She's had some bad experiences and isn't eager to have a boyfriend. She's not like other girls." Billy looked up from his guitar with a lopsided smile. "And be careful around her, Dude. She's not as tough as she wants you to think."

Jeff's long legs stretched out before him. He crossed them and his booted foot bobbed. Eyes fixed on the orange sky, he rubbed his chin.

Billy knew Jeff. And Jeff was restless.

The next evening, when Jeff entered the barn to check out the horses, pleasant humming came from the far stall. He stopped.

Cassie.

He approached, boots clicking on the barn floor. At the stall door, he stopped and watched as Cassie groomed a sleek, brown mare. When he rested his forearms on the door, the humming stopped.

She stiffened.

"Hi there," he said.

Without looking at him, she continued combing. "Have you found an apartment yet?" Forced lightness laced her voice.

"I have a few leads," he said. "Is this your horse?"

"Yup."

"What's her name?"

"Ginger."

"That's a good name. How old is she?"

"Four."

Jeff paused, eyes roving with admiration over the sleek, brown mare. "She has good lines."

Cassie smiled and looked away. "Thank you. I think so."

"I hear you just finished your second year at the university."

"Yup."

"What are you studying?"

"Animal Science."

He flashed a smile and chuckled softly. "That fits."

Cassie stopped combing and looked up. "What's that supposed to mean?"

He chuckled again. "Don't be so touchy. I didn't mean anything bad. I just remember you being very interested in animals. Do you want to be a vet someday?"

"I don't know," she said. "I just like studying animals. I'm not sure what I'll do with it."

She finished grooming Ginger and then filled the feeder with fresh hay. When she was younger, Jeff hadn't noticed that she moved with such grace. She was quite striking. Actually, beautiful with those dark eyes, flashing in his direction. He loved to see her smile, a rarity when she knew he was watching. White teeth and clear olive skin shone from a face framed with dark wavy, shoulder-length hair. Dimples appeared on either side of her smooth cheeks when she smiled. She definitely got that wide smile and those dimples from her father. He noted the cleft in her chin when she glanced up. He remembered that. It fit her spunky personality. She certainly had changed. She was tall, slender and well . . . nice—

"Was there something you needed?" Cassie interrupted his reverie.

He looked away and shook his head, suppressing a smile. "No, I'm fine." His staring must have made her uncomfortable. She was definitely dismissing him. "Are you coming in?"

"Not for a while. I've got work to finish up here."

He shrugged, turned on his heel and left.

Cassie watched his jean-clad, athletic figure as he swaggered, yes that was the word for it, out of the barn and headed for the house. She smiled slightly. He wore those good looks easily.

"Charmer!" she said aloud, "But no way am I going to fall for it. I can spot it a mile away."

Early the next morning, Cassie rose to exercise her horse before breakfast. With shopping to do in town, she wanted to get some riding in first. Leading Ginger out of the barn, she noticed Blackfoot's empty stall. Was Billy out riding this early?

Cool wind whipped through her curls as she galloped Ginger toward her favorite knoll. Out of the corner of her eye, movement caught her attention. It was Jeff on Blackfoot, headed towards her. At the top of her knoll, she reined Ginger in, keeping her still as he drew near. Grinning, he rode up beside her and tipped his hat.

"Yo, Cassie!"

She stiffened. "Listen, I want to set the record straight. I don't want to be your friend. I also don't date."

Jeff's brow lifted. "Whoa! Did I *ask* for a date?" He leaned back on his mount and scowled. "Do you have to treat me as though I have leprosy just because I'm friendly? What is it with you, anyway?"

She backpedaled. "I'm sorry," she said, looking away. "I guess that wasn't very nice. It's just that I don't trust you and everyone else seems to think you're part of our happy family."

"Don't trust me? What did I do?"

"It's not you. Let's just say I don't make friends with men. It doesn't work."

"Did someone break your heart?" Blue eyes twinkled, peering at her curiously.

"That's none of your business. But no. It seems guys get the wrong idea about me and I don't like it."

"I see." With a teasing smile, his face lit in amusement. "I suppose they fall in love with those big chocolate eyes. Then they throw themselves at your feet and pledge to be your servants to the death."

Cassie smiled wryly. "Something like that. Only when I tell them I'm not interested in getting serious, they get mad and tell all their friends I am the Wicked Witch of the West."

"That is a tough one. Can I help?"

Eyes lighting with mischief, Cassie sat back in the saddle. "Maybe you can. Don't fall in love with me and don't be my 'friend' either. I have friends and they're girls, thank you very much."

He saluted. "Scout's Honor!"

She threw back her head and laughed. "I don't recall you ever being a Boy Scout."

Suddenly she was off, calling over her shoulder, "I'll race you to the creek!"

Jeff kicked his heels and chased her down the hill and through the green pasture.

　　　　　　　ɞ ﹩ ﹩ ɞ

Laughter caught Linda's attention while she hoed the garden in the bright sunshine. From under her wide-brimmed hat, she looked up to see Jeff and Cassie walking toward the barn, side by side, conversing in low tones. Cassie giggled.

It seemed her daughter had relaxed over the last few days. Jeff paid quite a bit of attention to her and despite Cassie's initial coldness, they were forming a friendship.

This was a switch.

Linda leaned on the hoe, smiling warily. "Lord, have mercy. I have a feeling we're in for some excitement around here."

⁊ ❧ ☙ ⁊

Two weeks later, Cassie returned from town to find strange cars parked in the driveway. There was always something going on at home these days. A basketball hit the side of the barn, shaking the old structure.

Raised male voices called out encouragement. "There it is! We're ahead!"

Curious, she crossed over and peeked around the corner.

Brandon Spears and Fred Johnson, former classmates of Billy and Jeff, had joined them for a basketball game. Joey and her father were playing as well. Stripped to the waist, the sun glistened off their sweaty bodies as they competed in the heat.

No one had noticed her presence. She folded her arms, leaned against the side of the barn and smiled. "I haven't seen this much testosterone at work in some time."

Her father huffed and puffed. "I think that's enough for me. I'm getting too old for this." At the side of the court, he rested with hands on his knees.

"Ah, come on, Dad! You'll make the teams uneven," Billy said.

Then Fred Johnson saw her. "Hey! Cassie could fill in!"

All eyes turned to her.

She looked down at her slacks, boots and pink knit top. "No way. I'm not dressed for this."

"Go change. We'll wait. We could use a breather anyway," Billy said, leaning forward and breathing hard.

Jeff looked unsure. Bandana tied around his head and dripping with sweat, he recovered his T-shirt and turned to face him.

"Billy, I don't think that's a good idea."

58

"Yeah," Cassie said, "I don't know—"

"Come on Cass, you play basketball." Joey said.

Cassie's eyes traveled across the court and met a glare from Brandon's dark gaze. Suppressed anger blazed at her before he turned away.

Did he think he could *intimidate* her?

She set her jaw. "Okay. I'll change."

Half an hour later, a commotion in the kitchen interrupted Ben's book work in the office. He emerged into the hallway in time to overhear an argument between Billy and Jeff. In the kitchen, Billy stood leaning over Cassie's elevated bare foot, ice pack in hand. Dressed in shorts, a large T-shirt and hair in a ponytail, she sat at the kitchen table, her reddened face pinched in pain.

"I told you it wasn't a good idea," Jeff said from the doorway. "Those guys were being too rough!" T-shirt wet with sweat, he wiped his dripping face on his sleeve.

Billy examined her swelling ankle. "She agreed to it! How was I to know Brandon was still upset?"

"Upset? About what?"

"I don't think he ever got over Cassie dumping him—"

Jeff straightened. "You mean he did it on *purpose*?"

"Calm down! I don't think it was exactly on purpose, but he didn't show much respect, shoving her around like that."

"Well of all the . . . You just stood there while he roughed her around, knowing he was bent on revenge? Why didn't you say something?"

"Stop it, both of you!" Cassie exploded. She lifted herself from the chair to stand on one good foot and hopped to the stairwell. "Drop it, will you? I'm fine!"

A sheen of tears in her brown eyes, she gazed up the staircase, a slight quiver in her lower lip betraying her.

Ben strode over with the ice pack.

"Hey Beautiful. Do you need help up the stairs?"

Cassie nodded, stilling her lip with her teeth. "Please."

He scooped her in his arms and carried her to her room, where he laid her on the bed. Gently, he flexed her ankle. "It looks like a sprain. Stay off it for a few days and it should heal." Ice pack applied, he sat on the edge of the bed. "Are you okay?"

She wiped away a falling tear. "No. I'm not. But I will be."

"You want to talk about what happened out there?"

She folded her arms. "No."

"Okay, Sweetie. Is there anything I can get for you?"

Hannah's head appeared through the open closet door. "Cassie? Are you all right? I was reading and I heard the commotion."

Cassie glanced her way. Hannah's adjoining bedroom shared a large closet with hers and she was usually careful to shut the door. For privacy. She heaved a sigh and lifted the pack from the enlarging ankle.

Hannah entered, eyes widening. "It's swelling."

"Yes, it's swelling." Cassie sniffled and grabbed a tissue. "Could you two please leave? I'll be fine."

Hannah turned to go, but Ben lingered.

"Guys can be immature about how they handle their emotions, Cassie. It was wrong of him to take his anger out on you."

"It's okay, Daddy. Please don't say anything to him." Her voice choked. "Just drop it! This whole thing's so embarrassing!"

UNTAMED BEAUTY

---

*Will the wild ox consent to serve you? Will he stay by
your manger at night?*   *Job 39:9*

It was so good to be back in Haywacah Valley.

Jeff had settled into an apartment in Wallua Crossing, but
continued attending church in Fishtrap. A tinge of fall color framed
the highway as he made the scenic drive that cloudy Sunday
morning. He opened the window to let in the crisp, cool air.

More than eight years ago he visited Fishtrap Family
Fellowship for the first time. He had been miserable. It was bad at
his girlfriend Ashley's party, but that wasn't the reason for the sour
mood that plagued him that day.

It was Billy's dream. About the dungeon.

A person could change? Could be free?

The possibility of freedom somehow frightened him. There was
predictability in his misery that lent its own security. Nevertheless,
he had to know more. He took the bait and promised to do
something he wouldn't otherwise do.

Go to church.

Church? He wasn't religious. He could never be good enough to be one . . . of *them*. Why had he agreed to go? Everyone knew who his father was and what he'd done.

In the parking lot, he got out of the car, but wanted to bolt.

"I don't know, Billy."

"Come on Dude, chill out," Billy coaxed. "They won't bite. I promise."

Inside, a presence, something he could not identify, had welcomed him. Sweet, refreshing and vaguely familiar, it felt good. Like home, or the one for which he'd always longed. His eyes began to fill and yearning swelled, but he determined to keep a firm grip on his emotion.

The people were different than he expected. Laughing and smiling warmly, they shook hands with enthusiasm. Many hugged and some even kissed. Jeff had never seen a group so open in expressing their joy and affection.

Children and adults danced freely with joy and waved colorful flags. They sang songs of love and joy to God, lifted their hands, knelt, closed their eyes and sometimes spoke out words and prayers. Happy and free, they looked as if they were truly enjoying themselves.

Could people be this happy in *church*?

They told stories of how God had heard and answered their prayers. Hope for the future overflowed in their conversations. They seemed to really believe in this God and believe he loved them. Love and acceptance passed from person to person, enticing him and arousing his curiosity.

Were these people for real?

Sam Wallace from high school shared that God had set him free. According to him, he got "blasted" by God's love and was no longer addicted to drugs and alcohol.

Sam?

Jeff had seen him at Brooke Donner's parties. Something had to be different for him to be here. Maybe a person could change.

And from that day forward, *he* had changed.

Jeff pulled into the church parking lot. Lifting his eyes to the mountains, he stepped out on the pavement, inhaled the fresh air and stretched.

Little Justin Moore ran straight for him and crashed into his legs. "Jeff! You came again!"

"Of course I came, Little Buddy. Did you think I could stay away? This is one of my favorite places in the whole world." Ruffling his silky blonde hair, he lifted him to sit on his shoulders.

Once again a familiar presence welcomed him when he entered the building. The group had changed since he had attended four years ago, but the atmosphere was the same. Love was still here. After greeting friends, he chose a chair in the front, close to the outside aisle.

Billy went forward and read from the Bible:

"Oh Lord, our Lord how majestic is your name in all the earth! You have set your glory above the heavens. From the lips of children and infants you have ordained praise because of your enemies, to silence the foe and avenger."

He picked up his guitar and began leading out in worship. A drummer joined and another singer, followed by children erupting in dance. Flags waved and tangible joy filled the room.

Jeff glanced at Cassie, sitting alone the other side of the room with crutches lying beside her chair. Arms folded, she stared straight ahead. Conversation with her had been strained since the basketball game. Actually, she wasn't talking at all.

Oh well, Cassie was Cassie.

He turned back to worship God.

Later, he stole another look. She stood with hands lifted, singing out in a sweet, clear soprano. Small tears leaked from the corners of her closed eyes.

While Pastor Evan was speaking, children gathered around her, sitting on her lap and cuddling close on both sides. She dipped her head and smiled at them, stroked their heads and whispered in their ears.

"God, she's beautiful," he said, "I may be sorry I promised not to fall in love with her." Amused at himself, he smiled and returned to the pastor's message.

⠦ ⠿ ⠿ ⠦

Linda climbed into bed after a long day, a concerned frown on her face. "Cassie's a little down lately, don't you think?"

"Oh, I don't know," Ben said, undressing beside the bed. "She seems fine to me."

"Ever since she sprained her ankle, she's more subdued, especially when Jeff's around. How long's it been? Three weeks?"

Ben pulled back the covers and climbed into bed. "Yeah, it's been a while. She was pretty embarrassed by that whole incident."

"That's probably it. Maybe it reminded her of all the hearts she's broken."

"Yeah, I suppose so," he said. "But most of those guys just tripped over their egos. It amazes me how presumptuous they were. How can they appear so confident and be so insecure?"

He turned to her. "Was I like that?"

Linda laughed. "Uh . . . Remember the first time you asked me out?"

Ben snickered. "Yeah, it was pretty bad. Good thing you were so patient with me."

"What about Jeff?" Linda said. "Seems like he's always here, even after moving into his apartment. I thought I saw a spark there. But I'm not sure now. I heard them talking today and I've never seen her so cautious."

"If she's cautious, it's for good reason. She's learning that guys have feelings that come with their attentions. But don't worry, Jeff seems more mature than the others. He can handle it. They'll be fine. Ben reached for the light. "He's good help. How do you know he isn't hanging around just because he likes the work?"

"I'm sure he likes the work *and* the company, Dear."

"Company?" Ben teased. "Who, Billy? They are great pals."

"Billy, of course." An elbow jabbed his rib.

"Ouch!" Ben laughed, turning to her. "You're a hopeless

romantic. How about it? Do I get a good night kiss?"

"How much of a kiss do you want?"

⁂

Blackfoot's hooves pounded the road late that Friday afternoon as Jeff headed back to the Watson's barn. His summer schedule at the university allowed him to work four days a week. That morning he drove to the ranch and planned to work two days, then go to church and spend Sunday afternoon with the family before returning home.

The harvest in full swing, Ben had hired Harold Sanders to help out. It was obvious he had a crush on Cassie. She seemed oblivious. Although she never responded to his stares of admiration, she showed subtle signs of awareness. Harold doted on her and eagerly agreed with everything she said. Though she took it in stride, he could tell she enjoyed it.

Jeff smiled. How many other ranch hands had she held in the palm of her hand?

A rain shower had interrupted the grain cutting. While waiting for it to dry, Jeff and Harold had ridden out to check on cattle. Jeff wanted to check the last bunch alone, so had sent Harold home early on Ginger.

At the barn, Ginger stood outside, still saddled. Jeff halted and dismounted. Why wasn't she put away? He'd sent Harold home over two hours ago.

Inside, Cassie's voice came from Ginger's stall. "There's a little more over there."

He glanced over the door and caught sight of her back. She pointed to a small pile of manure in the corner. Shirtless, panting and sweating, Harold was mucking out the stall, shoveling manure and filling a wheelbarrow in the center.

Jeff stopped to marvel. Ben had told her to clean the stalls that morning. She was certainly taking advantage of an eager admirer. He shook his head and chuckled, leading Blackfoot to his stall.

Did he have to take his shirt off?

"That'll do," Cassie said.

Ginger's stall door creaked. Harold's grunts, accompanied by squeaking from the old wheelbarrow, faded as he exited the barn.

Jeff removed Blackfoot's saddle and put it away. Slowly, he rubbed him down, listening.

Footsteps reentered the barn, leading Ginger to her stall. The stall door creaked.

"Cassie?" Harold said.

"Hmm?"

"Uh . . . I was wondering if you would go with me to the Harvest Swing Dance tonight. I know it's late notice, but uh . . . would you?"

"Tonight? . . . What time?"

"It starts at seven-thirty."

"Uh . . . sure," she said. "I guess so."

Harold scrambled out of the stall to retrieve his shirt. Jeff peered over Blackfoot's stall door in time to see him throw it on eagerly, beaming with anticipation.

"Great!" he called over his shoulder. "I'll be back at seven to pick you up." And he was gone.

A man isn't always aware of his motives and sometimes it's good to analyze them. Jeff didn't bother.

He expelled a breath.

This was ridiculous.

Something had to be done.

Crossing over, he opened Ginger's stall. Curry comb in hand, Cassie groomed her horse, casually humming a tune. She didn't acknowledge his presence.

The stall door slammed and she jumped. Her eyes flew to him. The humming stopped.

Arms folded across his chest, he spread his feet. "What do you think you're doing?"

Surprised, she lowered the brush. "Grooming my horse. What do you think?"

"I thought you said you don't date."

"Oh, that!" Eyes widening, she lifted her chin. "It was a private conversation. Can't you mind your own business?"

"Are you really going out with that kid?"

"What do you mean, 'kid?' He's older than me. And he has a name! Besides, I don't see that it's any of your business."

"I recall someone telling me she didn't date and didn't have 'friends' of the opposite sex. So what's this all about?"

Dark eyes flashed. "Since when is 'having fun' outlawed?"

"It's obvious he has a crush on you! You're not taking him seriously."

"How would you know?"

"Oh, come on Cass, having him do your chores for you? He follows you around like a puppy-dog. You order him around like a slave! You and I both know you're fooling yourself!"

Cassie stopped grooming. The currycomb landed on the shelf. Nose in the air, she stomped over, dumped hay into the feeder, pushed Jeff out of the way, slammed the stall door and stormed out of the barn.

He followed.

"For your information, I did not have him do my chores. He offered!"

Startled, Hannah looked up from weeding the flowerbeds.

Joey turned off the lawn mower and watched their procession through the back yard.

Jeff and Cassie ignored them.

"He is a Christian and unbeknownst to you, I just may be interested in him. Why not?" Cassie shut the door and yanked off her boots.

Jeff caught the door before it hit him. "Cassie, you're going to regret this."

In the living room, Ben lowered the newspaper, Linda's jaw dropped and Billy's eyes went wide as Cassie stormed through the house with Jeff at her heels.

She stopped at the foot of the stairs. "So what if I do?" She turned to her father. "Daddy, would you tell him this is a free country and I'm allowed to make my own mistakes?"

Jeff was right on it. "Then you do admit it is a mistake?"

Arms at her sides, she tightened her fists and released a long hiss. "Leave me alone!" Escaping up the stairs, she disappeared down the hallway. The bedroom door slammed.

Jeff scowled at the empty staircase.

Awestruck, his audience remained silent.

Recovering, Ben exchanged a look with Linda. Eyebrows raised, a small smile teased the corners of his lips. "Well, she's not *subdued* now."

Jeff flopped on the couch beside Linda and groaned. "That went well."

Ben chuckled. "What was it all about?"

"Cassie's going with Harold to a dance tonight."

An eyebrow lifted. "And?"

"It's obvious he's all wrong for her."

Smirking, Ben leaned back in his chair and rubbed his chin. "I believe you're in over your head this time, Son."

Suppressing laughter, Billy and Linda nodded at each other. Billy strummed a chord on his guitar. Soon, he went back to the song he was playing for his mother.

A twinkle in her eye, Linda turned to Ben. "Maybe the 'storm' after the 'calm' is upon us."

Jeff grunted, rose and left the room.

≈ ❦ ❦ ≈

Cassie stood trembling.

"He has a lot of nerve!"

She paced at the foot of the bed. "What gives him the right to butt into my affairs? . . . How dare he judge me? . . . What a know-it-all! He has no respect!"

She flopped backward on the bed and clenched her teeth. "I'm definitely going out tonight and it's none of his business!"

Back on her feet in a determined bounce, she opened the closet, yanked out her bathrobe and headed for the shower.

≈ ❦ ❦ ≈

A mosquito landed on Cassie's neck and she slapped it. In the old grain truck, she waited for the combine to finish its rounds. Lifting a shirt sleeve, she wiped perspiration from her forehead and reached for a water bottle.

It was hot.

Conscripted for the harvest crew, her plans for the day were cancelled. Harold called in sick and Jeff was in Seattle, moving his mother back to Wallua Crossing.

Driving grain truck certainly gave her time to think. The high pitched humming of another mosquito pierced the silence. She swatted her ear, rolled her eyes and heaved a sigh.

Jeff was right, she supposed. She shouldn't have gone out with Harold. It was no fun. In fact, it was miserable. She had to tell him she wasn't interested before things went any further.

Now his feelings were hurt.

"Sickness" was not the reason he couldn't come to work. Her forehead fell to rest on the grimy steering wheel and she groaned. The palm of her hand struck the dashboard and a cloud of dust billowed in her face.

"A . . . Achoo!"

Brow furrowing, she scowled. "God, I knew it wasn't a good idea, but I'm getting impatient. I never get to go out anymore. Please give Harold the courage to come back to work!"

Her thoughts turned to Jeff and his passionate interference in her decision. Even though he might be right, he still had no business butting in. Who did he think he was, anyway? Even Mom and Billy didn't question her about the date. It'd been a year since she'd gone on anything remotely resembling a date.

Since Brandon Spears.

Cassie straightened, grabbed the steering wheel and set her mouth. "Jeff offends me," she said.

A gentle nag in her conscience yielded to steely pride.

Over the weekend, Cassie had purposefully avoided Jeff. The whole family noticed. Especially her mother. Sometimes it was hard living at home with everyone watching her every move. There were just too many opinions.

She lifted her chin. "It's my life!"

⁂

From the front yard, Linda Watson watched the game. In the nearby field, Cassie, Billy and Jeff played baseball with the neighbor children. Linda rolled her eyes. Cassie was obviously avoiding Jeff. She wouldn't even look at him. And when she did acknowledge him, it was with sarcasm.

Ben and Billy just laughed off the whole affair, but it bothered Linda. Admittedly, the situation between Cassie and Jeff was a bit awkward, but when was the girl going to grow up? Jeff had only expressed an opinion, although forcefully. It was about time she got a bit of what she dished out to others. She could at least be polite.

It was embarrassing. Especially on a day like this.

She turned her attention back to her guests, who were scattered in lawn chairs around the front yard.

The harvest was complete and it was a good one. The ranch buzzed with activity. A large picnic table, covered with various yummy dishes, invited all the neighbors to come and join the celebration. Several smaller tables were spread across the front yard and smoke rose from barbeques in the back, where meat sizzled.

The Watson family tradition was to host neighbors and friends for a celebration after the long, hot days of cutting wheat, barley and oats. Ben's parents, Leonard and Cassandra, had come to help.

Men played horseshoes by the stables and tended the barbeques while women visited in the front yard. Children gathered for the annual neighborhood baseball game. Neighbors came and went.

The party was winding down and Linda stood spooning left-over baked beans into a small plastic bowl. Her mother-in-law cleared a table nearby.

Joey appeared, a wide grin on his face. "Hey, Grandma! Grandpa won at horseshoes again!"

"Of course he won." Ben's mother laughed, gathering trash

into a large bag. "He's had a lot of years to practice."

After grabbing another piece of chicken and gobbling down a few more cookies, Joey scurried back to join the men.

"He's sure growing like a weed lately," Cassandra said.

Linda smiled. "That he is. I have a hard time keeping enough food around to fill him up."

Cassandra glanced at the baseball field. "What's going on with Cassie and Jeff?"

Linda pretended ignorance. "Cassie and Jeff?"

"There's something brewing between those two. I can feel the energy in the air."

Linda laughed. "There's energy all right! At this point, it's friction."

Ben's mother chuckled. "I did notice some sparks."

"Yeah, she hasn't been too happy with him for a few weeks now."

"Why not?"

Linda glanced up from her work, a lopsided smile on her face. "He doesn't act the part she expects from a devoted admirer."

Cassandra peered at Linda, dark eyes gleaming in interest. "*Is* he a devoted admirer?"

"Oh, I don't know. I thought he was at first, but who knows now?" Linda shrugged and turned to fold up the last of the tablecloths.

Cassandra grabbed the other end. "What happened?"

"He got upset with her for going on a date with Harold."

"Harold Sanders?"

"Yeah. He insisted Harold was all wrong for her."

"Well, I agree with that. But it's funny he would express an opinion, don't you think?"

"Cassie didn't think it was funny. That's when the fireworks began. And he didn't back down. They stormed through the house yelling at each other. It didn't seem to matter that we were all watching."

Cassandra's eyes lit up. "That must have been something to

see. You've had some excitement around here, haven't you?" She scanned the field nearby, watching Cassie and Jeff gather the baseball equipment. "I noticed she was rather short with him."

"Yeah. She's short with him," Linda said. "That's for sure."

Ben's mother smiled. "It doesn't seem to bother him too much. In fact, I just saw her stick her nose in the air and walk away. He just stands there, shaking his head and smiling. It's kind of a bewildered smile, but it's a smile none-the-less."

"Nah, it doesn't bother him. He isn't offended by her that easily. But, it bothers me. Why couldn't I teach her to have more respect?"

Cassandra studied her granddaughter, striding in from the field. Arms full of baseball equipment and shaking his head, Jeff followed.

"How interesting . . ."

SAVING SASSY CASSIE

Endure hardship as discipline; God is treating you as
sons.   *Heb. 12:7a*

Cassie was avoiding him.

Outside the science building, surrounded by friends, she smiled and joked as if she didn't have a care. But Jeff knew better. His mouth twisted in a crooked smile. He just couldn't keep his mouth shut about Harold, could he?

Classes had resumed at the university and Jeff only visited the Watsons for dinner after church on Sundays. Cassie was conspicuously missing. She now shared an apartment with a friend in town to save travel time and expense.

Jeff was happy with his new job. The renewed relationship with Billy and Ben also pleased him. He had missed them. Maybe the torment of his past was behind him.

Most things were certainly going well, but he was disappointed about Cassie. He didn't think she'd stay offended for so long.

The Watsons had invited Jeff and his mother to celebrate Thanksgiving the next week and they were planning to go. Maybe when he saw her again, it'd be better. At least she was civil to him around her parents.

Friday evening, Jeff drove downtown to a prayer room. Young adults, college and high school students gathered to pray for their city and the surrounding area. Earlier, he and Billy had attended. They were encouraged and challenged. But Billy was at a conference in Portland, so Jeff decided to go without him this time. It was a good place to spend time with God. When he entered the building, music played from another room.

> *Give us clean hands, give us pure hearts.*
> *Let us not lift our soul to another . . .*
> *Oh God, let us be a generation who seeks,*
> *Seeks your face, oh God of Jacob . . .*[1]

Jeff stepped into the room and began to pray. Moved by the music, he raised his eyes and worshiped.

After laying down concerns about his new job and his troubled relationship with Cassie, he came to peace. The worship was deep and satisfying. However, late in the evening, Cassie returned to his thoughts. It wasn't time to think about her, he was there to worship, but the heaviness and burden for her increased.

He prayed for her.

Linda bolted up in bed. The clock on the headboard rudely announced twelve-thirty A.M. Her heart pounded.

"What's wrong, Lord? What's this fear about?"

Cassie.

Linda prayed for her daughter.

Half an hour later, she was still awake. Though she had prayed, the alarm in her spirit would not silence. She turned to her fitfully sleeping husband.

"Honey, are you awake?" she whispered, hand resting on his side.

Irritated, Ben turned over in bed and groaned. "No, I'm trying to sleep. Most people are doing that at one o'clock in the morning."

"Sorry, but I can't shake the feeling that Cassie's in some kind of trouble. She's been on my mind for half an hour or more. I prayed for her, but I can't get peace. Will you pray with me?"

Ben chuckled. "Can't you pray when other people are awake?" However, he knew from experience there was only one way to get back to sleep. He sat up.

"Father, you know what's going on. Keep Cassie safe . . ."

⁘ ⋺ ⋲ ⁘

Jeff looked at his watch and yawned.

One o'clock.

On the way home, he missed a turn and found himself on a street he normally didn't travel. His headlights flashed on a yellow Toyota, surrounded by other cars.

Is that Cassie's?

Curious, he drove around the block and looked again. It was hers all right. The dent on the rear fender was a give-away. He smiled, remembering her recent encounter with a fencepost.

In the shadows behind the car, ragged overgrown shrubs surrounded a rundown house. Craggy dead twigs hung over gloomy windows.

It was Riley Cote's place! A notorious rebel Jeff knew in high school, Riley hosted drinking parties and was repeatedly in trouble with the law.

What was she doing there? He had to check it out.

He parked on the other side of the street and loud arguing accosted him when he opened the pickup door. He hesitated.

At the darkened front porch, a voice shrieked above the drone of a television.

"Let go of me!"

Male laughter followed. "Yeah, sure! You know you like it. Hey Tyler, bring some of that stuff. Cassie here needs to loosen up!"

Another shrill voice pled, "Riley, leave her alone! Cassie's my friend! She doesn't drink!"

"Ah, come on, what's she, religious or something? Think she's too good for us? Come to think of it, she does look pretty good."

A chorus of harsh, raucous laughter echoed through the door.

Stomach churning, Jeff knocked hard.

No answer.

He knocked harder. At last, the door partially opened and a dark haired girl appeared, eyes wide.

"Yes?"

"Is Cassie Watson here? I noticed her car out front."

She opened her mouth.

"Nobody's here by that name," a male voice mocked from inside.

Fuming, Jeff peered in the door. The stench of alcohol and cigarettes assaulted him, but he pushed past the girl and forced it open. Four unkempt guys lounged around a TV. Empty beer cans, trash and dirty dishes littered a grimy carpet and a haze of smoke hung over the eerie glow of the television.

"I heard her voice and I know she's here."

No one moved.

"Do you want me to call the police? She's under age and you're drinking."

"Go right ahead," a mocking voice said. Riley emerged from the hallway clenching Cassie tight against him and wrenching her hands behind her back. "Carson! What the hell you doing here?"

"Jeff!" Wide with fright, Cassie's dark eyes searched his. She struggled to get free, but Riley held her fast.

Laughing in drunken arrogance, Riley glanced down at his captive prey. "She came here by her own free will."

"Let her go," Jeff said.

"Why should I? You just want her for yourself?"

"Let her go . . . Now!"

Baring scum-covered teeth, Riley sneered. "Make me. I got as much right to her as you. It's my house."

A big man, about two-hundred and seventy-five pounds, he held her in a tight grip, ignoring her attempts to break loose. Cassie kicked him in the shin with the heel of her boot and Riley twisted her arm in response. She yelped.

Restraining himself no longer, Jeff leapt forward and landed a fist squarely on the offender's nose.

Riley reached for his face.

Seizing the opportunity, Cassie broke free and ran for the door.

Blood pouring from his nose, Riley raced after Jeff, grabbed his arm, swung him around and belted him in the left eye. Stunned, Jeff bent over, but shook himself and returned two swift blows to Riley's soft belly. When Riley doubled over, Jeff grabbed Cassie's hand and fled the house.

"What about my car?" she yelled as he pulled her across the street.

Jeff pushed her into his pickup, jumped in and slammed the door.

Foul language punctuated by obscene gestures pursued them from across the street. Riley ranted under the street light, fist in the air and nose bleeding down to the belly of his dingy white T-shirt.

Shivering, Cassie wrapped her arms tightly around her waist. "I left my coat in there!"

"Get it from your friend later!" Tires squealed as Jeff sped around the corner.

A few blocks away, he pulled over, took a deep breath and collected himself.

Cassie turned to him, voice quivering. "Are you . . . okay?"

"Yeah." He gripped the steering wheel and steeled himself against a trembling rage. He turned to her. "How about you? Did he hurt you?"

"No. I'm fine."

"We'd better go back and get your car. Tell you what, give me the keys. I'll get it." Hand extended, he waited.

Cassie gasped. "I left them in my coat pocket."

"Do you have another set?"

She nodded. "In my apartment."

At her apartment, Jeff waited in his pickup for Cassie to fetch the keys. Anger resurfaced and he fumed. "I can't believe she would set foot in a place like that. Ben would be—"

An idea struck.

Wrapped in a thick sweatshirt with keys in hand, she returned and climbed into the pickup. Without a word, Jeff drove back to Riley's house and parked a block away.

"Give me the keys," he said.

Cassie hesitated. "Are you sure? You're the one he punched."

"Of course I'm sure. Hand them over. I'll meet you at my place."

"Where's that?"

"Elm Tree Apartments."

"Be careful, okay?"

Jeff nodded curtly and reached for the door handle. Quietly, he exited the pickup, crept up to the Toyota, climbed in and sped away. Cassie followed in his pickup.

Jeff had already parked the car and was waiting when she arrived. He darted over to the driver's side and jerked the door open.

"Move over."

Taken by surprise, Cassie moved. He got in, started the pickup and pulled out of the parking lot.

"Where are we going?"

"I'm taking you home."

"What about my car?"

"It'll be fine where it is."

"Wait. I need it tomorrow!"

"You'll survive without it."

"What? Take me back!"

He pulled out onto the highway and headed north.

"Hey! You're going the wrong way!"

Jeff glanced at her. "I'm taking you *home*."

"You can't do this! I don't want to go home tonight!"

"Too bad . . . You're going."

"Jeff, stop the car! Right now!"

Jaw clenched in determination, he focused on the highway.

She tried another approach. "Jeff, I'm sorry about your eye. Don't you think we should go back and put some ice on it or something? It looks like it's swelling. You probably shouldn't be driving."

"This is not about my eye and you know it! What in the blazes were you doing at that house?"

"I took Kylie home and she invited me in."

"You had no business there. Are you out of your mind? Those guys are bad news!" Jeff turned to face her briefly in the darkness. "Do you have any idea what could've happened if I hadn't shown up?"

She stiffened. "He was just trying to scare me. I probably would've gotten away."

"Are you crazy? He certainly didn't let you go that easily!"

She huffed. "That's because he was showing off for you."

Flipping dark curls over her shoulder, she gazed out the side window. "How did you happen to turn up there anyway?"

Jeff glanced at Cassie's dark silhouette at the other end of the seat. Nose in the air, she exuded indignation. Exhaling slowly, he gathered a little patience.

"You were on my mind tonight. I just happened to drive by and see your car. I had to stop and investigate, especially when I realized whose house it was. I can't believe you would go there. And at this hour of the night!"

Her chin lifted. "I was fine."

"You were *not* fine! I could tell you were scared and for good reason!"

"Would you quit yelling at me? I'm sorry you got mixed up in the whole thing. I didn't go there to drink. I was with Kylie! Would you calm down?"

"Calm down? You act like it was nothing! What's with you lately, anyway? You know, I was just thinking about how I used to get so upset when your father spanked you. I thought he was too hard on you. Well, I was wrong about that! He should have spanked you more. You don't have a lick of sense!"

Cassie inhaled sharply. "That's a fine thing to say! Why do you always know the best way to insult me? You—"

Bright red and blue lights flashed in the rear-view mirror.

Jeff looked down at his speedometer.

"Uh-oh. Uh . . . Jeff, I think it's you he wants," she said. "You were going a little fast."

Jeff had been on a high horse and the force of gravity was unforgiving. His anger and frustration at Cassie turned to fear. For himself, his driving record, his bank account, but mostly his pride. He pulled to the side of the road.

Cassie winced. Two hundred fifty-five dollars was a shocker, especially for a guy with a perfect driving record.

Ten minutes later, they were back on the highway in heavy silence. Finally, she cleared her throat.

"Sorry."

No response.

"Jeff?"

He drove on, staring straight ahead.

"Plead for mercy from the judge. I'll bet he'd at least reduce it for you."

He didn't respond.

She leaned over in the dark pickup and looked into his stony face. "Are you okay?"

Jeff took a long, deep breath and let it out slowly. "Yeah, I'm okay."

The heated conversation had lost its steam and neither Cassie nor Jeff said much the rest of the way to the ranch.

Confident footsteps running up the stairway woke Linda from a sound sleep. Startled, she shook Ben's arm.

"Ben, someone's in the house! They're upstairs!"

The footsteps thumped back down in the same confident manner.

Ben chuckled. "Sounds as if they know their way around." He

turned over as if to go back to sleep.

"Ben, the refrigerator door opened. Someone's in the kitchen!" The suspense was too much. She scrambled out of bed and reached for her robe.

"Are you coming?"

"Yeah, I'm coming." He yawned and swung his feet over the side of the bed.

Voices from the kitchen greeted Linda when she opened the bedroom door.

"Ouch! I don't think that's gonna help!"

"It's swelling. You've got to get ice on it. Do you want to see out of it in the morning?"

"I think it's too late for that."

Linda peered into the kitchen. From the hallway, she observed Cassie and Jeff at the kitchen table. A small towel full of ice in her hand, Cassie leaned over, trying to apply it to Jeff's face. Backs toward the door, they were unaware of her presence.

Ben came up behind her. "What's going on around here? It's two o'clock in the morning!"

They jumped at his thundering voice and Jeff's head collided with Cassie's.

"Ouch!"

Rubbing their heads, they groaned.

"What in the world happened to you?" Ben said, noticing Jeff's eye.

Jeff and Cassie looked at each other. Neither answered.

"Well?"

They remained silent.

Sensing the tension, Ben backed off.

"I see," he said. "Jeff, you take the guest room. Everyone get to bed. We'll sort this out in the morning."

Cassie let out a pent up breath.

"Jeff, the sheets on the bed are the same ones you slept on last time you were here," Linda said. "We'll see you in the morning."

She followed Ben back to the bedroom.

"I wonder what that was all about. Did you see the look on their faces?" Linda laughed beneath her breath while climbing back in bed. "There's got to be a story behind this one. I have a feeling our prayers were needed tonight.

EATING CROW

Awake and overstimulated, Ben wrestled with a myriad of thoughts and questions. Finally, he threw his feet over the side of the bed. "It was my idea to go back to bed, but it didn't do me much good," he muttered.

Dim morning light revealed Linda's curled form and soft, regular breathing. Sleeping peacefully. How did she do it?

He pulled on jeans, socks and boots, then wandered over to the closet to find a shirt. On the way to the bathroom, he said, "I should've sat everyone down and dealt with Jeff and Cassie last night. Oh well, at least Linda's getting some sleep for us."

Slumbering household left behind, Ben ambled out to the enclosed front porch. Though it was after seven o'clock, the sun was just rising. A fresh, thin skiff of snow sparkled in the lawn and frosted the trees.

Glancing to the far end of the porch, he startled. Jeff sat there, bundled against the cold.

"Jeff! I thought you'd still be sleeping after such an eventful night."

Jeff looked up. Purples, reds and blues had begun to darken his upper left cheek below a tightly swollen eye. "It was because of the eventful night I couldn't sleep."

"Hey, come out and help me with the chores," Ben said. "Maybe you can satisfy my curiosity." He chuckled. "How did you happen to bring my daughter home at two A.M.? And looking like you had a run-in with Rocky Balboa?"

Jeff stood and followed him to the barn.

"What happened?"

"I'm not sure myself."

"You can start talking while I feed the horses," Ben said, busting open a bale of green hay.

⁂

Cassie awakened after a fitful night's sleep to a dim and chilly November morning. Her upstairs room was cold. She snuggled under the covers and stared at the ceiling in the morning quiet. Memories from the previous night flooded her thoughts, harsh realities hitting her conscience. She grimaced, squeezing her eyes shut. Both palms flew to cover her face and she groaned.

"What's Daddy going to say?"

Bold claims in the heat of argument came back to haunt her. She was *fine*? Sure, she was fine, struggling to get free, with that big fat bully's arms around her and his drunken breath blowing in her face.

The fact was, she was never so glad to see anyone in her life as Jeff busting through the door, demanding her freedom. Why couldn't she have just *thanked* him? It could've been even slightly romantic, him rescuing her from distress and all. But no, he had to start yelling at her.

She moaned. He was right. It was stupid of her to go into that house at all, let alone after midnight. It could have been really bad. Riley definitely had evil intent. He could have *raped* her.

"Oh my God! Why do I do these things?" she said, pulling the

84

covers over her head.

"What's happening to me, Lord? Jeff brings out the *worst* in me. Now he must think I'm an idiot. Why else would he say I should've been *spanked* more? That took a lot of nerve. I keep telling myself I don't care what he thinks. But I do. That's why he makes me so mad!

"I was embarrassed when he heard what happened with Brandon. I was mad when he confronted me about Harold. Now he rescues me from Riley and we have a big fight!

"I want him to think well of me, but I say and do things that make him think even worse of me. I just can't seem to help it. What's wrong? Why can't I let go of my pride?"

Cassie poked her head out from under the covers and her gaze returned to the ceiling. She continued softly, "There's something about Jeff. He *bugs* me." She rolled her eyes. "It's probably from hanging around Billy and Daddy . . . He's a bit overpowering and definitely not safe. Not like other guys. They treat me nicer.

"But I was sure glad to see him last night." Tears threatened. "Oh, I don't know!" She groaned again, threw herself on her side and yanked the covers up under her chin.

"Sometimes I think he likes me," she said, her voice choking. "He said he was thinking about me last night.

"But my other friends wouldn't dare talk to me the way he does. He doesn't respect me!

The whole scene from the night before haunted her. "I'm so confused!" The covers came over her head again, and Cassie gave in to tears of frustration and humiliation.

"God, why are you so distant? I haven't heard your voice in so long. What happened?"

Incidents over the last few months flooded her memory. A stubborn attitude, brushing aside the gentle prodding of her conscience, taking up offenses and entertaining rebellious thoughts. The excuses were gone and the dam broke.

Her body shook with sobs.

A soft knock sounded on her door.

"Who is it?" Cassie said, her voice hoarse.

Her mother entered, wearing a thick, warm robe and fuzzy slippers.

"Good morning, Dear." She crossed over to Cassie and stopped short. "You've been crying."

Cassie nodded and grabbed a tissue from the box on her headboard.

Her mother sat on the edge of the bed. "Tell me what happened last night."

Cassie blew her nose. It was difficult at first, but soon she spilled the whole story, including her worries about what her father would say. But she didn't share her concern about Jeff.

"So, Jeff got that black eye rescuing you?"

"Yes, but afterwards he was rude to me." Cassie's voice quivered. "He forced me to come home, against my will. Then he insulted me."

Her mother looked at her sidelong. "Sounds like he was pretty upset."

"Yeah, he kept yelling at me."

"He fought for you, Cassie. Did it ever occur to you that maybe he was concerned for your safety?"

Cassie winced.

Her mother continued. "He was probably afraid for you. Fear often comes out as anger. How about you? Weren't you afraid?"

"Yeah, I was afraid, but afterwards, when Jeff started yelling at me, I got defensive. For some reason it's easy for me to get angry with him." She sniffled and grabbed another tissue.

"I noticed."

Cassie looked up. "What do you think I should do? I feel bad, especially about the speeding ticket."

"Apologize to him," her mother said. "Thank him for rescuing you. I'm sure thankful he came when he did. It was an answer to my prayers! Lord knows what could have happened. You need to know that last night I woke up at twelve-thirty. I couldn't sleep. I felt like you were in danger, so I started praying. Finally, about one-o'clock, when I still couldn't get peace, I woke your father. He and I prayed together. Then I finally slept."

Cassie's eyes went wide. "Really?"

Her mother nodded. "God was watching out for you, Cassie. It wasn't by chance Jeff came driving by and saw your car there."

Cassie frowned and her voice choked with congestion. "I'm sure you're right."

Her mother placed a hand on her shoulder. "Cassie, talk to Jeff."

Cassie wrinkled her nose. "I'll think about it."

"I know you'll do the right thing, Sweetie." Her mother stood. "I wouldn't worry too much about your father. After all that, I think he'll be really thankful just to know you're all right."

❦ ❦ ❦

Jeff finished his story about the speeding ticket while Ben fed the cows.

"That sure took the wind out of my sails," he said. "I think God was trying to tell me something. Here I was hopping mad and scolding Cassie for her recklessness and I was going twenty miles an hour over the speed limit!"

He grimly stared ahead.

Ben chuckled and turned his attention back to the gravel road.

"You're probably right, but cheer up. You look pretty rough this morning. It should arouse a little sympathy for you. If not from Cassie, at least from Linda."

Jeff snorted and turned away. "Cassie could care less."

"Then why was she hovering over you last night in the kitchen?"

"Guilt."

Ben laughed outright. "If you think it was guilt, then you don't know Cassie. Incidentally, in case she never thanks you, I want to thank you for getting her out of that mess. It sounds like it was a close call."

"You're welcome," Jeff said. "Are you going to deal with the situation?"

"Is that why you brought her home?" Ben laughed again. "I suppose I could talk to her about it. But I'm sure the consequences are enough. I don't think she'll be going into strange houses with girlfriends late at night from now on. And you have a black eye and a speeding ticket to remind her."

Jeff frowned and scratched his head as they pulled up to the house. "I don't think that'll make much difference to Cassie."

"Don't worry about it. You'll see." Ben led Jeff through the back door into the utility room where they hung up their coats and washed their hands.

In the kitchen, Linda finished the preparation of a large breakfast and Cassie set the table. Joey and Hannah were already seated and waiting.

Hannah jumped up to greet him. "Jeff! We didn't know you were here!"

Joey sprung to his feet. "What happened to your eye?" he asked. "Did you get in a fight? What's the other guy look like? Did you hurt him bad?"

"Joey, sit down," Ben said.

Cassie looked at him. Eyes widening, she swallowed, turned away and busied herself.

"Good morning," she said to the napkins she folded.

"Morning." Jeff pulled out a chair at the table and sat, following Ben's lead. Linda brought out a plate piled with pancakes and another of scrambled eggs.

Jeff sat up straight. "Sure looks good."

"Thank you," Linda said, smiling.

She and Cassie joined the family at the table.

"When does Billy get home?" Jeff asked.

"He'll be home next week," Ben said.

After a prayer of thanks, they began to eat.

Linda chattered on about the upcoming holidays and the plans for Grandma and Grandpa Watson to join them for Thanksgiving while Jeff and Cassie sat in thick silence.

Jeff couldn't help but notice a small smile playing on the

corners of Ben's lips.

He's enjoying this.

Jeff studied Cassie's averted face.

Had she been crying? She definitely lacked her normal spark.

After breakfast, no one lingered at the table, but rather pitched in to clear it. Jeff retreated to the living room.

"Did you win?"

"What?" Jeff turned to see Joey at his heels, eyes sparkling with curiosity.

"The fight!"

Jeff smiled, face throbbing in the effort. "You might say I accomplished what I set out to do."

"I knew it! There *was* a fight!"

"Joey, leave it alone." Ben said, coming up behind him.

"Ah . . . Dad. Something happened to Jeff. Why does it have to be a secret? Cassie must know about it. She's really grumpy. Why can't I know?"

Ben laughed and ruffled his hair. "Go get started on your chores, Son."

Joey retreated, disappointment clouding his face.

"If you'll excuse me," Ben said. "I need to get some accounting done." He disappeared down the hall.

Jeff looked around the empty living room and sighed. Maybe a ride would clear his head. He turned back, retrieved his coat and hat and strode to the barn. He was preparing to mount Blackfoot when Cassie appeared.

"Jeff, I need to talk to you."

He searched her face. At least she didn't look armed for battle.

"Do you want to go on a short ride with me?"

"Sure. I'll saddle Ginger."

He waited outside the barn until she reappeared, leading her horse. They mounted and ambled out of the barn-lot, side by side on the snow-covered hillside.

"I lied," Cassie said.

Surprised, Jeff looked at her out of his good eye. "You lied?"

Cassie kept her gaze fixed on the horizon. "Yes, I lied. I was not fine last night. I was scared to death before you showed up and I was really glad to see you.

"I got defensive when you started yelling at me. Uh . . . I'm sorry you ended up with a black eye and a speeding ticket . . . Thank you for what you did."

Jeff pulled up Blackfoot. "You're *apologizing*?"

Ginger halted a few feet ahead and Cassie looked over her shoulder. "Yes. I'm apologizing. And don't look so shocked. I can do that from time to time. Are you going to forgive me?"

Jeff nudged his horse forward. "Of course I will, but with one condition."

"What's that?"

He came alongside her and smiled. "You forgive me for being so hard on you last night."

Cassie flashed a grin. "Consider it done."

Without warning, she dug her heels into Ginger's sides, galloping off toward the pasture.

"Come on, let's ride! It's cold out here!"

❧ ❧ ❧ ❧

Jeff drove his pickup into the parking lot of his mother's apartment complex. It was Thanksgiving and they were going to the Watsons for dinner. He smiled when he thought of the last time he was there.

"At least this time I can drive with both eyes," he said aloud, looking in the rear-view mirror. His cheek remained discolored and the white of his eye was bright red, but he could see out of it.

He turned off the ignition and leaned back in the seat.

"Lord, Cassie can be so sweet. I like being with her. I can't wait to see her again." Memories from the weekend came to mind and he smiled.

After staying over Saturday night, he brought Cassie back to town following the Sunday dinner. Recalling how they had joked and laughed together, he pictured her smiling at him. Joy surged through him. He chuckled.

"I think I'm in trouble." Dismissing the thought, he opened the pickup door and started for his mother's apartment.

"Mom, are you ready?"

"I'm upstairs! I'll be there in a minute!"

A large, colorful fruit salad sat on the kitchen counter, covered in cellophane.

"Is this salad supposed to go?"

His mother came down the stairs, pulling on a coat. Lightly streaked brown hair pulled back from her face revealed smiling, blue eyes. She was an attractive woman. The black slacks and soft green sweater accentuated her trim figure. He turned, kissed her on the cheek and received her embrace.

"You look nice, Mom."

She smiled. "Thank you. And yes, the salad goes. How are the roads?"

Salad in hand, he started for the door. "They're a bit snowy, but not bad. We may be in for a storm later today."

In the car, his mother laughed softly.

"What's so funny?"

"I had the most bizarre day yesterday," she said. "Two clients of mine are neighbors in the same apartment complex. They're constantly at war. Nancy keeps track of everything that happens at Maude's house and vice versa. Nancy can barely walk. Yesterday I found her out in the hall, dragging herself to Maude's door. She was sure Maude had stolen her coupons out of her newspaper."

She laughed. "The day before, she accused her of stealing her house keys. The care-giver found them sitting on her counter fifteen minutes later. Of course she'd forgotten that whole incident."

She shook her head. "Maude does the same thing . . . I hope I'm not like that when I get old."

"Mom, you'll never be like that," Jeff said. "You don't worry about those kinds of things anymore."

"You're right. I have changed."

Cassie set the hot dish of sweet potatoes on the table. Her mother took off her apron and pulled out a chair.

"Gather round! It's time to eat!"

People shuffled to find seats around the large makeshift table in the living room. Steam rose from a plate of carved turkey, a mound of mashed potatoes and a pile of hot rolls. A colorful display of salads and vegetables also graced the table. They joined hands, forming an unbroken circle. All grew silent and looked to her father for further instructions. He glanced at grandpa across the table.

"Dad, would you give thanks for the food?"

"Father, I thank you for your many blessings and provisions. Thank you for the family you blessed us with, the great food and the hands that prepared it. You're so good to us." He paused. "Good food, good meat, good God, let's eat!"

Chuckling erupted around the table and they reached for the food.

Cassie raised her eyes and met Jeff's blue gaze across the table. A warm, pleasant feeling surged through her. Grandma Watson, at her right, raised an eyebrow.

While they ate, Billy, at her left, described the conference he'd recently attended. Jeff listened intently, but found Cassie's eyes at just the right moments to share a smile.

Cassie peeked at Grandma and detected a knowing look on her face. She was a hopeless romantic. At seventy-four, she was in great health and full of energy and ideas. She also had a great imagination.

"Let's all take a minute to give thanks for at least one thing God's done for us this year," her father said, late in the meal. He leaned back in his chair and pulled out a Bible from the nearby shelf.

"Why don't we start with you, Hannah? We'll go from youngest to oldest."

Hannah cleared her throat and blushed. "I'm thankful for my family," she said, "and for my new friend Katelyn."

Everyone turned to Joey. "Uh . . . I'm thankful for all the food."

Soft chuckling rippled around the table.

"Cassie?"

She paused. "I'm thankful to be home." Stealing a peek at Jeff, she continued, "And for God's mercy."

"Jeff?"

A hint of curiosity in his eyes, he returned Cassie's glance. "I'm thankful to be back in Haywacah Valley."

"I'm thankful for good work and a great family," Billy said, "And for having Jeff around again."

"How about you, Molly?" her father said. "We'll just assume you're younger than Linda."

Her mother stifled a laugh. "Go ahead, Molly."

"I'm thankful for my new job." She smiled at Jeff. "And for a wonderful son."

"I thank God for good health and great friends," her mother said. "Ben?"

"I'm thankful for my beautiful wife."

"I would hope so," Grandpa said. "She's certainly done a good job of putting up with you. With all of us, for that matter."

"It's my turn," Grandma said, smiling. "I thank God for the love of a wonderful family."

Grandpa cleared his throat. "It's great to be here. I appreciate all of you. And I thank God for a wife that still loves me and puts up with me. You young men should take note." He winked. "Like I've said before, it's a good idea to marry up. It's the Watson Way."

Cassie felt her grandmother nudge him under the table, but he ignored her. "Worked for me! I—"

"Leonard," Grandma said. "That's enough."

"Okay! Okay!" Grandpa grinned. "See what I mean? She keeps me in line, doesn't she?"

Everyone laughed. Cassie shared the laugh with Jeff. It seemed he was looking into the depths of her soul.

Her father put on his glasses and opened his Bible. "I'm going to read from Psalm 107.

> Give thanks to the LORD, for he is good;
> His love endures forever . . .
> Let them give thanks to the
> Lord for his unfailing love
> and his wonderful deeds for men . . ."

Alone in the kitchen with Grandma, Cassie helped wash up the last of the dishes.

Grandma smiled mischievously. "Cassie, I noticed Jeff couldn't take his eyes off you during dinner."

Cassie turned to stack a bowl in the cupboard, laughing softly. "Grandma," she said, "Don't get any ideas about Jeff and me. Most of the time, all we do is argue. Right now we have a truce, but I don't expect it to last long."

Grandma laughed. "That's how it was with your grandfather and me," she said. "If you can't trust them enough to fight with them, then you can't trust them enough to fall in love with them. I figure if they still love you after they've seen the worst in you, then it's a love that'll last."

Cassie wiped off a pan with the dishtowel and turned to her. "Did you and Grandpa fight a lot?"

"Are you kidding? When I first met him, I thought he was the most stubborn and arrogant man on earth. He always had an opinion about what I should or shouldn't be doing. I was pretty stubborn and independent myself and didn't appreciate it at all. Now I know I wouldn't have been happy with anyone else. The other men were too weak and soft for me and would've let me run everything. I'm sure they would've checked out after a while."

After rinsing the last pan, she pulled the plug in the sink, turned to Cassie and winked. "Even though I've had to train him," she said, "I've needed him. He's always had lots of energy and opinions. We are a good match. I think I would wear most men out." She smiled mischievously. "You know, we can still have a good argument to this day, but making up is the best part of all."

Curious, Cassie tilted her head. "Weren't you afraid he didn't respect you?"

Grandma's eyes lit with amusement. "Oh, yes, the thought did occur to me. But respect is not what I thought it was. Bowing prostrate in my presence was not what I needed.

"Love was what I wanted. And love requires enough trust to speak the truth and enough hope to persevere. Your Grandpa respected and honored me enough to have a fair fight. That earned my respect."

"Grandma, do you really think Jeff's *interested* in me?"

"Humph. Of course he's interested. Cassie, any guy who thought he had a chance would be interested in you. You're the best!"

TENDER MOMENTS

*For great is his love toward us, and the faithfulness of
the LORD endures forever.* Psalms 117:2

Jeff observed the family scene in the living room.

Ben and Billy were discussing politics. Grandpa and Joey
played checkers and Linda and his mother were chatting about
somebody's health problems. Hannah, nearby, listened intently.

Cassie and Grandma emerged from the kitchen. Grandma
joined Linda and his mother, but Cassie lingered in the doorway,
hesitating.

Her dark eyes found his, beckoning him with questions in their
chocolate depths. He rose from the chair and approached, sinking
his hands in his pockets.

"I could use some fresh air. You want to take a walk?"

Cassie flashed a smile. "Sure."

They found warm coats and boots in the utility room and
escaped out the back door.

Cassie paused. Lacy flakes of snow danced in the yard light,
floating to the ground.

"Isn't it beautiful?"

Melting snowflakes shimmered in her hair and her dark eyes sparkled.

"Yeah," Jeff said.

Beautiful? That's for sure.

They meandered toward the barn, turned on the lights and stopped at Ginger's stall. Cassie crooned to her, petting the horse's velvety nose.

"Hey, girl. I've missed you lately." The horse nickered in response and tossed her head. "Sorry. I didn't bring you a treat."

Awkward silence overtook them.

Finally, Jeff broke it. "How's school?"

"School's fine. Finals are next week. I've really been hitting the books." Cassie turned and leaned against the stall door. "How's your work coming?"

Blackfoot nudged Jeff's shoulder and he turned to stroke his soft muzzle. "It's going well, though I'm pretty sure this isn't what I want to do for the rest of my life."

"Oh? What are your dreams for the future?"

"I don't know if I should tell you. You might think I'm crazy."

Smiling, she faced him, arms folding across her chest. "Try me."

"I'd like to do something with youth," he said. "I helped coach a basketball team and did some camp counseling for teenage kids while I was in Seattle. I really enjoyed it.

"It may be a long time from now, but I'd like to have my own ranch. I've thought of working with troubled teenage boys. I remember how it was for me when I was young and how much your father did for me. I'd like to do the same for others. There's a lot of hurting kids out there."

Her soft eyes met his. "I think it's a great idea."

Surprised, Jeff's heart pounded. "You do?"

"Of course I do." Cassie unfolded her arms and ran her palm over Ginger's sleek neck. "You're great with kids."

"Thanks. I've been praying about it and I think that's where

God's leading me. What about you?"

Cassie frowned. "Oh, I don't know. I'm not sure what I'm going to do." She continued petting her horse. "I wish I knew what God wanted."

"Are you talking to him?"

"A little," she said. "I've been so busy with school lately. It seems like a long time since I felt close to God." She turned, dropped her thumbs to her pockets and let her eyes travel out the open door to the falling snow.

"Are you and God okay?"

"It's better this week." She gave him a brief, sidelong glance. "My attitude hasn't been the best the last few months. I think you noticed. After you brought me home last week, I had a little talk with Jesus and let go of some offenses."

Misty eyes rose to meet his, her voice catching. "If it hadn't been for you the other night, I don't know where I'd be . . . Thank you, Jeff."

He swallowed. "You're welcome."

She turned back to Ginger. "I have more peace and joy than I had, but I need more. There's got to be more."

"There's always more," he said. "God wants to fill us to overflowing every day."

"I haven't been pursuing God lately, Jeff. I've been off doing my own thing. What happened last week made me realize just how far off I've been."

"You're forgiven, Cass."

She looked up. "How do you know?"

He smiled. "'If we confess our sins, he's faithful and just and will forgive . . .' You confessed, so you're forgiven."

Her eyes held his.

Was this the Cassie he knew? All independence and feistiness? What was that in her eyes?

Need?

It surprised him.

Intrigued him.

It also scared him.

She looked away, placing her hand on the stall door. "Thank you."

Jeff reached out and covered her hand with his. "Cassie?"

Her eyes flew to his again. In the soft light of the barn, he studied her with his hand warming hers.

She had always been so strong and independent. Even tough.

But, now she was . . . soft. *Vulnerable.*

A surge of protectiveness welled up from within, surprising him.

He heard himself say, "Would you come with me to the Prayer Room next Friday night? It's a good place to get in touch with God."

She looked at their joined hands. With his thumb, he stroked her smooth skin.

"Uh . . . I've heard about it. What's it like?"

"The presence of God is thick there . . . I think you'd like it."

"Sure. I'll go with you," she said. "I'll be done with finals by then."

Jeff smiled. "Can I pick you up around seven?"

Cassie returned his grin. "I'll be waiting."

※ ❦ ❦ ※

On the way home to Wallua Crossing, his pickup headlights cut through falling snowflakes to icy pavement. Cautiously, Jeff drove, deep in thought.

"Jeff, you're falling for that girl," his mother said from the seat beside him, breaking the silence.

"Huh?" He shook himself.

"Are you all right?" she asked. "You've hardly said a word since we started back home. I said you're falling for that girl."

"Who, Cassie? . . . Don't worry, Mom. I'm fine. Cass and I are friends."

"Friends who make eyes at each other across the table and go for moonlight walks?"

"Make eyes? You're imagining things, Mom."

She looked at him sideways. "I'm not imagining anything and you know it," she said. "How do you feel about her?"

He shrugged. "Oh, I don't know. I admire her, I guess." He laughed softly. "But she also infuriates me. She gets under my skin like no other girl I've ever known."

"Sounds like love to me."

"Love? I don't think so. Her life's so different from mine. She's always been protected. She's had everything she's ever wanted. I'm not sure we understand each other." He grimaced. "Besides, I don't think I'm the type of person Ben and Linda are looking for in a son-in-law." A pain stabbed Jeff's heart when he said this. But he ignored it.

"Then why are you pining for her?"

"Pining?" He laughed nervously. "I'm not pining for her."

"You were thinking about her when I broke the silence, right?"

"Yeah . . . I was . . . but we were just there."

His mother smiled knowingly. "I would guess that you spend a lot of time thinking about her."

"I'm planning on taking her to the Prayer Room next week. That's all, Mom. She needs a touch from God."

"Uh-huh . . . I'm praying for you, Jeff. Sooner or later you're going to have to face your feelings."

They were pulling up to her apartment, so she didn't press the issue. She grabbed her salad bowl and Jeff walked her to the door.

"Jeff, thank you for taking me. I had a wonderful time," she said, hugging him tight. "And don't sell yourself short. I'm so proud of you, Honey."

❧ ❦ ❧

The next morning, Cassie's closet door opened partway and a blond head peered around it. "Cassie, can I come in?"

"Sure, Hannah. What is it?"

Cassie laid aside the book she was studying. It was not early, but no one in the house seemed in a hurry to rise after such a full day of celebration.

Hannah, barefoot and still in her nightgown, padded to where

Cassie had pulled back the covers. She crawled into the warm bed with her older sister. They cuddled a few moments like they did when Hannah was little.

Cassie leaned her head against Hannah's blond curls. "What's on your mind, Sweetie?"

A troubled look crossed Hannah's young face. "Do you think I'm pretty?"

Cassie was surprised. She leaned back to look at her younger sister and admired her soft, smooth skin, button nose, brown eyes and silken curls. Almost thirteen, Hannah was growing up.

She hugged her close. "Of course you're pretty. You're beautiful."

Hannah's eyes clouded with skepticism. "Do you really mean that or are you just saying it because you're my big sister and you're supposed to be nice?"

Cassie laughed. "Have you ever known me to be nice just because I'm supposed to be?"

"Not really," Hannah said. "But I wish I looked more like you."

Cassie's eyes widened. "Hannah! You're beautiful the way you are. Those blond curls and deep brown eyes! Why would you want to look like me?"

"All the boys like you. Even Jeff. I saw the way he looked at you yesterday across the table. He doesn't even notice me."

Smiling, Cassie squeezed her sister to her side. "Sure, he notices you. You're one of his favorite people."

"Not the way he notices you."

"He's twelve years older than you are, Hannah. He adores you like a little sister."

"Do you think anyone will ever fall in love with me?"

"Of course. Who could resist you? You're not only prettier, but much sweeter than I am. Have you noticed there haven't been many guys around here lately? They might like me for a little while, but once they get to know me, they run. I guess I'm scary." She growled furiously, playfully pinching Hannah around the waist with her fingers. "You won't have that problem."

Hannah giggled, snuggling close. "I've missed you lately."

ಜ ೨ ೩ ಜ

Cassie stood in front of her apartment window the following Friday, waiting for Jeff to arrive. She turned to her roommate, Kristy, who lounged nearby, watching television. "I'm a little nervous about this."

Kristy twirled a long strand of hair with one finger and lifted her eyes to Cassie's worried face. "Is this the guy who rescued you from Riley Cote?"

"One and the same."

"Why are you nervous, then? He sounds safe enough. Besides, you've practically known each other all your lives."

"He's my older brother's friend. When we were younger, they were quite a unit and didn't want the 'kid sister' tagging along. For that reason I didn't like him."

She paused. "I've gotten over that. He's a great guy . . . A little bossy, I suppose. I think I'm nervous for other reasons . . . Oh, here he comes. I'll go get my coat." She darted to the bathroom, ran a brush through her hair and reapplied her lip gloss. The doorbell rang.

She headed for the bedroom to get her coat.

"Is Cassie ready?"

"Cassie, he's here!" Kristy called from the front room.

She met Cassie coming out of the bedroom. Eyebrows raised and blue eyes wide with appreciation, she whispered, "He's waiting at the door. Wow! What's your problem? He looks good to me!"

ಜ ೨ ೩ ಜ

Jeff parked on a side street downtown. Several cars were in front of the Prayer Room. Cassie opened the door, but hesitated. Jeff quickly came around the pickup, took her hand and helped her to the sidewalk.

He sure knew how to treat a lady.

It was nice, but made her a little uncomfortable. She was perfectly able to get out of a pickup by herself.

They walked to the door of the Prayer Room and Jeff opened

it. Soft music greeted them. They were in a small, lighted room with shoes lining the floor. Coats on hooks covered the walls. Warm hands took her coat and she yielded again to Jeff's easy manners.

After hanging their coats, Jeff removed his shoes and Cassie followed suit. The music came from another room. Cassie hesitated, searching Jeff's face. He smiled and took her arm.

"Come on, you're going to like this."

Nearly a dozen young people looked up briefly, as they entered. Some sat on chairs with heads bowed and some knelt. Others sat on the floor or lay on the carpet.

A slender young man greeted them with a warm smile and fiery eyes, vibrating with life. "Jeff," he whispered, so as not to disturb the others. "Glad you could make it."

He shook Jeff's hand and hugged him, then turned to Cassie. "Your friend?"

"This is Cassie. She's Billy's sister. Cassie, this is Matt."

Matt nodded and motioned to the center of the room. "Glad to have you. We're starting with a time of worship."

Cassie looked around. A large cross stood in the far corner of the dimly lit room. Hand painted drawings and writings covered the walls. Prayer requests, poems, inspired words and scripture verses were scrawled on a scroll of paper lying on the floor. Candles glowed in one corner, communion elements were set up in another. Large pillows lay scattered about. Cassie found a pillow and space on the floor where she could lean against the wall. Jeff slid down beside her.

Music poured from the C.D. player and she sang along.

> *In your presence there is everything,*
> *That I need for my soul.*
> *There is healing and forgiveness,*
> *As we reach out to you and be made whole . . .* [2]

After about an hour, she relaxed and focused. All her concerns spilled out in prayer. Awareness of those around faded. Tears flowed as she felt the weight of God's presence. A peace filled her and she knew . . . God was with her and he loved her.

> *For it's your kindness, Lord, that leads us to repentance,*
> *Your favor, Lord, satisfies,*
> *Your beauty, Lord, makes us stand in silence,*
> *And your love, it's better than life.*[3]

Later, people began praying for each other. Matt produced a vial of oil and passed it around. They prayed for healing, rubbing the oil on foreheads, necks, arms, and feet. Sweet fragrance filled the air, along with words of encouragement and scripture verses. People moved about the room. Some laughed, others cried. They worshiped and communed with God.

About midnight, Jeff nudged Cassie. "It's late. Do you want to go home?"

Covered in a blanket of peace, she lay on the carpet.

Her eyes opened. Everything was clearer and more intense. Colors were brighter. She inhaled deeply. Even the air felt cleaner.

"Not really, but I suppose we must." Rising to her feet, she stumbled and caught herself.

She giggled. "I can hardly walk!" She grabbed Jeff's hand.

They laughed. A warm, rich laughter, only known by those who share in the presence of God. The entire drive back to her apartment, they couldn't stop laughing. He pulled into the parking lot, put the pickup in park and turned to her.

"You were really into it."

"It was wonderful. I needed that." Cassie paused, leaning toward him in the dark. "Are you coming out tomorrow?"

"No, I've got things to do at home. I'm going to be really busy at work the next few weeks."

"You are planning on coming for Christmas, aren't you?"

"I don't know. I can't think clearly right now."

Laughter overtook them again.

She reached for the door handle, giggling.

"Wait! I'll walk you to the door." He went around the pickup, opened her door and took her hand. She leaned into him, still giggling. His arm went around her. Thus, he led her to the apartment, both continuing to laugh.

Everything seemed funny.

☙ ❦ ❧

Jeff couldn't sleep. Visions of Cassie at the Prayer Room flashed across his mind. She loved God. She stirred him. Perhaps his mother was right and he was falling in love with her. The thought agitated him. Anxiety gnawed his soul.

What would Ben and Linda think?

What about Billy?

Something about this thing with Cassie scared him.

Jeff you're one in a thousand.

Coach Bower's words had kept him going, even though he still had trouble believing them.

One in a thousand?

He turned in bed. "Father, Cassie's beautiful. She's exciting. I could never be bored around her. She's wonderful, but is she for *me?*"

This was stupid. They just liked each other. It's not like he was ready to propose.

"Maybe I will go to Watson's for Christmas."

☙ ❦ ❧

"Hello, Cassie?"

Two weeks before Christmas, Jeff found himself on the phone.

Home for Christmas break, Cassie was busy helping with preparations for Sunday's Christmas program. He hadn't really talked to her for two whole weeks. It seemed an eternity.

"No, this is Linda."

"Oh. Hi, Linda. This is Jeff. Could I talk to Cass?"

"Cassie!" Linda called out. "The phone's for you! It's Jeff!"

"Hello?"

"Hey, Cassie. How would you like to go to the Prayer Room with me again tonight? I'll come out and get you."

"You'd drive all the way out here to pick me up?"

"Sure. I was thinking I could come out early and we could get a hamburger in town before going to the prayer meeting."

She giggled. "Are you asking me out on a *date*?"

Jeff went silent, remembering his promise from the previous summer. Though in jest, he had promised. He swallowed.

"Jeff? Okay, then are you asking me to go as a *friend*?" she asked, a teasing lilt in her voice.

He cleared his throat. "I'm not a Boy Scout. Remember?"

She laughed. "I'd love to go."

He relaxed. "I'll be there about five."

"I'll be ready."

The windshield wipers squeaked and swished, back and forth in the rapidly falling rain. Visibility was poor and the wipers barely kept up with the downpour.

Jeff was lost in disturbing thoughts. The pickup hit a large puddle in the road and he slowed, shaking himself. "Lord, I know exactly what I'm doing here. This is a date. And I want more than friendship. This Prayer Room thing is just an excuse to be with her. I like being with her. Is that bad?"

He went silent, his left foot bobbing. He turned on the radio and cranked it up.

Cassie greeted him at the door with a bright smile. In a cream-colored sweater and brown slacks, she looked beautiful. Without inviting him in, she quickly grabbed her coat and marched straight for his pickup, hopping over small puddles in the driveway.

"Hey, slow down!" He hurried to catch up. "Chivalry isn't dead."

At the passenger's door, he gave her a courtesy hand up into the cab, laughing under his breath. He circled to the driver's side, climbed in and started back to Wallua Crossing.

Jeff listened as Cassie chatted about her biology class. He laughed at her theatrical accounts of debates with her professor. It seemed the guy didn't know what to think of her different views. Her boldness and confidence surprised and delighted him. For the time being, he forgot his misgivings, sat back and admired her animated beauty. Enjoying her amusing and entertaining recollections of class debates and discussions, he laughed with her.

The Prayer Room was great for Cassie, but Jeff found himself distracted. This was a bad idea. He couldn't worship God when she was there with him. He couldn't think about anything but her.

About eleven o'clock, he suggested they leave.

Cassie was again enjoying herself and continued giggling on the way home. Halfway back, he reached over and took her hand in his. She fell silent.

"Thank you for taking me again. It was wonderful." She squeezed his hand.

"Yeah . . . it was," he said, savoring the moment.

Jeff drove into the Watson's driveway and parked the pickup near the front porch. Cassie reached for the door handle.

"Whoa! When you're with me, I walk you to the door."

Cassie pulled her hand back. "Sorry." She giggled.

Jeff went around the pickup and opened the door. "May I?" She took his extended hand and slid down onto the driveway. A full moon shone through dark, moving clouds. The storm had broken and the sky was clear, leaving the air crisp and cold.

Hand in hand they started for the lighted porch.

At the front door, he halted. He let go of her hand and faced her, gazing down into her smiling face. A strong urge to take her in his arms coursed through him, but he held back. Gently, he took her hand, raised it to his lips and kissed the softness of its back, still searching her gaze.

"Cassie, I . . ."

"Yes?"

Lowering her hand slowly, Jeff pulled back. "Never mind. It's late. I've got a long drive home."

"You could come in and use the guest room for the night," she said, eyes shining.

Jeff let out a short laugh and briefly looked away. "I think not."

"Goodnight, then." A cheery smile on her lips, her eyes locked with his. Then, she rose on tiptoe and kissed him on the cheek.

"Uh . . . goodnight." Hiding his feelings in silence, he stood stock still, heart pounding.

Turning, she opened the door and with a smile over her shoulder, disappeared.

On the drive home, Jeff contemplated. Why hadn't he kissed her? She was willing. She had given him all the signs. What was wrong with him?

⊰ ❦ ⊱

"Jeff, we need to give them an answer." After talking with Linda on the phone, his mother nagged him once again. He still hadn't told her whether he wanted to go to the Watson's for Christmas.

In the living room of his mother's apartment, Jeff sat reading the newspaper, stocking feet propped on the coffee table. He sighed. "I suppose you're right." He set the newspaper down and looked at her. "What do you think?"

"It's up to you. I'm sure *I* will enjoy myself. You're the one with the excuses. What's bothering you? You've always enjoyed yourself at the Watsons . . . It's Cassie, isn't it?"

Jeff didn't answer. Disturbed, he rose from the couch and wandered into the kitchen for a glass of water.

She followed. "What's troubling you?"

"I don't want to talk about it."

"Are you and Cassie fighting?"

"No, Mom. We're not *fighting*." He leaned back against the kitchen counter, stared at the glass in his hand and twirled it with the tips of his fingers. "I think that's the problem. It was easier when we were."

"I see." She turned away, a knowing smile on her face. "What do you want to do then?"

Irritated, he gave in. "Oh, go ahead. Call Linda. Tell her we'll come." He placed the glass on the counter, ambled to the front door and prepared to leave.

"By the way Mom, I haven't done any Christmas shopping yet.

Could you help me?"

His mother appeared with the phone, ready to dial. "How about Saturday?"

"That would be great. Should I pick you up about ten o'clock?"

"Sure. I'll see you then." She followed him to the door and kissed him on the cheek. "Don't worry, Honey. It'll be fine."

He opened the door and left.

THE DARK FEAR

*For you did not receive a spirit that makes you a slave
again to fear ...*   *Rom. 8:15a*

"Oh, Jeff. It's beautiful! Thank you!"

Cassie jumped up off the couch and threw her arms around his neck. Jeff's face went hot with embarrassment, but he returned her embrace.

"I thought it would look good on you," he whispered into her ear.

Everything looked good on her.

"Thank you for the pocketknife," he said, stepping back to see her smile. "I really like it."

Her face glowed. "You're welcome."

He looked around. No one paid much attention and that was just as well. Of course there was Grandma, whose twinkling brown eyes didn't miss anything.

Exchanging gifts with Cassie wasn't as awkward as he had feared. The whole family seemed to take it as an expected and natural occurrence. So far, things were easier than he thought they'd be, the mood light, happy and festive. Warm laughter rang out in the living room where wrappings and empty boxes lay strewn over the carpet. Family members embraced as they gave and received joyfully.

Full of wonder and delight at the gifts they received, Joey and Hannah laughed with joy. They also thrilled, watching others open gifts.

Jeff was enjoying himself. Occasionally, he caught Cassie smiling at him. That smile of hers was a heart-stopper and it seemed his dropped into his shoes every time it flashed his way. He was in deep water just looking into those sweet chocolate eyes.

After dinner, Billy and Joey emerged from upstairs wearing sweat pants and old sweat-shirts.

"Hey, Jeff, come out with us for a jog!" Billy said.

Jeff hesitated. "I didn't bring any clothes for that. You got some extra?"

"Don't worry about it," Billy said. "We'll fix you up."

He followed Billy upstairs.

Soon they reappeared, laughing at Jeff's "sweat suit." The dark red pants barely met the tops of his socks and the orange sweatshirt didn't reach his wrists, but laughing, they decided it fit him just right. Cassie and the others gave their humorous appraisal before they were out the back door and off.

A few hours later, Jeff rose from the table after finishing a game of cards. "Well, Mom, it's getting late."

His mother covered a yawn and glanced at her watch. "Oh my! You're right!" She rose to her feet. "It's been a wonderful day. Thank you so much for inviting us."

Jeff started for the entryway and Cassie followed. "Hey, Jeff, did you go to the Prayer Room last week?"

"No, not last week." His back to her, he bent to pull on his boots.

She continued from behind. "I'd like to go again. Are they carrying on over the holidays?"

"Not as regularly, but there's usually someone there." He straightened and faced her.

"When's a good time to go?"

"This next Friday night they're having worship again."

Just then, Grandpa appeared in the living room. Face lit with a mischievous smile, he raised his voice. "Hey, look at that! The two of you are standing under my mistletoe!"

On the ceiling directly above, they spotted the offending article. An old, worn plastic sprig of mistletoe hung pitifully over the entryway by a piece of string and some scotch tape.

The rest of the family converged, filling the entryway with laughter and expectation.

Cassie stood glued to the floor, eyes wide and face red. "Grandpa!"

"Go on, kiss her!" Grandma said, laughing. "Even though it's plastic, it still counts."

Jeff looked down at Cassie's blushing face, his eyes searching hers. Their brown depths shone in anticipation. And . . . a hint of shyness? But she certainly didn't look opposed to the idea. Smiling, he shrugged his shoulders. Gently, he moved his hands to either side of her head and lowered his lips to hers. He kissed her soft lips, lingering a few seconds . . .

It was better than he had imagined. Head rising, he noted Cassie's wide smile and his heart skipped. Turning to the audience, he lowered his hands and smiled.

"Is that sufficient?"

He looked over the laughing, cheering group. Hannah and Joey jumped up and down yelling, "Way to go, Jeff!" Grandpa, Grandma, his mother and Linda all grinned and laughed. However, one face in the back of the group wasn't smiling. Billy's. And where was Ben?

His smile faded. "Come on, Mom. We've got to go."

Cassie lay in bed, arms wrapped around herself in ecstasy.

"He kissed me!" she said into the darkness. The tenderness of his warm lips on hers and both his hands holding her head, lingered. She smiled. "I don't care if it was a product of one of Grandpa's practical jokes. I know a real kiss and that was a real kiss!"

She giggled. He felt her kiss him back, too. She was sure of it. "Oh God! It was wonderful!"

Cassie closed her eyes, letting out a long pleasure-filled sigh. Her heart was doing funny things lately when Jeff looked at her. It had to be happening to him too. She never imagined it would be Jeff, but she felt something wild and exciting when he was around. She trusted him and respected him more than any other guy she'd ever known. It just felt *right*!

But why was he frowning when he left the house? The way he kissed her, he had to have liked it as much as she did.

He was sure a hard one to figure out.

Cassie didn't hear from Jeff for the rest of the week. She drove to the Prayer Room Friday night, but he never appeared. Blessed, but distracted, she couldn't help worrying.

Where was Jeff?

Sunday came and he didn't come to church.

Should she call him? She quickly dismissed the thought. Not yet. It may seem too aggressive, especially to someone like Jeff. The kiss wasn't exactly his idea and he hadn't said anything. Billy said it irritated him to have a girl call unless he had declared himself.

Classes at school resumed after the first of the year and Cassie kept an eye out for Jeff at the university. After another week of silence, she was really worried. She even mentioned it to her mother.

"Mom, I haven't seen Jeff for almost two weeks. Have you heard from him?"

"No, I haven't. Maybe he's busy with work. He'll probably be at church tomorrow. Don't worry."

Cassie had a feeling something was terribly wrong.

During worship, Cassie looked around.

He still wasn't there.

This was more than she could stand. She rose to leave for the bathroom. While returning to her seat, she saw him slumped in a chair in the back row, arms folded.

He looked away, avoiding her eyes.

What was his problem?

Sam Wallace went over and sat with him. They whispered something to each other and Sam chuckled.

This was torture. Maybe she should watch babies in the nursery. She couldn't worship in these circumstances.

Many people shared that Sunday, expressing excitement about what God was doing in their lives, but Cassie was distracted. She finally tuned in to Pastor Evan's sermon.

> ". . . God wants us to trust him fully and to leave all our cares and worries with him. Worry doesn't equal love. It doesn't prove you love anyone. In fact, the Bible says, 'Do not fret, it only leads to evil.' Turn away from worry and cast your cares on Jesus. You can trust Jesus. Don't let worry and fear rob you of your joy."

Well, she knew who that sermon was for.

At the end of the service, she glanced back.

He was gone.

⁊ ❦ ⁊

Fear had raised its grisly head, no longer to be denied. Jeff's good judgement and logical thinking was clouded at best. Established facts had little meaning.

He drove back to his apartment and turned off the engine. Leaning back in the seat, he considered what the pastor had said.

Suddenly, he turned angry. "Sure . . . don't worry," he said aloud, his voice laced with skepticism.

"What a mess! What was I thinking? I don't want to hurt Cassie and I don't want to lose my best friend or the only person who's ever really been a father to me." A deep groan escaped. He gritted his teeth.

"Billy knows me. He knows where I've come from. It's obvious he'd like someone better for his sister. I should have been warned off. He's been trying to discourage me concerning Cassie all along."

"And Ben. I'm sure he's not impressed. Linda's fine with it, but everything's good with her. She's a woman."

He twirled the car keys on his index finger. Picturing the scene at the Watsons at Christmas, he could still see the frown of disapproval on Billy's face.

"I'm damned if I do and I'm damned if I don't!"

He growled.

"God, what do I do now? I had no business falling in love with her!" He opened the pickup door and threw the keys across the parking lot.

Talk to them.

"And what am I supposed to say? 'I'm in love with your daughter. So what do you think?'"

Go talk to them.

"I don't think so!"

He slammed the door and went after his keys.

Sleep came hard that night as Jeff wrestled with his thoughts. Visions of Cassie kept going through his mind. Cassie grooming her horse. Cassie smiling at him. Cassie's dark eyes flashing in anger. Cassie trying to put ice on his eye in the middle of the night. Cassie looking up at him in the barn, eyes misty and vulnerable . . .

Would he ever get her out of his mind?

The following day he saw her talking with friends, smiling and animated. She had no shortage of male admirers.

Maybe he was imagining things. Why would she take him seriously? Why would she care for him?

Studying her from a distance, he brooded . . .

❧ ❦ ❧

Later that day, Cassie stood in her apartment kitchen scrambling eggs for dinner.

The front door slammed and Kristy strode into the kitchen, carrying a load of books. With a loud thump, she dumped them on the table.

"Cassie, I saw Jeff staring at you today." Kristy turned to her, placing her hands on her hips. "I've never seen such a look of torture on a guy's face. So, what happened? What did you do to him? That poor guy has it bad—"

"Really? When was that?" Cassie looked up briefly from her cooking, feigning disinterest. She hadn't taken Kristy into her confidence concerning her feelings for Jeff, but was glad for the information.

"It was at noon today when we were hanging out at the fountain. Did you dump him or something?"

"No, I didn't *dump* him!"

"Then what happened?"

"I don't know!"

"Then why don't you find out? You're moping around here like a lovesick puppy! And don't try to tell me you don't care!"

"It's not that simple!"

Cassie returned to the Prayer Room that Friday night. On the verge of tears, she poured out her heart to God in worship and prayer. "Oh God! I'm so confused! What should I do? I'm worried about Jeff."

Cast your cares on me.

"Okay I give it all to you, Lord. All my feelings and all my desire to understand. My dreams and my future are yours."

A heavy snow fell that night and because of the bad roads, Cassie decided not to go home for the weekend.

Jeff couldn't sleep.

Old feelings of self-doubt resurfaced with a vengeance.

He turned over, tormented by disturbing thoughts. Pushing the pillow over his head, he finally fell into a troubled sleep.

It was the dream again. The same dream he had after his first visit to the ranch, almost ten years ago.

At the Watson table again, everyone smiled as Billy's mom served him a big bowl of hot chili. Cheddar cheese melted in a yellow puddle on top. Delicious smells wafted to his nostrils as she filled his plate with hot bread, salads and desserts. His mouth watered. But when he lifted his fork, the food disappeared before reaching his lips. Desperate, he tried to eat faster, but without success. Hunger gnawed and his stomach growled. The warm laughter changed to jeering. Hands like scorpion claws, snapped at him and faces morphed into snake-like monsters. They mocked him, chanting with forked tongues, "Not enough! Not enough! . . . Not for you! Not for you! . . ."

Jeff awoke trembling, blankets twisted in a heap.

Further sleep evaded him. He turned over and groaned.

༄ ༉ ༈ ༄

"Hey Carson, what's up?"

Jeff swallowed. Billy was on the phone.

"Not much."

"Well, I haven't seen you around lately. You weren't at church last week, or at the Prayer Room. Are you okay?"

"Uh . . . Yeah, I'm okay. Just busy with work and stuff."

Silence.

"Sure . . . I don't buy that. You got a girlfriend or something?"

Jeff let out a harsh laugh. "No. Don't worry. No girlfriend."

"Well, I had to call to say goodbye. I was hoping to see you at the Prayer Room last night, but you didn't show. I'm going to Spokane for a couple of months to work for my uncle on a remodel project. I'll be back the second week of March."

"Okay. Thanks for calling."

"Jeff, keep in touch, okay?"

"I'll try . . . I gotta go."

"I'm praying for you, man. Give me a call . . ."

༄ ༉ ༈ ༄

Linda found Ben in the living room, sitting by the fireplace, reading. She sank into the couch and sighed. "Honey, have you noticed Jeff lately? He seems upset about something. When he comes to church, he sits in the back and looks withdrawn and unhappy. I'm worried about him."

Ben put down the newspaper and looked at her. "There does seem to be something bothering him." He gave her a crooked smile. "I wouldn't be surprised if it had something to do with our daughter."

Linda rose and crossed over to his chair. "Why don't you talk to him?"

His face dropped. "I don't think so. It's best not to interfere in these things. If he has something he wants to talk about, he'll come and ask." Bristling, he lifted the paper.

Linda scrutinized him. "I don't think he will. It's like he's avoiding us. Every time I invite him over, he makes an excuse."

"Linda, leave it alone," he said. "Give him some time. He probably has something he's working out with God." Pretending to be absorbed in the paper, he turned a page.

"Honey, I think Cassie likes him. And he likes her, too."

Ben threw the paper down on his lap. "I know! But I'm having doubts about all this. I'm not sure—"

"Ben, Jeff's been a great blessing to us. You love him. What's wrong with you? You knew he and Cassie were getting close. You saw this coming. I thought you were all for it!"

She lowered her face and searched his averted gaze.

"Ben?"

He turned to her. "I was, but I just don't know anymore. I didn't think he'd just check out! On the rare occasions that I do see him, he won't even look at me. I don't like it . . . It's like he's hiding something."

"Well, talk to him!" she said. "It's not fair to assume things. Remember Randy McDuffy? We were all impressed with him. He always looked so good. Raised in a Christian home, always there at church and quick to quote scripture. He faked it real well, didn't he? Now he's in prison for molesting his own niece!"

"But he was always so polished and smooth, " Ben said. "He

never let down his guard. No one really knew who he was."

"That's the point. We know Jeff. And we know he can at least admit when he's wrong. He's not doing well and he's not faking it!"

Ben let out a long breath. "You're right. I do know him . . . and love him . . . And he's been good for Cassie."

Pausing, he studied the flames in the fireplace, then hit the arm of the chair with his fist. "This whole thing messes with me. Why can't he just come out and tell me what's going on? We've had some good talks. Am I so unapproachable? I thought he trusted me!"

"I don't know, Honey." Linda gently shoved the paper aside and settled herself on his lap. "We could at least pray for him."

Ben sighed. "I suppose. Go ahead and pray. I'm listening."

※ ❦ ❦ ※

Fear had taken a captive. Those watching from the sidelines were tested and Ben was no exception. He tossed and turned. The peaceful, regular breathing of his wife's uninterrupted sleep irritated him.

He groaned.

Surrendering, he got up, grabbed his Bible and retreated to the living room. In the darkness, he groped for the lamp switch and sank into his recliner.

"Father, there's something wrong with Jeff. He's obviously avoiding us and he looks depressed. What's wrong?"

Ask him.

His Bible fell open to the book of James and he read:

"My brothers, if one of you should wander from the truth and someone should bring him back, remember this: Whoever turns a sinner from the error of his way will save him from death and cover over a multitude of sins."

"Father, I don't want to do this. I think it has to do with him and Cassie and I don't want to get involved."

Ben leaned back and closed his eyes. A storm raged within.

"This is Cassie. My daughter. I can tell they like each other."

He frowned. "Should I seek him out? Should I try to help him? I don't know . . . What if I help him with Cassie and he . . . I could make things worse!"

He opened his eyes and stared into the darkness. "He's a man! He can rise up on his own, can't he? I'm bad at this. I'm no counselor!"

Memories from years ago came back.

He was with Jeff's father, John. John had withdrawn and started drinking. Again. He couldn't seem to quit. The old feelings of agony and worry for his friend returned. Repeatedly he had asked God to deliver him. He had felt so helpless.

The last time he confronted John, he tried to convince him to come back. Ben had found John downtown one afternoon, eyes red, clothing rumpled and smelling of alcohol. The hard look in his eyes alarmed him. After coaxing him into the cab of his pickup, he tried to reason with him. "John! You've got to believe that Jesus has the answers. Turn away from this stuff and look to him. You're going down, man!"

John leaned back and sneered. "That's easy for you to say! You don't understand. Life's easy for you. Everything's hard for me!"

"No, I don't understand, but Jesus says there's nothing impossible for him."

John had let out a harsh laugh. "So, where's the impossible that's happening because of Jesus? Where is it, Ben? I don't see it. Do you? One bad thing after another keeps happening to me and I'm tired of begging God for help.

"I go to church and they tell me to be good and try harder. Well, I can't be good and I'm done trying! They tell us to go out and share our faith. Who'd want to be like me? Nobody! I'm miserable! Those church people, they ain't like me. They're all fixed up and pretty. If they have problems, they're able to get through them. I just can't."

The old heartache returned as Ben revisited the dark shadows of his memory. He had forced the issue and challenged him.

"John, you've got to believe! Rise up in faith! I know the

church has been weak, but you could be part of the solution."

John turned angry. "You go ahead and be a solution yourself! I'm done with church and all the games people play! I feel like a hypocrite! I'm tired of faking it! I feel worse after going than before! At least if I stay away, I'm not pretending everything's okay. Like they do!" He jumped out of the pickup and slammed the door.

"That confrontation did a lot of good," Ben said to himself. "He didn't speak to me again. Until the end. Fifteen years later.

"I'm glad he finally turned back to God. But meanwhile, Molly and Jeff went through hell." The clock on the mantle continued to tick, punctuating the heavy quiet. Ben stared into the darkness, fighting with himself. Fear, doubt and disappointment assaulted him.

"I can't deal with this," he said, dragging himself back to bed. "Not yet."

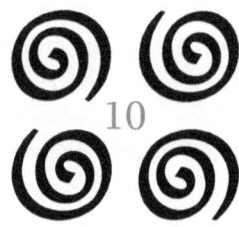

FAINT HEARTS

> *. . . but you received the Spirit of sonship. And by him*
> *we cry, "Abba, Father."*   Rom. 8:15b

"Ben! You've got to get over here! I'm afraid your father's going to kill himself!"

The frantic voice on the phone pierced Ben's sleep-muddled brain. Shaking himself awake, he sat up in bed. "What's going on Mom?"

"Your dad wants to fix our yard light and is too stubborn to admit he shouldn't climb the ladder! Remember what happened last time he got on a ladder? And you know how hard it is for him to ask for help. Could you just 'drop by' this morning?"

"Sure Mom, I'll be there in a few hours. Distract him somehow, but keep him off the ladder!"

Later, Ben followed his father into his parent's house. "Brrr! That wind is cold!" he said, shivering and stomping his feet. "It's certainly too windy to be out there working on a ladder, but we got it done."

"Come on in and I'll make you some lunch," his mother said from the kitchen.

"Sounds good to me, especially if it's warm in there."

Ben sat at the kitchen table and waited for lunch. After an attempt at small talk, he finally confronted his father. "Dad, were you really going to do that by yourself? That light has got to be at least fifteen feet up there!"

After an uneasy silence, his father looked down sheepishly and cleared his throat. "You're always so busy," he said. "I didn't want to bother you. I thought I should at least give it a try."

"You know your dad, Ben. He never asks for help," his mother said.

"Dad, last time you got on a ladder, you fell five feet and were laid up for a week. And it could've been a lot worse!"

"Well, what good am I if I can't even fix my own stuff?" His dad pushed himself out of his chair, crossed over to the adjacent living room, picked up a magazine and sank into his recliner.

His mother tried to break the tension. "By the way, how's the romance coming?"

"What romance?" Ben asked.

"You know, Cassie and Jeff."

Lowering the magazine, his father brightened. "Yeah, did my mistletoe work?"

"Oh . . . that. I'm not sure we have a romance."

"What's the problem?" his mother asked. "They sure had eyes for each other at Christmas. Did Cassie chase this one off too?"

"I wish it were that simple. It seems Jeff's struggling with something."

Furrowing her brow, his mother continued stirring the soup at the stove. "You're close to him, Ben. Have you asked him what's wrong?"

"No. I haven't."

She glanced over her shoulder at her son, eyebrows raised. "He might need some help."

"If the kid can't fight the dragons, he won't get the maiden."

His father snickered from the recliner. He raised his magazine. "Faint heart never won fair lady. I had to do it alone."

"Yeah, Leonard, but it wasn't a pretty sight. If it weren't for God's mercy, we'd never have gotten together. It still bothers me when I think about the time when I came home from school and you wouldn't even acknowledge me. You left me there standing by the car to carry in my own luggage! We were engaged! You were so insecure in front of your family. Afraid to let them see you express any affection toward me. And you're still too proud to admit it. You—"

"Ah, Cassandra!" His father threw down the magazine. "I thought you forgave me for that. I said I was sorry! That was over fifty years ago!"

Ben chuckled. "Maybe I'd better call your pastor and have him help you two sort this out."

Hands on her hips, his mother took a stand between him and his father. "My point is that you can't expect a young man to fight his battles alone, when neither one of you did that well yourselves. And you each had a father to support you!"

"Wait a minute! Don't bring *me* into this!" Ben said.

"From what I remember, you weren't exactly Mr. Confident when you were pursuing Linda."

Ben fiddled with the napkin holder.

"Okay. Maybe I should consider helping the kid out."

Flipping through the magazine, his father snorted. "Good luck! If I were you, I wouldn't get involved. From my experience, he probably won't appreciate you butting in."

His mother frowned and returned to the stove. "Maybe you're right, but I think it's sad. He's such a nice young man. And Cassie really likes him. He's the first one to really stand up to her."

She gave him a long, knowing look.

"Ben, sometimes it takes a father."

He didn't respond.

"Have you asked anyone for advice?"

"I don't know who I'd ask," Ben said.

"How about Pastor Evan, or the men's group you were so excited about?"

Ben winced. "They're all so busy with their own stuff."

His mother smiled sweetly, a teasing light in her eyes. "The apple doesn't fall far from the tree, does it Son?"

Friday afternoon, Cassie parked her yellow Toyota in the driveway of her grandparents' small house. Mid-March sun warmed the air and after the cold week before, she was glad for the promise of spring. It had been a long winter for many reasons. Popping out of the car, she jogged to the front door.

Grandpa opened it. "Cassie, my girl! What a pleasant surprise! Come in!"

After giving Grandpa a hug and kiss, she turned to Grandma who emerged from the kitchen wearing an apron and wiping her hands on a dishtowel.

"Grandma, I just had to come to visit. How've you been?" Cassie asked, embracing her and kissing her on the cheek.

"I've been well, Sweetie. What an honor to have you come! I was just finishing up the lunch dishes. Have you eaten?"

"Yeah, I already grabbed a sandwich."

Cassie followed Grandma to the kitchen. Grandpa returned to his recliner and his magazine.

"Then have a cookie."

"No thank you I—"

Cassie checked out the scrumptious creations under her nose. Her grandmother nudged her and smiled.

"Well, maybe just one."

Grandma set the plate of cookies on the counter and busied herself scrubbing out a frying pan. "How's school?"

"Wow! These are great cookies, Grandma! School's fine. I just finished my finals. Spring break's next week."

"What are your plans for the break?"

"I'm going home this afternoon. I plan to help Mom and Dad and do some riding."

"I'm sure you miss your horse," Grandma said, smiling.

Cassie started her second cookie. "I do."

After a long pause, Grandma cleared her throat. "So, how's that boyfriend of yours?"

Cassie choked. "Grandma, he's not my boyfriend!"

Grandma laughed. "You can't tell me that two people flirting with each other like you did over the holidays didn't have some feelings for each other. What happened?"

"That's just the point. *Nothing* happened!"

Smiling deviously, Grandma lifted her brow. "I detect some strong emotion there. But you wanted something to happen. Right?"

Groaning, Cassie turned away.

Grandma studied the side of her face. "Do you like him?"

A voice called from the living room. "Leave the poor girl alone, Cassandra! The guy's a fool if he's not crazy about her. Why, if I was a young buck—"

Grandma turned. "Quit eavesdropping, Leonard! This is a private discussion."

Cassie couldn't help smiling at the two of them, but remained silent. She picked up a towel and began drying dishes.

"Cassie?"

She glanced wistfully out the kitchen window. "I thought I liked him, but evidently he's changed his mind about me."

"How do you know that?"

"He won't even talk to me. He avoids me."

Grandma wrinkled her brow. "Is he happy?"

"No, he's not happy. He's changed, Grandma. Something's wrong."

"Have you asked him what it is?"

"No." Cassie shoved a glass pan in the cupboard and slammed on the lid.

"Hey, be careful with that!" Grandma straightened and looked at Cassie. "This bothers you more than you want to admit. How serious are you about him?"

"Oh, I don't know." Cassie looked away.

"So far, he's the only guy I could really trust. He knows me well. He has faith in God. I respect him. I didn't think I would, but I miss him." Cassie choked back the rise of some unexpected emotion and cleared her throat. "I guess it just didn't work out—"

"What do you mean, 'it didn't work out?'" Grandma folded her arms and stared at her bluntly. "He's not dead or married yet. Fight for him."

"Grandma, I don't know how to fight for him."

"Does he know you like him?"

Cassie nodded. "I'm sure he knows. That's not the problem."

"Hmm . . . " Grandma reached for a broom and began sweeping the floor.

"Something scared him off, Grandma. And this time I didn't mean to do it. I have no clue what happened." Cassie took a seat at the kitchen table and fiddled with the ornate salt and pepper shakers. Lips pursed, her eyes flashed. "The problem is he won't fight for *me*!"

Grandma gave Cassie a sly look. "You can think of something to do about that. Can't you?"

"What do you mean, Grandma? If you think I should try to make him jealous, forget it. I'm through playing games or dating guys when I'm not interested."

Grandma moved away, continuing to sweep the floor.

"I've seen Jeff in a few situations," she said. "He's not afraid of you. He's a fighter. He wouldn't have gotten this far in life if he wasn't. Maybe there's a way to bring that fight out."

Frowning, Cassie grabbed the dustpan, dropped to the floor and held it for Grandma. "I can tell you one thing. Every time I think about this, I get mad."

A mischievous smile lit Grandma's face. She leaned back on the broom and winked. "Maybe your anger is there for a purpose."

Cassie left her grandparent's house deep in thought. "Lord, I really don't know how to fight for Jeff. Please help. I've prayed for him, but nothing's changed. He's backed off. Something's definitely bothering him."

You backed off too.

"I know. But what else can I do?"

Communicate.

"What?"

Tell him how you feel.

"I don't think I can do that," she said. "Besides, that's not my job. The guy's supposed to declare his feelings first."

Back at her apartment, Cassie packed what she needed to go home for the week. Humming a tune, she threw her duffle bag into the backseat of her car and took off. Car windows halfway down, fresh spring air tossed her curls and soothed her troubled thoughts. She inhaled, flipped on the radio and began to sing.

The yellow Toyota bounced into the long driveway of the Watson ranch thirty minutes later. Cassie gasped.

Jeff's blue pickup was parked by the front porch.

She hesitated.

Bag in hand, she looked up just in time to see Jeff come out of the house and grab his luggage from the bed of his pick-up. At the sight of his athletic figure and dark good looks, her heart raced. How she missed those twinkling blue eyes. And that flashing smile.

Their eyes met.

No smile.

He nodded curtly, then turned away to enter the house.

She froze.

Grandma was right. This was no time for timidity. She pursed her lips. It was one thing for him to ignore her, but he was not going to give her the cold shoulder in the presence of her own family. Not if she had anything to do with it.

It was time for a new strategy.

Head high, she flipped her hair over her shoulder and marched toward the house with new resolve.

At the front door, she announced, "Mom, I'm home!"

"I'm in here, Cassie!" Her mother said from the kitchen.

Without hesitation, she pressed on, straight for the kitchen and her mother.

She stopped. Jeff sat at the table, lounging in the chair with his long legs stretched out before him. Duffle bag at his feet, he turned a glass of water with his fingers, staring at its contents.

Facing him boldly, she dropped her bag.

"Hi Jeff!" she said with forced flippancy. "You don't look too good. When was the last time you got your hair cut?"

Her mother gasped.

No one breathed.

Jeff's eyes flew to hers, before darting away. Darkness and torment dwelt in their blue depths. He forced a nervous laugh, eyes returning to stare at his water glass.

Glancing briefly at her mother, Cassie caught her disapproving look.

She cleared her throat. "I'll be up in my room unpacking."

She crossed over, kissed her mother on the cheek, picked up her bag and fled.

Upstairs, Cassie pushed her bedroom door open with her foot and tossed the bag aside. She stood with her back against the closed door and exhaled slowly. "This isn't going to be easy. But I refuse to allow things to go on as they are. He's not going to give me the silent treatment in my own home."

After unpacking, she ran a brush through her hair, applied fresh lip-gloss, returned downstairs and bounced into the kitchen.

Jeff had left her mother alone.

"Where's Hannah?" A smile pasted on her face, forced cheerfulness laced her voice. "Anything I can do to help with supper?"

At the sink peeling carrots, her mother gave her a sidelong glance, questioning and scolding at the same time.

Cassie sighed, crossed over to the kitchen table and fell into the chair Jeff had occupied earlier. "Mom, this is between Jeff and me. You wouldn't understand. What's he doing here anyway?"

Her mother turned and faced her squarely. "What do you

mean, 'What's he doing here?' Your father invited him! We needed some extra help this week. He always helps out when he can and usually enjoys himself when he's here. What's going on with you two anyway? Come on, Cassie, making comments about his looks in that snitty little tone of voice? You sounded like you were trying to pick a fight."

"Maybe I was," Cassie said. "Mom, would you please leave this between the two of us?"

"I don't want to interfere in your affairs," her mother said. "But Cassie, remember, he's our guest."

"Don't worry, Mom. I'll try to remember."

For a moment, she sat silent, studying her mother, busy preparing supper.

She stiffened. "But you have to admit, he hasn't looked good lately. All he does is frown. And he does need a haircut!"

THE PRECIPICE

Better is open rebuke than hidden love.   *Prov. 27:5*

"So, Jeff, what have you been up to lately?" Cassie asked, her fork full of salad. "You sure have been making yourself scarce."

Billy had returned from Spokane just in time for dinner. He looked at Jeff. His friend's presence was a pleasant surprise, but he sat stiff, avoiding Cassie's gaze. It was good to see the guy, but was he all right? It was like he wanted to crawl under the table.

"You must be hiding something," Cassie said, a teasing lilt to her voice.

Surprised, Billy met her eyes.

He recognized that glint. This was not exactly friendly teasing. Something was up.

"Jeff?" she said.

His mother threw a desperate look to his father.

"That's enough, Cassie," his father's soft voice interjected.

Billy cleared his throat. "Uncle Dean says 'hi.' He's thinking about doing a project in Wallua Crossing. He thought maybe you and I could help out some this summer, Jeff. Make a little extra money."

Jeff grunted.

"So, what do you think?"

His father shot a glance at his mother, a slight smirk on the edge of his lips.

"Jeff?" Billy looked directly at him, intent on a response.

The poor guy looked like he was going to throw up.

Jeff shook himself. "Huh?"

"Don't you think it's a good idea?"

"I think it's a great idea," Joey interjected from across the table. "I'll help."

"What?" Jeff said.

Billy grunted and turned away. "I get the feeling you're not listening."

Jeff turned pink. "Sorry. I think I need some fresh air." He picked up his plate and utensils, set them on the kitchen counter, retrieved his jacket and took off out the back door.

Billy looked at Cassie. She didn't seem to be paying any attention. He took a deep breath and let it out slowly. She must be up to her old tricks again. Puzzled, he studied her. He'd never seen her so insensitive. It was obvious that Jeff was in bad shape. He'd tried to talk to him on the phone a few times in the past three months, but Jeff was evasive.

Something was wrong.

He finished his supper. After clearing off his dishes, he grabbed his sweatshirt and followed his friend.

"Jeff, what's going on? Are you ever going to tell me what's eating you?"

Jeff leaned against the barn, face troubled and distant. After staring in silence at the sun setting over the mountains, he picked up a stick and whittled aimlessly with his pocket knife.

"It's Cass, isn't it?"

Jeff looked up briefly, then returned to whittling.

He looked . . . tortured.

"I knew it," he said. "You've been down lately, haven't you?

Don't go getting all worked up over her. There are other fish in the sea. Come on, let's play a game of ping-pong."

Jeff scowled and dropped the stick. Slowly, he folded his knife, put it back in his pocket and followed Billy to the shop.

The sun was beginning to light the eastern sky that morning, when Jeff left the house and entered the barn. After throwing the saddle on Blackfoot, he led him out, stopping around the corner to tighten and adjust it.

The back door opened and Cassie appeared, but didn't see him. At the barn door, she jumped.

Their eyes met.

"Hi, Cassie."

"Well at least I see you can still talk."

He turned and tightened the cinch with a jerk.

Cassie approached and stood behind him. "Jeff, this is stupid. What's wrong?"

"Who said anything's wrong?"

"It's obvious," she said. "You've been avoiding me for three months. You've been avoiding everybody. What's bugging you?"

Setting his jaw, he lifted himself into the saddle.

"It's none of your business."

Cassie gasped. "Oh. I see." Eyes filling, she turned swiftly away, opened the barn door and disappeared inside.

Jeff winced, "Cass, wait." But she was gone.

He shook his head.

I didn't really want to talk anyway.

Not knowing what else to do, he mounted the horse and galloped out of the barn-lot, stopping to open and shut the gate. Remounting, he didn't stop running the horse until the far end of the pasture. After opening another gate, he led the horse to a grassy hillside and tied him to a tree.

The sparkling green valley stretched before him, lit by the dawning sun. Snow-capped peaks crowned the velvety softness of new grass on the hills. Crisp mountain air filled his lungs. He let out a long breath, crossed over to a large rock and sat.

"Valley of Peace," he huffed. "'Peace, peace', they say. But the war's still on . . . there is no peace."

My peace I give you . . .

God.

A deep internal longing returned, simmering in his soul.

He looked up. "Father, here I am."

Leaning over, he picked up a stick. "She was hurt. But I can't tell her what's wrong." The stick flew through the air. "Why can't she just leave me alone?"

This wasn't working. But what else could he do? These were his friends and they needed his help. And he needed them. It might be difficult, but it was better than being alone. Or getting wasted. And God knew he was close.

Too close.

He and Cassie would just have to get over it. Ben would never approve. And for good reason.

When you feel like you're sliding, resolve to stay connected.

How many times had he heard Ben say that? It had helped him in the past. He'd even taught it.

Well, it wasn't so easy to do.

Especially now.

His stomach clenched. And drinking and drugs? Of all people, he knew it was a pit that had no bottom. But he wanted to run. To escape. To hide.

Maybe people were right and he was damaged goods.

Or maybe he was too proud to accept his lot in life, take what was given him and be thankful.

Why did he continually want something he couldn't have? What went wrong?

He had been happy and done well.

He had resolved to stay connected.

Now he was barely hanging on.

And so alone.

Linda Watson sat on her front porch, gazing out toward the sunrise. "Oh, Lord, what a week this has been! We've all been so busy and tense. Please give us peace. Especially me. Watching this drama between Cassie and Jeff is wearing me out."

And a full week it had been. Between working cattle, spring plowing, fixing fence and house cleaning, the days and evenings were completely full. Cassie helped outside and also assisted her mother in feeding the crew. She seemed to be enjoying herself in a forced sort of way.

But Jeff wasn't.

Linda was tempted to take him aside and ask what was wrong, but held back. He seemed to be making an effort to relate to the family, but he was avoiding Cassie. And it was not that he didn't care. The tortured looks he sent her way gave her a clue. There was a growing tension between them and Jeff was not in his usual form.

It was probably best she stayed out of it.

"Something's going to happen," she said.

"I agree."

Startled, she turned to see Ben approaching her chair, carrying a fuzzy blanket.

"Warm enough?" He laid it over her lap. "I thought you might need this."

"Thank you. It's chilly this morning." She snuggled under it and smiled. "I was praying about Jeff and Cassie."

"No need to tell me who you were referring to." He settled himself in the chair next to her and snorted. "It's like a volcano building pressure and getting ready to explode."

"Thanks to Cassie," Linda said. "She keeps fueling the fire. I've never seen her so determined to harass someone like she is Jeff."

"That's for sure, but it's been a long time since I've seen Jeff so withdrawn and depressed. I think she's trying to crack his shell."

"She might as well use an ax for all her tact," she said. "I could hardly believe it yesterday while we were working cattle. She wouldn't leave him alone. I thought he was going to bolt a few times, but he seems determined to stick it out. What do you think is troubling him?"

"I'm not sure, but I can guess."

"Why don't you talk to him?"

"I'm waiting for the right opportunity." Ben scratched the top of his head. "Besides, I don't like meddling in this kind of stuff."

Puzzled, Linda turned to look at him. "What kind of stuff?"

"You know, Jeff and Cassie," he said. "I don't know. It's just awkward."

"Ben, something serious is going on with him and it's much more than a problem between him and Cassie."

"That's what Evan said."

Linda's eyebrows rose. "You talked to Pastor Evan?"

"Yeah."

"Really?" she said. "You must be desperate."

A short laugh escaped Ben's lips. "You might say that. I visited with him on the phone last night and asked him to pray for us. He's concerned about Jeff too."

"What did he suggest?"

"I confided in him about my dilemma and he thought I should talk to him anyway. I tried to get him to deal with this, but he said I was the man for the job. He said he'd pray for me, but I was the one with relationship and I should handle it. He said if I love the kid, I'll have faith that God will work it out."

"So when are you going to talk to him?"

"Like I said, I'm waiting for the right opportunity."

Linda looked skeptical. "What has God told you about this?"

Ben went silent.

"Probably more than I'm willing to admit," he finally said. Crossing his legs, he leaned back in the chair and rubbed his chin.

Linda wagged her head. "Well, you'd better start listening."

Scanning the wet landscape, he heaved a sigh.

Linda reached for his hand. "Father, please take care of this situation with Jeff and Cassie. Bless them with the desires of their hearts. And please, give Ben his opportunity soon."

Sounds of stirring within the house interrupted their morning interlude. They entered the house to prepare breakfast and a sleepy-eyed Jeff stood at the kitchen counter, micro-waving oatmeal and buttering toast.

He turned and acknowledged their presence. "Morning," he said. "I wanted to get an early start on the fencing."

Linda turned towards the refrigerator, hiding a smile.

And get out of here before Cassie gets up.

"That one section on the west eighty is pretty bad and going to take a lot of work."

Ben sat at the kitchen table. "Sounds good."

As soon as Jeff settled himself to eat, Cassie bounced into the kitchen. "Looks like a beautiful day!" She smiled with gaiety and forced cheerfulness. Predictably, she focused on Jeff. "How are you this morning, Jeff?"

"Fine," he said to his oatmeal.

"Daddy, what's on the agenda?" She crossed over to the kitchen cupboard and pulled out a frying pan.

"I figure Jeff and Billy can finish fixing fence while you and Hannah prepare Mom's garden spot. Joey and I will feed. Then I'll help him do some mechanic work on the tractor."

Cassie turned to Jeff. "Do you guys need a lunch?"

He ignored her.

"Jeff?" She walked over to where he sat.

Suddenly, Billy interrupted. "A lunch would be great." His eyes met hers in a look of warning.

Cassie frowned. "Okay. I'll pack it for you." She turned and opened the refrigerator.

❧ ❦ ❧

The late afternoon sun cast long shadows in the trees as Jeff hammered the last staple for a section of barbed wire fence. "Billy, I'm going to follow this section up the hill and check it out. I think I can get it if you want to go back and start the feeding."

"Are you sure?"

"Yeah," he said. "If it needs a lot of work, we'll come back tomorrow and finish. Go ahead and take the pick-up. I'll walk back. It's not that far. Besides, that section is easier to walk than drive. If I can't fix it, I can at least figure out what we'll need to get it done."

"Fine with me," Billy said, turning to leave. "See you at dinner."

Retreating into hard work and a fog of passivity, Jeff had found a certain safety, but Cassie was making it difficult to stay there. Increasingly agitated, he wanted time alone. To think.

Along the fence-row, he prayed, "God, what am I doing here? I knew it would be tough, but this . . ."

He trudged up the hill. Around the bend, he came to a basalt cliff with a severe drop-off. Jeff didn't normally have a fear of heights, but there was something about this cliff and its loose shale that unnerved him. He shuddered.

At the top of the rocky cliff, the fence was in complete disrepair. His life seemed like that fence, barely functional and hanging on the edge of a slippery slope.

It was a bad place to have a fence down. A cow or calf could slide over the edge. Posts were hard to drive here, so it took some creativity to keep the fence in shape. He pulled one upright, propped it with rocks and stapled the sagging wire, trying to make do. They would have to come back the next day with more materials.

Clattering hooves crossing loose shale interrupted his thoughts. His head shot up to see Cassie on Ginger, coming straight towards him.

"Cassie, what are you doing out here?" he asked as she passed.

Dark eyes bored into his. "I'm out for a ride."

He turned back to his work, rolled his eyes and let out a long, deep breath.

Not again.

He'd seen that look before.

She was on a mission.

His back to her, he continued hammering and pulling sagging

wire, avoiding the inevitable. He heard her stop, dismount and tie her horse to a tree.

From behind, she spoke. "I see you've got some problems here."

"I'm going to have to come back to fix this right," Jeff said. "More posts and braces are needed. It'll definitely need some work before the cattle are turned in."

"Jeff, what's wrong?"

"I suppose the snow broke the fence down," he said.

"Don't give me that! You know what I mean. What's wrong?"

"I can't tell you right now."

"You can tell me. You just won't!"

He turned around and faced her.

Hands on her hips, she challenged him. A ponytail pulled her hair from her face, emphasizing the set of her tilted chin and the determined flash of her eyes.

He wasn't going to get out of this easily.

"Okay, I won't then." He turned to tack the wire to another post.

Suddenly, she was across the fence, facing him from the other side.

"Cassie! Get back over here! It's not safe! The rocks are loose!"

"I want to talk to you."

"Talk away. But get back over here!"

"No. I want you to look at me when I'm talking to you."

He stood still. She had stepped back . . . Close to the edge. His heart tightened. "Cassie—"

"This whole thing stinks. And I mean really stinks!" She folded her arms. "You've changed, Jeff. And not for the good. I think you're listening to the devil. You used to be so full of life and now you smell like death! What happened to you?"

"Cassie, come away from the edge," he said, his voice sharp.

"No! I want you to listen to me. Why do you insist on taking this dark cloud with you wherever you go?"

What did she know about what he was going through? He threw down his tools.

"Dammit, Cassie!"

"Oh . . . strong language? Impressive!" she said with fake shock and admiration. Feet spread, she maintained her stance. "Damn what? Why not *damn* this passive thing that has a hold on you?"

Jeff tossed his gloves to the ground. "Get over here," he said, eyes finally fixed on hers. "Shut up and get back over here!"

Now that she had his attention, Cassie moved away from the edge and closer to the fence-line, face close to his. "I thought you had dreams," she said. "I thought you were different from other guys. I thought you were a fighter and would fight for what you wanted. But no. You gave up! You're sliding into a pit. You're choosing to do so!"

Jeff set his jaw, fists clenching at his sides. "That's enough, Cassie. Get back over here!"

"And if I don't?" She swiped her face with the back of her sleeve.

His nose came within inches of hers. "I'll come over and get you and you won't like it."

Her chin lifted. "Oh? Why not?"

His thumb pointed over his shoulder. "I'll take you to that log over there and turn you over my knee!"

Her eyes rolled before returning to lock with his. "You wouldn't dare."

They stood staring at each other, faces close. A sad, dilapidated barbed-wire fence sagged between them. For a moment, the humor of the situation struck him. Thumbs in his pockets, he looked down at his muddy boots, a small smile playing at his lips. He drew back.

But she would have none of it. She pressed on.

"Jeff, the way you're acting you're no better than your father."

His head shot up.

"I know you don't drink or do drugs, but why not, for all the misery you're in?"

"Cassie, I'm warning you—"

"Why not go the full distance and drink yourself to death like he did? After all, what kind of life—"

That did it. He grabbed her arm and lifted one leg to straddle the sagging fence. She struggled against him, but his arm moved to clench her waist and the other one went under her knees to toss her to the other side. In the process, the leg of her jeans snagged the barbed wire. She bent and attempted to free herself, but he grabbed her from behind.

"Jeff! Let go of me!" Cassie dug at his hands with her fingernails, trying to pry them loose.

The sound of ripping denim didn't distract him when he pulled her away. Tossing her over his shoulder, he headed for the trees.

"Put me down! Put me down!"

Fists pounded and legs flailed, but Jeff ignored them. At the log, he slid her down to stand in front of him without letting go of her arm. Dodging her kicks, he held her at arm's length, retaining his grip. A downward glance caught the defiance in her flashing eyes. Trying to yank her arm loose, she fought with all her strength.

"Let go of me!" she screamed. "Don't you dare!"

The sharp toe of her boot caught him in the shin and he flinched. He turned her around, pulled her closer and spread his feet, arms tight around her waist from behind.

Gritting his teeth, he lowered himself to sit. Roughly, he forced her over his lap face down and braced his left arm over her upper body, wedging her between his thighs to protect himself from flailing boots.

He hesitated.

"Jeff! No! Don't do this! Stop!" She fought against him, feet kicking and fingernails clawing.

"I'm not stopping now!" he said. "I warned you, remember?"

Pent-up anger and frustration broke loose. He freed his right hand and started landing blows to the seat of her jeans with his palm.

"Ouch! . . . You're hurting me! . . . Jeff! . . . Stop!"

For a short time, she squirmed and fought, but it only served to feed his anger. Finally she went silent, surrendering to his superior strength. He continued.

Until his anger was spent.

Or did he stop because of the burning pain in his hand?

He tossed her on a soft bed of rotted fir needles.

"Now get on your horse and go home!"

He stepped back, his breath coming in deep, rapid gasps, his face hot.

A rumpled heap on the ground, Cassie lay quiet, then slowly rose to her feet. Mustering up a bit of dignity, she brushed off her jacket and jeans and shook the needles from her bedraggled pony tail. Chin quivering, she glared at him.

"You . . . JERK!"

Eyes full, she gritted her teeth as angry tears escaped down her face.

"Don't you ever touch me again!"

She hurried to Ginger, pulled the reins loose, jumped into the saddle and galloped home.

THE DUST SETTLES

See to it that no one misses the grace of God and that no bitter root grows up to cause trouble and defile many.   *Hebrews 12:15*

Jeff watched Cassie's retreat in silence. He dropped down on the log and stared blankly at the trees where she had disappeared.

Grim reality struck. The adrenaline rush ebbed away and his head fell into quivering hands. A deep groan escaped from the depths of his soul. "Oh, God! What have I done?"

Slowly he rose, returned to the fence line, and picked up the gloves and tools he had tossed aside. He hung them on his belt and pocketed the extra staples.

Long pliers flopped against one thigh and a hammer handle beat against the other as he descended the fence row. Thudding boots and jangling tools were the only witnesses to his torment. He emerged from the trees, looked toward the sky and growled.

"I give up," he said. "I'm sick of this whole thing . . . I've failed. I just can't do this and I'm tired of trying!"

He was such a fool. Why did he come back here anyway?

Getting wasted would have been easier.

Okay, maybe not in the long-run.

Long-run? Who cared about the long-run?

What a mess he'd made. He didn't want to lose the Watson's friendship, but how could he face them now? And Cassie . . . the little twit!

Trudging down the fence line, Jeff vented. Who was he trying to fool? He didn't belong with these people.

What happened back there? She touched a nerve and he'd lost it. Why did she have to bring up his father? She knew that was a sore spot. She had no right to talk to him like that.

"This is hell!" he said. "Why can't she leave well enough alone? She has no *respect*!"

But why should she respect him? He'd been rotten to her. He'd ignored her and avoided her. He'd been downright rude. He'd tried everything to put her off. But what else could he do? He wasn't qualified for a good woman anyway.

And now she'd never forgive him. Let alone Ben or Billy.

Jeff stopped.

Tall trees, like sentinels, guarded the barn in the growing shadows.

The ranch.

A long, tortured breath escaped his lips. He spied his blue pickup in the driveway. Right where he left it.

I want to just—

But that wouldn't help.

Cassie or no Cassie, they were like family.

And Billy was his best friend. They hadn't rejected him yet. Shoulders squared, he released another breath. "I'm done running.

"All right God. Cover me, I'm going in."

Resigned to their fate, his boots marched on.

⁂

Jeff quietly entered the back door and left it ajar.

Linda appeared. "Hello, Jeff. It's about time for dinner. Here, I'll get the door." After closing it, she returned to the kitchen.

He removed his coat and boots, rolled up his sleeves and washed his hands. While lathering his forearms, he heard Linda call from the other room, "Billy, would you go upstairs and tell Cassie dinner's ready?"

Jeff swallowed hard and looked toward heaven. He slowly rinsed and dried his hands, then headed for the table. Ben and Linda went silent when he approached. Hannah and Joey both looked at him, worried expressions on their faces.

Moments later, Billy entered the kitchen wagging his head. "I don't know what the trouble is, but Cassie's pretty upset. She says she's not hungry."

All eyes turned to Jeff.

He studied his glass of water.

Ben thanked God for the food and each passed their plate to Linda, who served them casserole from a large dish at her end of the table.

Jeff focused on his food.

"Hey, Jeff," Joey said. "What happened to your hand?"

Jeff glanced down. Red scratches covered the tops of both hands. He gulped. He hadn't even noticed!

"I don't know. Must've done that fencing."

Taking a deep breath, he tried to relax, but was suddenly aware of throbbing in his shin. His face went hot.

I've got to get out of here!

"How'd the fencing go?" Ben asked.

Without looking up, Jeff forced the food down. He gulped. "Fine. There's still a few spots at the top of the rock ledge that need some help before you turn the cows in, but otherwise it's all done."

"Good. You and Billy can finish it in the morning."

"Uh . . . Actually . . . I'm thinking I need to leave tonight."

Ben's brow lifted. "Oh? Any particular reason?"

Jeff looked up.

All eyes were on him.

He cleared his throat. "Yeah . . . well, it's kind of personal . . ."

Billy interrupted his brief pause. "Cassie."

"Billy, let him talk!" Linda said.

Eyes again focusing on his plate, Jeff poked a green bean with his fork. "He's right. It's Cassie."

Ben leaned back in his chair. "When are you going to tell us what's up?"

Jeff winced, then looked up. "You'll probably want to hear Cassie's version first."

After exchanging puzzled frowns, questioning gazes returned to Jeff.

Ben shrugged. "Suit yourself," he said. "So, you've decided to leave tonight?"

"I think it's best."

Jeff excused himself and headed for the stairs.

⊱ ❧ ❦ ⊰

Billy watched his parents retreat to the porch.

A worried frown on her face, Hannah began clearing the table.

A somber Joey headed out the back door.

Billy sat at the table. Left alone. Ankles crossed and hands in his pockets, he stretched his legs under the table and leaned back in the chair, taking a moment to think. Exasperated, he let out a long breath, rose and climbed the stairs.

Thumbs in his pockets, he leaned against the doorframe and watched Jeff finish packing.

"Look, Jeff," he said, "I consider you one of my best friends. You and I both know you haven't been doing so well lately. What'd you do, lose your head over my little sister?"

Jeff looked up from stuffing the last of his clothing into his bag. "That's right."

He pushed past Billy and strode down the hall. Billy caught up to him and placed a hand on his shoulder.

Jeff stopped and turned.

"Hey man," Billy said. "We'll get through this . . . I'll be in touch."

Nodding blankly, Jeff turned around, descended the stairs and

146

disappeared out the front door.

"Cass? It's Billy."

"Go away!"

"I'd like to talk to you."

"Go away!"

"Come on, Cass," he said through the bedroom door. "Can I come in? Are you dressed?"

Cassie buttoned the top of her pajamas. "Oh, all right. Come in."

Cautiously, Billy peered into the room. "Are you okay?"

"No."

"What's going on?" he said, shutting the door behind him.

"Oh, nothing. Just had a big fight with your best friend, that's all." She sniffled and turned sore eyes back to her book.

"What did you do, ride out to where he was fixing fence?"

"Yeah," she said. "That I did."

"Cassie, why don't you leave him alone? You've been harassing him all week. Can't you see he's in love with you?"

Her eyes darted to his. "Did he tell you that?"

"Not exactly." He lowered himself to sit on the edge of the bed.

She returned to her book. "I didn't think so."

"Does the idea bother you so much?"

Groaning, Cassie threw the book down, turned toward the wall, and pulled the blankets over her head. "I don't know what I want anymore," she said from under the covers. "Besides, now I've made things worse. He hates me!"

"I doubt that . . . What happened?"

Cassie let out a long breath, shoved down the covers, sat up and folded her legs. "That's a good question," she said. "It's the weirdest thing ever. I thought I was really starting to like him. In fact, I was beginning to believe I was in love with him. Then he just—"

"Whoa! Wait a minute! You mean you *like* Jeff?" Billy stood and paced the floor, running a hand through his hair. "Why didn't you tell me?"

"Billy, are you kidding? You didn't know? It's obvious to everyone else!"

"How was I to know? You've been a brat this week, badgering him—"

"I was trying to get him to come out of it. He's not okay. Haven't you noticed?"

Billy stopped and faced her. "Yeah, but I thought it was because he liked you. If you like him, then what's the problem?"

She folded her arms. "Like I was about to say, he shut down. He won't talk to me or anything."

Sighing, he flopped into the overstuffed chair in the corner. "I have a feeling I've made this thing a whole lot worse, Cass. I've been discouraging him about you. I didn't know you were interested."

"Billy, how can you be so socially retarded?" She shrugged. "Oh well. It probably doesn't matter that much. Everything's so confusing with him."

Cassie sniffled, grabbed a tissue and blew her nose. Voice congested, she continued, "It probably wouldn't have worked out anyway."

"Cass, I'm sorry about this. I haven't connected with you in a long time. I guess I kept thinking about my other friends who liked you—"

She held up a hand. "I know, I know. Please don't! Don't go there."

"Would you like me to say something to Jeff about this?"

"No. Not now. I don't know what I feel anymore."

Billy rose and walked over to the bed. "Whatever happens, Cass, you're still my little sister. You let me know if I can do anything to help, okay?"

Cassie nodded. "Thanks, Billy."

Leaning over, he kissed her on the cheek. "I love you, Sis."

She sniffled. "I love you too."

A soft knock sounded at the bedroom door.

"Come in," Cassie called from her bed.

Her father opened the door. "Hey, I didn't know you had company," he said, peering at Billy through the open door.

"I was just leaving."

Cassie grabbed his hand and squeezed it before he left the room.

Her father sat in the corner chair, which Billy had just vacated. "Are you okay, Sweetie?"

"A little better."

"Do you want to tell me what happened?" Leaning back, he made himself comfortable, crossing his ankle over his knee.

"I don't know, Daddy," she said. "Why don't you ask Jeff?"

"Jeff thought I should hear your version first."

Cassie straightened. "Oh, he did, did he? That sounds just like something he would say. 'Let Cassie tell you what happened. Don't ask me—'"

"Whoa!" her father said. "Hold on! I do want to hear your version first. I think it's time you tell me what's going on."

"Why don't you get Jeff in here too? I'd like to know myself!"

"He left."

Cassie's eyes widened. "He left?"

"Yeah. I thought I'd go see him tomorrow."

Her face fell. "Oh. Did he say anything before he left?"

"He was upset about something between you and him. He said it was personal."

Groaning, Cassie sank down in the bed.

"Oh, Daddy! I really blew it! I lost my temper and said some really mean things. Grandma said to fight for him, but I got a little carried away."

"Grandma? You talked to your *grandmother* about this?"

"Yeah. I visited her before coming home and she said I should fight for Jeff. I guess I fought *with* him instead of for him."

"I see." He rubbed his chin. "Go on, I'm listening."

"I thought God told me to tell him how I felt. But I don't think what I said was exactly what he had in mind. Anyway, I said some really mean things and uh . . . Jeff, he . . . Daddy, he might have changed his mind about me before, but now I think he hates me!" Voice shaking, a tear spilled down her cheek.

"Changed his mind?"

She swiped the tear with her pajama sleeve. "We . . . uh . . . were getting really close over the holidays. You noticed, didn't you?"

"Yeah. I noticed."

"I thought I . . . was falling in love with him. I never told him. But all of a sudden he shut down and started avoiding me. He liked me, Daddy. And he knew I liked him. But something happened.

"We talked about everything. He was strong. I trusted him. He was there for me. He made me feel special. He was wonderful. Then . . . nothing!" She choked back another sob.

Her father rose from the chair, walked over to the bed and sat beside her. "When did this all start going downhill?"

"Right after Christmas. Then he got depressed or something." She reached for another tissue.

"I noticed that too."

"What do you think's wrong?" she asked, wiping her eyes.

"I can only guess," he said. "So, what happened today?"

"I rode out to the fence where he was working . . . and we . . . had a confrontation." She looked down and twisted the tissue.

"A confrontation?"

"Yeah. I'd call it that."

Glancing to where her jeans were hung on a hook, her father asked, "Is that how you ripped your jeans?"

Cassie paled. The jeans! She hadn't thought to hide them!

She fiddled with the tissue and cleared her throat. "Uh . . . my jeans got caught in the barbed wire where he was working and he, . . . uh, pulled me away from the fence while we were arguing and uh, ripped them."

He studied her. "I get the feeling you aren't telling me

everything."

She looked away. "No, Daddy. I'm not. I confronted him and got . . . a little carried away. He got really mad and we had a . . . uh, fight." Sniffling, she stared at the twisted tissue. "It was pretty intense."

"I can imagine." He fell silent. Then his calloused hand lifted her chin and turned her face to his. "Are you going to be all right?"

"Yeah, Daddy. I'll be okay."

Dropping his hand, he rose to his feet. "Are you sure you don't want anything to eat?"

Cassie shook her head. "I'm fine right here for tonight."

"How about if I send your mother up with a cup of tea and some toast?"

Cassie giggled softly. "That would be nice. I guess it's her turn to visit the 'patient.'"

Smiling, he kissed her on the cheek and turned to leave the room.

"Daddy, don't tell him."

He stopped and turned back. "Don't tell who?"

"Uh . . . You know . . . Jeff. When you talk to him, don't tell him I'm in love with him. I may have changed my mind about that. I don't want him to know."

Her father smiled and opened the door.

"Your secret's safe with me, Sweetheart."

"Thanks, Daddy."

HEARTS RETURN

They will be my people, and I will be their God, for they
will return to me with all their heart.   *Jeremiah 24:7*

Blankly, Jeff stared at the highway, slouching in the seat. His right hand gripped the steering wheel and the opposite elbow hung on the edge of the window.

He passed a slow moving truck.

Suddenly, the palm of his hand struck the steering wheel. "The cat's out of the bag and it's about time! I'm scared to death, but at least now something has to give!"

Both hands grabbed the wheel. "God, I'm just not strong! I'm sick of trying to be who you want me to be. I'm always trying to be somebody I'm not. I'm a . . . poser! I'm tired of faking it!

"Who did I think I was hanging out with the Watsons or falling for someone like Cassie? But you told me to go back. Was that just to show me how weak and corrupt I am?

"I'm so ashamed. I keep polluting myself. I feel dirty. Rotten! My heart's sick! But I'm not strong enough to quit. And if Ben hadn't called me to help on the ranch, I'd probably be drinking right now. That's what I want to do. After all I've been through. After all I've promised myself. What's wrong with me?

"And why did I get so angry? I hit Cassie! I wanted to hit her harder! I swore I'd never do that to a woman. I thought I had dealt with this thing with my father, but I guess not. I'm just like him! Maybe I should never marry. But I'm so alone! Oh God, Please, forgive me! . . . Help me!"

Eyes blurring with tears, his breath came in painful gasps and it was difficult to drive. Spotting a turnout, he pulled off the road and parked.

Unwelcomed emotion gripped him like a giant octopus and his chest constricted. The pressure steadily increased. Tentacles of hidden grief squeezed tighter and tighter, forcing tears from his eyes.

Forehead collapsing on the steering wheel, he gasped for breath. "What a waste . . . these last few months . . . have been! I thought . . . I was delivered . . . from this garbage!"

Years of restraint gave way and gut-wrenching sobs convulsed through his body . . . His failures . . . His frustrations . . . His weaknesses . . . His anger . . . His father . . . His mother.

Jeff.

He looked up. "God?"

Return to me, Jeff.

"But I can't . . . I can't do it."

Let me do it.

"Let you do it?"

Surrender.

"Okay . . . I give up."

The pressure immediately eased. Jeff heaved a ragged sigh and wiped his face with his flannel shirt-sleeve.

Will you let me go deeper?

"I don't know, Lord. What do you mean?"

Will you let me rid you of the root and not just the fruit?

Closing his eyes, Jeff leaned back. "Sure," he said. "I've ruined everything. Do what you want. I'm done."

In the silence, his heart opened to God. Grief subsided and peace enveloped him. Peace he hadn't known for months. When his eyes finally opened, the sun had sunk behind the mountain, but his heart was light.

Light!

A long breath escaped. He started the engine and turned on the lights. "Thank you, Jesus," he said, and pulled back onto the highway.

⁂

The door to Cassie's bedroom opened and her mother entered, bearing a tray laden with buttered toast, a boiled egg and a cup of tea. "How's our patient?"

"Better." Cassie sat up in bed and smiled. "I should try this more often. I haven't received so much tender loving care in a long time. Actually, I feel a lot better."

After gathering pillows and propping them behind Cassie's back, her mother placed the tray on her lap.

Cassie immediately reached for a piece of toast.

Her mother sat on the side of the bed. "We've been praying for you, Cassie. And for Jeff. What happened this afternoon?"

Cassie choked. The toast was suddenly too dry and she reached for her tea. "Trust you to get right to the point."

After taking a sip, she remained silent, twirling the teacup with her fingers.

Her mother waited.

"Mom, did Daddy ever spank you?"

"*Spank* me?" She laughed. "Not really. He may have come close a time or two, maybe a slap on the bottom when he thought I was a little too sassy." She paused. "But no, he's never really spanked me."

Cassie huffed. "I didn't think so. He respects you too much to do something like that."

"So that's what happened?" Her mother studied her. "He spanked you?"

Cassie nodded. "He was well provoked, Mom, but that's what

he did."

"I can imagine," she said. "Did he hurt you?"

"Well, sort of. It stung for a while, but that's not the point. I've never been so humiliated in all my life!"

Her mother smirked. "That couldn't hurt."

"Mom!"

"Cassie, some of the things I've heard you say, I wouldn't have dared say to a young man, especially at this stage of a relationship."

"But Mom, don't you think this is over the edge? Should I forgive him?"

"Of course you need to forgive him," she said, "for your own sake. As for it being over the edge, that's something only you can decide. Talk to your grandmother. I've heard tales about her courtship with your grandfather. It was pretty wild."

Cassie smiled. "It must've been. I can guess what she'd say."

"Did you tell your father about this?"

Cassie shook her head. "No. I couldn't bring myself to tell him. Jeff can tell him. He can confess his own sins."

"Are you sure he'll tell him?"

Cassie nodded and took another bite of her toast. "He'll tell him."

"I don't know what your father will think. But it probably won't set too well with him. He's pretty protective."

"I know."

Her mother smiled. "He also surprises me sometimes."

❧ ❦ ❧

Early Friday morning, Jeff opened the door of his apartment and stepped out into the crisp air. A cool breeze blew and he inhaled the fresh, clean aromas of spring. After sinking into a lawn chair near his front door, he zipped up his jacket and pulled out his Bible. This morning he felt different. Though it was a cold, overcast day, the warmth of hope rose within him.

He opened his Bible and read:

"There is no fear in love. For perfect love drives out fear, because fear has to do with punishment. The one who fears is not made perfect in love."

If there is no fear in love, why was he so afraid? What was he missing?

His eyes lifted from the Bible. Purple and white crocuses poked sturdy heads through soggy dead foliage. Budding trees promised new life and birds chirped from their perches. Smells of wet earth embraced him.

"Father, I know you love me and I want to love others, but fear is consuming me." Jeff frowned. "It's driving out love. "

What do you fear?

"Shame. Failure." He paused. "I'm afraid I'm not good enough."

Good enough for who?

"Ben, Billy, Cassie . . . even you."

Who said you weren't good enough?

"It's obvious. My family's messed up. I don't even know what normal is. I'm so insecure. I'm angry. Half the time all I want to do is get drunk. Escape. I really lost it with Cassie. And I don't even want to read the Bible or go to church anymore!"

"And the pornography. I let myself get addicted. Again. Most of the time I don't even care. It was bad before, but after all this time and all you've done for me—"

Do you remember when you first came to me?

"Yeah."

Did I love you because of your great qualifications?

"No. I had none. It was only because of your mercy and grace."

Then why are you looking to your qualifications now?

Jeff paused.

"But how I was raised affects me. Ben and Billy don't think I'm good enough for Cassie. Not for a permanent relationship. Ben never has really trusted me. And for good reason. I'm damaged goods."

Do you believe I want to bless you with the best?

"I've been taught that, but—"

Then why do you hang on so tight to so little?

Jeff exhaled. "I don't know . . . I guess I don't really believe it. Help me."

He continued reading, "We love because he first loved us."

"So, love for others only comes from receiving your love? How can I get more? How do I receive more?"

He leafed through his Bible and came to a passage he had underlined several years earlier.

"'Be careful how you listen, because to him who has, more will be given and to him who has not, even what he has will be taken away.'"

He set his Bible aside. Elbows on his knees and head in his hands, he stared at his feet.

What was this all about? He was confused.

Leaning back in his chair, he closed his eyes.

A clear picture formed in his mind. He sat beside a great banquet table, holding a crumb of bread with his right hand. The luscious food was at his left elbow. Focused on the crumb, he squeezed it tightly in his fist, while pushing the table away. His hand opened and he looked for the crumb, but it was gone.

Faint music brought him back. How long had he been sitting there? Shaking himself, he listened. His phone!

Quickly, he stood and reached into his pocket.

"Hello?"

"Jeff, it's Ben."

His heart stopped, then raced. He swallowed. "Oh . . . hi."

"I'm coming over this afternoon."

"Oh?" he said, forcing a superficial calm. "What time?"

"About one-thirty."

"Uh . . ." Jeff's mouth went dry. "Okay."

"Great. See you then."

Heading for the door he glanced at his phone. Eight-thirty. He had five hours. Maybe five hours left to live! Letting out a short laugh, he braced himself. "I'm going to face this, even if it kills me.

"God help me," he said, surveying his apartment. The disarray certainly reflected his recent state of mind. "Where do I start with this mess?"

Arms loaded with a stack of old pizza boxes and other trash, he headed for the recycle bin.

༒ ❦ ❧ ༒

The sun had not yet penetrated the thick, gray clouds when Cassie awoke. Thoughts of the previous day closed in on her as she lay in bed, staring at the ceiling.

She groaned. "Lord, are you upset with me? I was mean to Jeff yesterday."

Unable to find relief in her rehearsal of the episode with Jeff, she sat up and reached for her Bible. Opening it casually, her eyes fell to an underlined verse.

Better is open rebuke than hidden love.

A surge of self-justification swept through her. She sat up straighter.

"Yeah!"

But her self-adulation was cut short.

"If it's so much better, Lord, why is everything such a mess now? And it's worse than ever. He was so mad, he spanked me!"

The absurdity hit and she let out a short laugh. "I can't believe he did that! He's always been controlled. Mr. Cool in a crisis. Levelheaded. At least somewhat mannerly."

She shook her head. "I provoked him, but how can I trust someone who treats me like that?"

Flipping the page, she spotted another verse and read it out loud. "Starting a quarrel is like breeching a dam, so drop the matter before a dispute breaks out."

"I think I broke the dam," she said.

At the next underlined verse, Cassie muttered, "Oh no, I'm in trouble."

"A fool's lips bring him strife and his mouth invites a beating."

Her Bible slammed shut and she plopped it on the bedside table. Eyes closed, she buried her face in her hands.

The look on his face across that fence had warned her.

She had pushed him too far.

158

But she was curious as to what he would do.

Now she knew.

It had never occurred to her she could end up so out of control. With a wry look of self-acceptance, she opened her eyes.

"I've always been an experiential learner. Jesus, have mercy on me!"

Arms folded, she lay thinking.

Suddenly, she sat upright.

"I'm glad I did it. Somehow I had to crack that disgusting passive attitude! At least now he's fighting back!"

Cassie got up and dressed. She was going for a ride. Fresh air would clear out the cobwebs. Give her another perspective.

⁂

Ben reflected on the events of the past week as he pulled his pickup onto the highway and headed for Wallua Crossing. The smell of freshly watered earth lingered in the air. Bright sun shone through fluffy white clouds in a deep blue sky. It was a cheery display, but his heart was heavy. Jeff's withdrawal, depression, passivity and obvious torment grieved him.

What hurt most was that familiar dark look. More than grief and hurt, that look incited *fear*. Ben had seen it before. On the face of Jeff's father, John.

John Carson.

Classmates all the way through school, he and John were close friends when they were young. Both came to know Jesus at summer camp. He smiled, thinking about the pranks they'd pulled in high school and the fun they had playing together on the basketball team, especially the year they won the state championship. They'd been friends into their twenties and had loved to brag about their exploits.

But John's father was an alcoholic and life wasn't easy. Abuse, rejection and insecurity hounded him. His parents didn't understand his decision to follow Jesus and mocked him openly, scoffing at his attempts to break out of the family mold. Ben had tried bringing John home when they were teenagers, but John and

Ben's father clashed. His father had tried, but just didn't have the patience for him.

John, retaining wounds from childhood, repeatedly failed in different areas of his life and soon lost heart. Misunderstanding the grace of God and the teachings of the church, he was convinced he wasn't good enough to be a Christian.

When John and Molly lost their oldest son in an accident, John became angry with God and started drinking, something he swore he'd never do. He isolated himself from all his Christian friends and turned his back on God. The drinking increased and eventually led to the accident that killed him.

A lump swelled in Ben's throat and he swallowed. Choosing between their friendship and following God was hard, but he had to let him go. All these years later, it still hurt to remember. Ben suddenly found himself angry. He gripped the steering wheel.

"Not this again, Lord. Where are you? Where were you for John? He was my best friend! Do we only get saved from hell and the rest is up to us? That doesn't sound like your grace. Does anyone ever get better?

"And now it's Jeff," he said. "Don't let him go down too! I know you're a jealous God, *visiting* the iniquity of the fathers on the children, on the third and fourth generation of those who hate you. But Father, you also show loving-kindness to thousands, to those who love you and keep your commands. Jeff doesn't hate you, he loves you. I expect you to show him your kindness!

"If I have anything to do with it, this visit, of his father's sin, will be short. I don't want to wait until he's facing death to see him repent!"

Rehearsing in his mind the times he had seen Jeff lately, he burst forth, "Father, I've left him alone too long. That look he has scares me. I—"

Pull over. I have something to say.

Eyes widening, Ben's heart raced. He slowed down, turned off the highway and parked at the side of the road. Quieting himself, he waited.

Finally, God spoke.

Jeff is my son. Is that not good enough?

"Of course it's good enough, but I'm not sure he believes in who he is. What good is it to be your son if he doesn't believe it?"

Do you believe in who he is?

"Of course I do."

Then why haven't you talked to him?

"I was afraid. He's not going in the right direction. I don't want that for my daughter. I didn't want to encourage him."

Do you believe he is my son?

"Yeah, but he's checked out. He's not doing well."

Do you believe he is my son?

"I believe he's your son, but his dad was an alcoholic and abusive. Sometimes he's so insecure. He's done really well considering, but it's hard when he has so much baggage."

How can my son have 'baggage'?

Stunned, Ben sat up. "Oh my God! He *is* your son! . . . If anyone is in Christ he is a *new creation*."

The old is gone, the new has come.

"I haven't believed! I've been regarding him from a *worldly* point of view. I wouldn't want someone telling me Billy had baggage."

Groaning, Ben winced. "I've been calling him 'Son,' but I've held back my full blessing and the affirmation he needs. I had confidence in him until he started having trouble . . . I abandoned him when he needed me most."

Why do you have faith in your disappointment?

Ben leaned back in the seat. It was no wonder Jeff had fallen and was unable to get back up. Tears moistened his eyes as he thought again of past disappointments with John.

"I did have faith in my disappointments. I focused on them and let them accuse you and your son, Jeff, believing for the worst."

If the worst happened, would you still be okay?

"Yes. I'll be okay, Lord. I trust you.

"I'm sorry for pulling back. I don't understand why these things happen, but I'll believe your words for myself and others. But I've failed him and I've failed you." Ben brushed away falling tears. "Father, forgive me!"

You're forgiven.

"Help me with Jeff. I don't know what to say. I'm not sure if he's the one for Cassie. But this really isn't about *them*, is it? It's about you and me." A wave of love swept over him and he chuckled. "I guess I'm the project.

"And I do love him. He's like a son to me. I want to affirm him. I want him to believe in who he is. And I know you want to deliver and heal him.

"Father, every good thing in my life is from you. I need you. Help me to bless Jeff and have faith for him. *He's* your son and I'll fight for him because *I'm* your son."

Studying the clouds in the blue sky, a song drifted into his mind and he began humming.

Soon he was singing softly.

> *This is the air I breathe . . .*
> *Your holy presence, living in me . . .*
> *This is my daily bread . . .*
> *Your very word, spoken to me . . .*
> *And I . . . am desperate for you . . .* [4]

Peace and confidence filled his soul, followed by a tangible joy. He turned on the ignition, pulled onto the highway and continued toward his destination.

PRUNING

*He cuts off every branch in me that bears no fruit,
while every branch that does bear fruit he prunes so
that it will be even more fruitful.*   John 15:2

"Hello?"

"Mom? It's Jeff."

"Yes, Honey. What's up?"

"I need you to pray for me."

"Are you all right?"

"Yeah, just nervous. Ben's coming over to visit. Please pray it'll go well and that I'll have peace and confidence. I need it!"

"That's great, Jeff. I'm so glad for you. Ben loves you. I know things have been rough lately, but it'll work out. I've been praying for this."

"It could be hard."

"You can do it. I'm so proud of you. Honey, you're stronger than you think."

"Thanks, Mom. I appreciate you . . . I think he's here. Got to go."

Ben approached Jeff's front door and rang the bell.

"Come in," Jeff said. He followed Ben into the room and left the door ajar.

He cleared his throat. "Do you want a glass of water or something?"

"Sure," Ben said. "That'd be great." He sat on the living room sofa and removed his boots.

Jeff disappeared into the kitchen.

Ben looked up. "Hey, it's pretty cold out there. You want me to shut the door?"

Jeff's voice came from the kitchen. "If you want . . . I guess I like the fresh air."

Chuckling, Ben closed the door. "I remember a time it seemed you always left doors open. I thought when you paid the heat bill that would change."

Returning to the couch, he leaned back and rested his feet on the coffee table.

After handing him a glass of water, Jeff perched on the edge of an overstuffed chair, ready to bolt.

"Sometimes I'm more comfortable with it open."

Feet returning to the carpet, Ben sat forward. "You want me to open it again? It's your house. You should have it your way. I can put my coat back on."

Jeff waved him back. "No. It's just a stupid habit. I'll be fine." He swallowed.

Arm over the back of the sofa, Ben raised his feet again and let out a deep breath. Inexplicable joy rose within him and he chuckled. "Relax, Son. I didn't come here to beat you up."

Jeff sat back, crossed his legs and drank from his glass.

His foot bobbed.

"Go ahead and tell me what's happening with you lately," Ben said.

Jeff uncrossed his legs and leaned forward. "Uh . . . I guess it's kind of a long story."

"I've got time."

He cleared his throat. "I'm not sure where to begin."

"Why not begin with my daughter. How do you feel about her?"

Jeff swallowed hard. "I . . . I think I'm in love with her."

"You think?"

A deep sigh escaped and Jeff leaned back in his chair. "I've been in love with her for a while now." He smiled ruefully. "I've been trying to talk myself out of it, but it hasn't worked."

"What do you have against her?"

Jeff's eyes widened. "Against her? I don't have anything against her!"

"What's the problem, then?"

Groaning, Jeff dropped his head into his hands and looked at the floor. "I . . . uh . . . You know how messed up I've been . . . and am. You know what kind of family I come from. I'm not the kind of son-in-law you want."

Ben went silent. Forearms on his knees, he peered at Jeff. Head hanging. Beat down. Defeated. This was not right and he was partially to blame.

"I thought you might be thinking that," he said. "Jeff, I need to tell you something. You're awesome. You've always been awesome and I love you. But my love hasn't been perfect. I should've come sooner. Would you forgive me?"

Jeff's tortured blue eyes widened with surprise. "Me? Forgive you?"

Ben nodded. "It scared me to see you checking out. Will you forgive me?"

Puzzled frown on his face, he shrugged. "Sure."

"Jeff, you are a son of God."

Jeff shifted, dropping his gaze. "Yeah, I know. But I guess I'm ashamed. You know how I struggle with my past." Wincing, he lifted his eyes. "And you know about the pornography."

Brow lifting, Ben studied him. "How is it with the pornography thing? I thought you were free of it . . . Are you?"

"No," he said. "The last few months I've slipped back into some old patterns and habits. After being free for six years, I thought I was over it, but now it's worse." He swallowed. "I feel like I want to throw up every time, but I do it anyway."

"How about drinking? And drugs?"

"I've been tempted," Jeff said. "That's the reason I decided to help you out last week. I was miserable. I wanted to go drink with some guys from work and I haven't wanted to do that for years. It scared me. In my recent state of mind, it would've been bad."

Ben leaned back on the couch, crossed his legs and rubbed his chin. "So let me get this straight. You didn't think you were good enough for Cassie. Or us. So you withdrew. Now you find yourself worse off than you were before, desiring things you were finished with years ago?"

Jeff forced a short laugh. "Yeah, that's about it. I've been praying about it and trying to do what's right, but I don't have the strength to resist. Sometimes I don't even try. I've thought about getting rid of my computer—"

"Jeff," Ben said. "If you trust in your will, it'll always fail you."

Jeff stared at him. "I don't know," he said. "I've heard of people who just decided to quit, and did. But I can't seem to make it work."

"Have you talked to anyone about this?"

"I've talked to God," he said. "He finally spoke to me."

"What did he say?"

"Yesterday, on the way home, I broke. I cried out to him. He asked me if I would let him take out the root this time, not just the fruit. Then this morning some scriptures popped out at me and I had a vision."

Jeff went on to describe his vision of the crumb and banquet table. "I think God was talking to me about my relationships," he said. "But there's this other garbage. I don't understand why I continually return to it. It's killing me. I've repented every way I know how and feel better today, but I'm afraid I'll go back to it again. I'm weak—"

"What do you think the root is?" Ben asked.

"I'm not sure."

Ben's eyes grew intense. "I think I know."

Jeff gulped. "You do?"

"Yeah."

"What is it then?"

"Jeff, who are you?"

"What do you mean?"

"When you think of yourself, what's the first word that comes to mind?"

"Probably 'screwed up,'" Jeff said under his breath.

"So you're a sinner?"

Jeff looked up. "Of course. We're all sinners."

"Who told you that you were a sinner?"

"I sin every day. I would be a liar if I said I wasn't."

"Jeff, who told you that you were a sinner?"

He shrugged. "I heard it in church. It's in the Bible."

"But is that who you are? Is that your profession?"

"My profession?"

"Yeah. What you do and who you claim to be?"

"Huh?"

"If you mow a lawn, does that make you a lawn mower? If you sweep a floor does that make you a broom? And if you sin, does that make you a sinner? You have a profession of faith, Jeff. Faith in who Jesus is and faith in who he says you are."

"But I'm compelled to sin, and God hates it."

Ben leaned back. "Okay. Tell me about your church in Seattle. What was it like?"

"It was a good church. I went there at first because of a girl. That didn't last long. But they had lots of programs for kids. I enjoyed helping out with the basketball team."

"What did they teach you?"

Jeff paused.

"They preached a lot on humility, the importance of leading a blameless life, keeping a clear conscience and being a good witness.

One thing they always said was they were 'tough on sin.'"

"Tough on sin? "

"Yeah."

"So what did you get out of it? Did you get closer to God?"

"Closer to God? I don't know. I learned a lot about the Bible. But I didn't read it as much as I should have. I was so busy with school and stuff."

"So you didn't get closer to God, they were tough on sin and convinced you that you were a sinner?"

Jeff stared at him. "You think I shouldn't have gone there?"

"I didn't say that. Church is what you make of it. There are no perfect churches and there's always a few bones to spit out. Billy told me about visiting there last year. It sounded to me like there was an emphasis on sin with a lot of 'be good and try harder.'"

Jeff stiffened. "So what's wrong with that? Aren't we supposed to be good and try to be the best we can be?"

"The sin message with 'be good and try harder' brings judgement," Ben said. "When are you ever good enough or trying hard enough? When your eyes are on sin, it's a comparison game and it's a lifestyle of judgement and strife, setting you against yourself and others. It either brings fear or pride.

"I've been recovering from this for years, Jeff. It's not the gospel of Jesus Christ. The gospel is not focused on sin. It's focused on love. It's scandalous. It's grace. It's the power of God. It's not like other religions. Buddhists, Muslims, Hindus and most religions have rules and teach you to be good and try hard. Some are extremely devoted. But there's no redemption there. I would venture to say that focusing on sin and trying hard hasn't helped you be good and it definitely hasn't helped you rest in God's favor."

"That's for sure." He wagged his head, looking down at his folded hands. "But this thing with Cassie has exposed—"

"Jeff, everything's suppressed when you trust in religion and law. Shame and guilt hide the bad stuff and false humility the good. That's why the 'be good and try harder' message doesn't work. It doesn't change the heart.

"When you keep your eyes on Jesus and stay in grace and freedom, everything grows. Good seed and bad. You know you're loved, so you're not afraid to see what's planted in your heart. The power of God sets you free to do what you want."

"Do what I want?" Jeff snorted. "No way! I would be totally out of control."

"Jesus did what he wanted. He didn't obey God because of fear of punishment or shame. He obeyed for the joy set before him. And we follow him."

"But he overcame temptation. I just can't."

"If you know the truth, you can. Jeff, you want to do what's right. But lies planted in your soul steal your hope for the future. Your will against them will not hold up forever. You might suppress them for a while, but eventually they'll come back and bite you. Get your eyes off your sin and onto Jesus. When bad desires show up, don't be afraid to confess them and give them to him. He'll deal with them. A mature Christian knows who he is and does what he wants."

"But I just keep blowing it—"

"Wait a minute, Jeff. When you accepted Jesus as your savior, you were born again. So you are no longer a slave, but a son; and since you are a son, God has made you also an heir. You were a sinner. Now you have a new identity.

"You have confessed Jesus as the Son of God. Now confess yourself as a son of God, bought by the blood of the Lamb, washed clean, totally forgiven, brand new. He loves you and he's pleased with you. Do you believe that? Are you telling yourself that? Are you making these good confessions of faith?"

"Good confessions?"

"You know, like, Galatians 2:20: 'I have been crucified with Christ and I no longer live, but Christ lives in me. The life I live in the body, I live by faith in the Son of God, who loved me and gave himself for me.'

"There are other verses that work the same way. Like; I have received him and believed in his name, so I am a child of God.

". . . He redeems my life from the pit and crowns me with love and compassion.

". . . He chose me before the creation of the world to be holy and blameless in his sight.

". . . I am justified freely by his grace through the redemption that came by Christ Jesus.

"Any scripture that the Holy Spirit shows you about your identity can be personalized and become a declaration of faith. It's like receiving his substance of power to help you stand."

"But, how can I say that when I keep on sinning?" Jeff said. "God hates sin. He wants me to be truthful and honest. If I'm humble, I admit it. I don't want to fake it."

"How's that working out for you? Sure, God hates sin, but only because it separates you from him and hurts you and others. Has dwelling on your failures ever restored you? And if you really were truthful and honest, wouldn't you have shared this with someone by now? Jeff, you haven't had the grace to tell anyone about this whole thing until you were backed in a corner. Is that how this 'truthful and honest' thing is supposed to work?"

He smiled wryly. "Not really."

"True humility is not only admitting your faults to yourself and God, but taking hold of the truth of who you are. Then you can deal with failures and even confess them to others. It's hard to admit faults without groveling in shame unless you know his grace."

Jeff looked at him. "So you think I grovel in shame?"

"Isn't that what you've been doing? Isolating yourself, escaping into fantasy and convincing yourself you're worthless? Berating yourself is false humility. It's rooted in doubt, fear and pride. It depends entirely on your own efforts and not the grace of God.

"Jeff, take hold of your identity with confidence. Jesus was humble, but never denied his identity. It made him strong. It'll make you strong too."

"So you think this is the 'root' God was talking about?"

"Yes, I do. You're having an identity crisis. You've clung to false beliefs about who you are. The devil has clothed you with shame and fooled you into believing it's yours to wear. The truth is, your heavenly Father has given you robes of righteousness. Anytime you accept shame as yours, you forfeit the grace of God. It may feel like humility, but it's really deception and will lead you back to sin."

"I guess you're right. I—"

"Jeff, you're not the only one who's being tested. Like I said, I was afraid when I saw you withdrawing. I didn't believe in you or have faith for you. On the way here, God showed me this."

"Really?"

Nodding, Ben smirked. "Yeah. We had a little talk. He reminded me that you're his son. He also told me I'd been giving in to fear, among other things.

"You're the real thing, Jeff. After today, you'll believe the truth about who you are, rather than these lies. I am going to stand with you, believing God for who you are. He'll remove this blanket of shame and restore you to your rightful place."

They both fell silent.

Jeff stared at him.

"Are you ready to pray with me?" Ben asked.

"I don't know," Jeff said. "I think I am."

Rising, Ben crossed over to where Jeff sat and put his hand on his shoulder.

"Holy Spirit, come and show us how to pray," he said. "Show us how to face these monsters of doubt, fear and pride."

He waited.

Jeff cleared his throat. "Father, help me believe your word about who I am. Forgive me for not believing what you say about me. I've listened to the accuser and believed his lies. I may sin, but I'm not a sinner. That's not who I am."

"Father, Jeff has confessed to me that he's polluted his mind with pornography. Your word promises: 'if we confess our sins, you are faithful and just to forgive us our sins and purify us from all unrighteousness.'

"Jeff, in the name of Jesus, you are forgiven."

Ben put his hand on the back of Jeff's head. "In the name of Jesus, and because of his confession, I erase these images that have been imprinted in Jeff's mind. I command his thoughts to be cleansed by the blood of Jesus.

"Now, Lord, show us any doors in Jeff's heart that are open to fear and how to shut them." Ben paused. "What comes to your mind?"

"My father used to say I hid behind my mother. He used to call me a 'wimp.'"

Ben paused. "Jeff, repeat this prayer after me.

"Father, I choose to forgive my father for cursing me with these words. . . ."

"I forgive him for suggesting I was not a real man. . . .

"I forgive him for accusing me of hiding behind my mother . . .

"I forgive him for calling me a wimp. . . .

"And I renounce the spirit of fear. . . .

"I renounce the belief that I am messed up. . . ."

"I just realized something," Jeff said. "Because of my father's words, I questioned my manhood. Pornography made me feel like one." Tears rolled and he groaned. "Temporarily."

Tangible peace settled in the room.

"Let's keep going," Ben said. "Repeat after me. I renounce the belief that I am not a real man. . . .

"I am your son. . . .

"Strong and powerful. . . .

"Nothing can take me out of your hands. . . .

"God has not given me a spirit of fear. . . .

"But of power, of love and of a sound mind. . . .

"I know where all this came from and I cast you down, accuser. In the name of Jesus! . . .

"The curse is broken! Father, thank you that Jeff is a new creature in Christ. The old is gone, the new has come. You've taken away all the shame. We remove this deception in the name of Jesus! Jeff is a strong man. Forgiven and free!"

Jeff wiped his face with his hand. "Lord give me the boldness to be who you've created me to be. I want the blessing! I want to let go of the crumb you showed me and receive your abundance at the banquet table. "I don't . . . feel worthy, but I believe you love me and I want your abundant life."

Jeff stood and left the room. He found a roll of toilet paper in the bathroom and blew his nose. When he returned, Ben stood and the two shared a long embrace.

Looking into Jeff's eyes, Ben said, "I know our relationship is sometimes difficult, Jeff, but I want to be there for you as a father. You'll want to receive from other men who are wiser and more mature than I, but I'd be honored if you considered me a father."

"I already do," Jeff said. "But thanks for asking."

Holding his gaze, Ben's dark eyes grew intense. "Listen to me, Son, you're going to do great things for God. You are his son. You're strong. You have what it takes. "

He paused. A smile spread across his face. "One more thing, about my daughter . . . You have my blessing to pursue her. Good luck!"

WELCOMED HOME

You . . . were enemies in your minds because of your evil behavior. But now he has reconciled you. Col. 1:21-22

Jeff's eyes widened. "You mean you'll have me? Knowing the truth? It may take me awhile to get over—"

"Of course I'll have you," Ben said. "And if you and Cassie don't get together, I still want you as a friend. You know, Jeff, there's nothing new revealed here. The stuff you confessed didn't surprise me. What hurt the most was your mistrust."

"I know," Jeff said. "And I'm sorry."

"You're forgiven. But I didn't trust you, either. If I had, I would've come sooner. Jeff, the fact is, you're awesome. Stay in right relationship and if this hasn't already passed, it soon will. Meanwhile, get to know Cassie better."

A broad smile spread across Jeff's face.

Then he remembered.

The smile dropped.

"Uh . . . Thanks Ben, but I'm not sure that's possible now."

"Why not?" Ben said, returning to the couch.

Jeff looked away. "After what happened yesterday, I think I blew my chances with Cassie."

Out of the corner of his eye, Jeff saw Ben studying him, brow contracted in puzzlement. He leaned back and crossed his legs.

"What *did* happen yesterday?"

Jeff faced him. "Cassie didn't tell you?"

"Tell me what?"

"We had a fight."

Ben chuckled. "So what's new? You've been fighting on and off since you came back from Seattle."

"Yeah, but I never spanked her before."

Ben sat up. "You what?"

Jeff froze.

So she didn't tell him.

"Did you say you *spanked* her?"

"Uh . . . yeah." Jeff winced. "She kept pushing me. I warned her, but . . . it just sort of . . . happened."

Ben rose from the chair and paced the room.

Jeff felt Ben's agitation, but an uncanny peace enveloped him. He waited.

Finally, Ben stopped in front of his chair.

Jeff avoided Ben's piercing gaze. "I . . . uh . . . guess it was the most violent and dramatic thing I could do to her without completely losing it. I didn't want to hurt her, but I had to do *something*."

Ben folded his arms, sighed and sank back on the couch.

Jeff continued to examine the carpet.

"So what did you do, lose your temper and wrestle her over your knee?"

"Yeah. She fought like a wildcat, but I won. Whatever that's worth."

"Bad idea, don't you think?"

"I was pretty worked up."

Soon he heard a soft chuckle. Looking up, he saw Ben trying to repress a grin. "It seems to me I remember a certain young man working for me who had very strong opinions against any form of physical punishment."

Jeff twisted his lips. "Yeah, I remember. But when it comes to Cassie, I surprise myself."

A short laugh escaped Ben's lips. "Don't we all?"

"Do you think I should apologize?"

"That probably would be a good idea." Ben looked at him quizzically. "Or do you think you were in the right?"

"Are you kidding?" Jeff said. "She was the one who was right. It's just . . . She was going for the jugular. She wasn't fighting fair. I warned her, but she wouldn't back off. It was like she was trying to provoke me into some kind of violent reaction.

"We were up there in the pasture, on top of the rock ledge. She hopped over to the other side of the fence and got near the edge of the cliff where the rocks are loose. I thought she was going to kill herself trying to get my attention. That's when I threatened her. I didn't really think it would come to that, but when she accused me of being just like my father, I couldn't just stand there."

Jeff swallowed. "I'm not trying to make excuses, but that's what happened."

Ben snorted. "Cassie's pretty determined when she gets her mind set on something. She can certainly push your buttons. In the future I suggest you calm down and get a grip before you act, especially with her. If you don't deal with your anger and fear, you'll do things you'll be sorry for later."

"That's for sure."

Smiling sheepishly, Ben shifted on the couch, head shaking. "I don't know what else to tell you. How you solve this is between the two of you."

"Do you think she'll forgive me?"

"I can't say," Ben said, "but it wouldn't hurt to apologize."

A long silence followed.

"You were under major attack, Jeff. I'm proud of you for sticking around as much as you did, even though you were only half there." He smiled. "Cassie would have none of it, would she?

Actually, I shouldn't be surprised. Linda and I knew something was going to happen."

"You did?"

"Yeah. It was quite obvious."

"You know, the devil will try to do this to you again, Jeff. How can you prepare yourself, so you don't get so blind-sided and beat down?"

"For one thing, I'm going to take your advice and start making declarations of faith about who I am."

"That'll certainly help," Ben sat forward. "Hey, is your Bible handy?"

"Sure."

After retrieving it from the bedroom, Jeff handed his Bible to Ben and returned to the chair.

Ben leafed through it and read:

"'Praise be to the God and Father of our Lord Jesus Christ, the Father of compassion and the God of all comfort, who comforts us in all our troubles, so that we can comfort those in any trouble with the comfort we ourselves have received from God.'"

"God comforts us through fellowship, Jeff. When you're ambushed by doubt and fear, when you're confused and can't connect with God, run to the Body. Run to those who believe in Jesus and the power of the Spirit. There is no shame, so be transparent.

"Your brothers in Christ have comfort and encouragement to give you. They'll remind you of who you are and encourage you to fan into flame the Spirit within you. This is fellowship. It's unconditional love. It's intimacy."

Ben found another scripture.

"But if we walk in the light, as he is in the light, we have fellowship with one another, and the blood of Jesus, his Son, purifies us from all sin.

"How do you walk in the light?" Ben asked.

"I'm not sure anymore," Jeff said with a short laugh. "I always thought that you walk in the light by knowing the Bible and the truth as revealed by Jesus. He is the light."

"Yes, he's the light," Ben said. "However, walking in the light is more than just knowing the truth about Jesus. *You* need to be known. Don't hide anything from Jesus or intimate friends with authority in your life. Keep your failures exposed. If you do this, you'll have fellowship and you'll be cleansed. Sin will lose its power over you.

"We were made for intimacy, Jeff. Without it we seek false comforts and cheap imitations. Sexual sin is false comfort. It's a cheap imitation of true intimacy. The devil's always willing to give you short-term pleasure to keep you from the real thing. He uses guilt and shame to deceive you into believing you're unqualified for anything better."

Ben leaned forward. "Sexual sin thrives in secrecy, Jeff. All sin does.

"When I was your age, I struggled with intimacy. Porn wasn't as easy to come by, but I found it. I gave it up when I got married, but during a difficult time in our relationship and a hard, lonely time in our church, I went back to it. I was guilty and miserable. One of the hardest things I ever did was tell my wife. It was a great risk for me, because I was sinning against her and I didn't know how she'd react. But I had to tell someone who could minister forgiveness to me. She was the only one I could trust at the time. God blessed me when I confessed it. We cried together, she forgave me and I was cleansed. I have faith for you too. You'll be fine.

"There's a blessing for those who confess their sin, Jeff. Not just to God, but also to each other. The Bible says to confess our sins to one another and pray for each other that we might be healed. It's boldness with God and one another that brings the blessings of God's kingdom. In this case, forgiveness, cleansing from sin, and healing."

"Do you think I should tell Cassie about the pornography?" Jeff asked.

"If you continue growing closer, you'll eventually tell her. She'll ask what happened. She already wonders. But I wouldn't be in any hurry to tell her. You need some distance between you and this problem. Wait a while. Walk out your victory in this. Go for the root issues. Form close relationships with men. Be transparent. It'll change you."

"Speaking of being transparent," Jeff said. "Can I ask you a question?"

Ben leaned back. "Sure. Go ahead."

"Why were you so easy on me when I was working for you as a teenager?"

"Easy on you?'

"Yeah. You were much rougher on Billy. I always wondered if you thought I was too weak to take it. Did you feel sorry for me?"

"It wasn't that," Ben said. "You were usually careful. Billy was the one who took chances—"

"But there were times I knew you wanted to chew me out and held back."

"You wanted me to be *harder* on you?" Ben said. "I was afraid you'd run. I didn't think you trusted me." He smiled. "Remember that time you and Billy lied to me about the squirrels?"

"Yeah."

"You took off out the door so fast. You didn't even stay for dinner." He chuckled. "For you to skip out on food, it had to be serious! I thought I'd scared you off. I was sure glad to see you come back the next morning."

Jeff laughed. "That was one of the best things that ever happened to me. I was scared, but I came back anyway. There was nowhere else to go."

Ben sobered. "Looking back, I wish I'd given you more affirmation and told you how much I appreciated you, Jeff. I yelled at Billy too much and I was way too gruff with everyone. I didn't give out enough praise. I was proud of you. You always did real well and were good help. You still are."

Jeff smiled. "Thanks."

⊰ ❦ ❦ ⊱

The family was at the dinner table when Cassie's father opened the front door. She looked up from her food.

"How'd it go, Daddy?"

"Real well." He settled himself at the table for supper, a closed expression on his face.

He was not going to tell her anything.

Alone with her father at last, she stood before his recliner after doing the dishes.

"Daddy? Did he tell you?"

His eyes lifted from the newspaper. "Tell me what?"

"Did Jeff tell you what happened up at the rock ledge yesterday?"

"Oh, that." He smiled. "Yeah, he told me."

"I knew he would," she said. "Well?"

Her father studied her. "Well, what?" He tossed the paper aside and patted his thighs. "Come here, Pumpkin."

She settled herself on his lap and he held her close, kissing her hair. "Did he hurt you?"

"Sort of, but not really."

"Did he scare you?"

"Who, Jeff? No . . . Well . . . maybe. I didn't think he'd do it!"

"Did you want me to do anything about it?"

"No."

He held her there, in silence, the top of her head nestled into his neck. "I didn't think so."

"Is he mad at me?"

"Huh?"

"You know. Jeff."

"Oh, Jeff."

He chuckled softly. "Honey, you'll have to ask him yourself. I don't think you want me in the middle of this."

She rose to leave and he lifted the newspaper.

"I love you, Daddy," she said from across the room.

He lifted his head. "I love you too, Cass."

"Hey, Jeff! It's great to see you!" Matt shook Jeff's hand and patted him on the back. "It's been awhile."

"Yes, it has." Jeff took off his shoes, removed his jacket and hung it on a hook. "Too long. It's good to be back."

Young people were scattered around the Prayer Room, calling out to God. Overwhelmed with longing, Jeff immediately laid face-down on the floor.

"God, you're so faithful to me. Thank you . . . Come to me again . . . I need you."

> *Draw me close to you,*
> *Never let me go . . .*
> *Help me find the way,*
> *Bring me back to you.*
> *You're all I want,*
> *You're all I've ever needed . . .*[5]

He poured his heart out to God, in prayer.

> *Father, father me.*
> *I need your love, I need your love,*
> *I need comfort, I need shelter,*
> *I need healing for my soul*
> *Take this fear that I surrender,*
> *Take me in, make me whole.*[6]

Peace enveloped him, just like when he was with Ben in his living room. An old, familiar feeling bubbled up from the core of his being.

Joy!

He chuckled. "Thank you Lord! You're so good!"

☙ ❦ ❧ ☙

Jeff opened his front door. Saturday morning had dawned bright and sunny. Singing birds echoed the joy dancing in his heart. He settled himself in the lawn-chair.

"What's in store for today, Father?" He leaned back. "What do you want me to do about Cassie?"

A verse popped into his mind. Quickly he found Matthew 6:25 where he had it underlined in his Bible.

"Do not worry about your life . . ."

At the end of the passage, something caught his eye.

"But seek his kingdom, and these things will be given to you as well. . . . for your Father has been pleased to give you the kingdom."

He had written a reference in the margin. He turned to it.

"For the kingdom of God is not a matter of eating and drinking, but of righteousness, peace and joy in the Holy Spirit."

He exhaled, smiling. "Thank you Father, for righteousness, peace and joy . . . and for loving me."

"So, should I talk to Cassie?"

Wait.

"But I'm in the kingdom. I'm forgiven and cleansed. I'm free."

Establish yourself in freedom.

Turning the pages of his Bible, he came to another underlined passage.

"So I say, live by the Spirit, and you will not gratify the desires of the flesh."

Jeff pondered Ben's comments about his need for distance from his recent bondage and stared at the trees in the courtyard.

"Will Cassie understand?"

Trust me.

"Okay Lord, I'll do it."

⁙ ❧ ❧ ⁙

Cassie sat to the side of the church, near the front with Hannah. Periodically, she stole a look over her shoulder, searching for Jeff. He finally entered with Joey. Head high and shoulders back, she hardly recognized him as the same person. A few weeks earlier he'd sulked in the back row, slumped in the chair, eyes downcast. But not now. Her father rose and embraced him warmly and the three of them conversed at the back of the room. Finally finding seats, they began to worship.

Her eyes turned to the front, where Billy led.

At least Jeff was speaking to Daddy.

With a small huff, she folded her arms across her chest and joined the singing. But she was more than a little distracted.

She peeked again and Jeff saw her. Their eyes met. She looked away. There was light in his eyes!

Heart pounding, she shifted in her seat. He was back! Now what?

Oh God, this is awkward!

The worship progressed and Pastor Evan approached the communion table. He read from the Bible:

> "'Therefore, if you are offering your gift at the altar and there remember that your brother has something against you, leave your gift there in front of the altar. First go and be reconciled to your brother; then come and offer your gift.'"

Looking up from the Bible he continued:

> "We come to the Lord's table to eat the bread and drink the cup. Here we receive the sacrifice he made for us.

> "Stop and think about it. Is there anyone here with something against you? Humble yourself. Make things right, if you can. Honor that person as a part of the body of Christ. We'll wait. If you have anything to clear up, now's the time to do it."

Total quiet settled on the church, the atmosphere charged. Cassie's eyes roamed and she searched the faces of the people. Cindy Harding rose from her seat, tears sparkling in her eyes. She crossed over to her husband, who sat on the other side of the congregation. Kneeling in front of him, she grabbed his hand and—

"Cassie."

She jumped. Turning, she found her face only inches from Jeff's. Her heart stopped.

His eyes searched hers.

"I'm really sorry . . . for everything. I had no right to treat you like that. Will you forgive me?"

She couldn't help noticing his smooth shaven face, neatly trimmed hair and fresh, clean smell.

"I didn't have any right to sp—"

"Yes. I forgive you," she said, shooting a glance toward her younger sister beside her. "I'm sorry too. I shouldn't have said those things. It was cruel. Will you forgive me?"

His intense blue eyes bored into hers. "You were totally right in all you said."

"No. I shouldn't have said it."

With a soft smile, he whispered, "Then I forgive you too." He turned and left, returning to his seat beside Joey.

Pleased, she looked at her younger sister, who beamed.

People moved around the room. Some were hugging, some crying. Soft music played in the background as they made things right with each other.

Pastor Evan rose from a front-row seat.

"Now," he said, "the Lord welcomes you to his table. Come. We want to serve you."

Gloria, his wife, appeared at the other side of the table to help.

Cassie stood up and walked to the line which was forming in the center aisle of the sanctuary.

Jeff came up behind her with his arm around her little brother, a peaceful smile on his face. Sky blue eyes twinkled with life and hope from his tanned countenance. Dressed in a black tailored shirt and new blue jeans, rarely had he looked so good.

He was okay now, it seemed, but what had happened?

SHARPENING

As iron sharpens iron, so one man sharpens another.
Prov. 27:17

Cassie avoided looking at Jeff.

It was good he was here. He was finally coming back to life. But she sure had a lot of questions.

The family gathered for dinner and he joined them, along with Sam Wallace. The guys laughed and joked, while together they planned a men's meeting for the afternoon.

Her eyes lifted, daring a peek. Was this men's thing his idea? He was certainly agreeable, grinning like that. How could he be in such a good mood with so many unresolved issues between them?

Her mother emerged from the kitchen bearing a large pitcher of water. "So you guys are going to be busy all afternoon?" she asked.

Her father scooped up a serving of potatoes for himself and passed them to Billy. "That's the plan."

"Fred Johnson and Jed Miller will be here in a bit," Sam said. "The others couldn't make it, but maybe next time."

"When do you expect them to show up?" her mother asked Billy.

"Oh, three o'clock or so," he said, grinning. "We thought we'd play a game of basketball first. You know, get ourselves all sweaty and tired, then do the heavy stuff."

Cassie looked up from her meal and searched Jeff's face. Was it her imagination, or did she detect a certain relief there? He seemed perfectly happy with the arrangement.

Jaw clamped, she remained silent. Hey, if he was fine with it, she was too. Maybe all she'd get was a simple apology with no explanation for the last few months of being ignored. Her chin lifted. Well, she was certainly not going to bring up the subject.

After finishing dinner, she excused herself and began cleaning the kitchen. Hannah followed and soon her mother joined them, humming softly. The guys moved to the living room, continuing their good-natured banter.

Unsettled, Cassie retreated to a familiar place. The barn and her horse. Ginger neighed softly in greeting, eager for her attention.

"Hey, girl. At least I know you care," she said to the horse as she rubbed her velvety nose and ears. After leading her out of the stall, she tightened the cinch, mounted and galloped away.

On top of her favorite knoll, she looked out over the valley. The sun peeked through white clouds. Spring was upon the land, the rolling hills covered with soft, new grass. A cool breeze blew over her face.

She took a deep breath and reigned herself in. Maybe she was jumping to conclusions. They had both had a very tense week. School would start the next day and he knew where she lived. He might be planning to talk to her later, away from the watchful eyes of her family.

She smiled.

This would be a good time to be patient.

Her eyes feasted on the expanse of green, grassy fields and she breathed deeply. Across the meadow, a horse and rider caught her attention, approaching at a slow gallop. Long, curly, blond hair flew in the breeze behind the small figure on Blackfoot. Hannah.

"Hey, Cassie," Hannah said, riding up alongside. "Are you okay now?"

"I'm fine."

Hannah peered at her. "I noticed you didn't look too happy at dinner. It's Jeff again, isn't it?"

"I can't get much past you anymore, can I?" Cassie said with a smile.

Hannah smiled back. "Well, it is kind of obvious. And who wouldn't notice that you two haven't been getting along lately? I thought maybe it would be better after he apologized this morning. Is it?"

Not wanting to confide too much in her little sister, Cassie nodded. "Yeah, it's better. I guess I was feeling a little left out with the guys planning this get-together and all. What are we girls supposed to do?" Cassie forced a laugh. "But we can think of something, can't we?"

Hannah looked at her doubtfully. "Is that what's really bothering you?"

"Of course. Well, some of it. How about a race?"

Later, when they returned to the barn, the pounding of a basketball shook the far wall. Shouts of encouragement rang through the air.

Cassie and Hannah rubbed their mounts down and chatted easily, enjoying the time together. Silence greeted them when they emerged from the barn. The guys had gone inside.

∙⁂∙

Ben watched Jeff pace the room.

Jeff wasn't satisfied. He had disclosed his struggle with pornography to the whole group, but Ben could see he had unfinished business. Some of the guys had left, but Ben, Billy, Jeff and Sam lingered.

"Do you want to sit down and tell us more?" Ben said.

Jeff stopped. His gaze traveled from Billy to Sam and back

again. "I think so."

He pulled up a chair and the four sat in a tight circle while he shared his feelings for Cassie and the depression that followed.

"I've been so alone in all of this," he said.

"Not so," Billy said. "You just thought you were alone. Sam and I have been praying for you. I remember asking what was up. Why didn't you tell me?"

Jeff grunted. "I guess I felt rejected. The way you acted, I was sure you didn't approve of me and Cassie."

"Well, I wasn't worried about Cassie."

Jeff's head jerked up. He frowned. "What?"

"I thought you were going ga ga over Cassie like all the other poor—"

Jeff jumped to his feet. "You were worried about *me*? This is worse than I thought! You think I need protection from your little sister?"

"What was I supposed to think?" Billy said. "It seems every friend I've had has fallen for her. They get rejected and then I lose—"

"You think I'm a real wuss, don't you?" Jeff clamped his jaw.

Billy slid his chair back. "No way, Jeff! Look, I didn't mean that."

Sam shifted.

Ben started praying.

Lord, don't let him run.

"You think I can't handle Cassie's rejection, don't you? And you're sure she'll reject me!"

Ben lifted an eyebrow. At least he was speaking his mind.

"Well, no," Billy said, "but I didn't know—"

"Uh," Ben cleared his throat. "Jeff, could you sit down? I didn't treat you right either."

Jeff sat.

Billy exhaled loudly.

A long pause ensued.

Ben leaned forward. There was more to this than he thought.

Give us grace here, Lord.

"I'm sorry, Jeff," Billy said. "You're right, I didn't treat you right. I just thought—"

"I was weak."

Billy winced. "I wouldn't put it like that. Come to think of it, you do stand up to her. I let you both down. Can you forgive me?"

Jeff sighed. "You're forgiven. But could you trust me?"

"I'll try." Billy smiled wryly. "Are you sure you don't need my help?"

Leaning back, Jeff twisted his lips. "I'll be sure to let you know when your *expertise* is needed."

"This whole mess wouldn't have happened if we'd been transparent with each other," Ben said. "We haven't been sharing. And we haven't relied on each other. I know I've been guilty."

Sam and Billy nodded. "We were too," they said.

Ben looked up. "Father, forgive us for the pride of self-sufficiency. Forgive me and my generation for teaching these guys they aren't men unless they can stand alone."

"Forgive me too, Father, I was too proud to seek help," Jeff inserted.

"This is not just our weakness," Ben said, to the group. "It's a spirit. An attitude."

"You know, I think we've all felt abandoned. It's this isolation and independence garbage. How about you guys? Do you feel it?"

"I guess so, but it's normal to me." Sam said. "How about you, Jeff?"

Jeff snorted. "That's a no-brainer."

"I know your father felt it, Jeff," Ben said, settling back in his chair.

"He did?"

"Yeah. He didn't have any family support and didn't feel safe enough to be transparent. I was his only close friend and he could barely talk to me. Did he ever tell you about his experiences at church?"

"He never talked about it unless he was drunk. And you don't want to know what he said then."

"I can imagine," Ben said. "He was pretty passionate. He was passionate about God and when he became disillusioned, he was passionate about that, too. Did he ever talk to you about his faith?"

"No. He never shared any of that with me. When anything personal came up, he would avoid the subject. If Mom tried to press the issue, he'd get angry. I had no idea what he'd been through. I assumed he didn't care about me or Mom, but that was probably not true. He told me a few things before he died, but otherwise, he didn't tell me . . . much." Jeff hung his head in his hands.

"I'm sorry, Jeff," Ben said. "But it doesn't surprise me. Rejection and mistrust, if ignored, eventually take over. Those were the bad old days."

"Jeff?"

When Jeff lifted his gaze, unshed tears stood in his eyes. He swallowed.

"Before your father died, I visited him in the hospital."

Jeff nodded.

"He was broken. The many wasted years and the fact that he wasn't there for you weighed on him. His failures as a father tormented him, but guilt and shame kept him from turning back. Until the end. When facing death, he and I prayed together. He was finally able to give it all to God and receive forgiveness."

A deep groan escaped and Jeff said, "I've tried so hard not to be like Dad, but I am!" Falling to the carpet, he landed on his knees and gripped his head. "Guilt and shame have been destroying me!"

Billy crossed over, knelt with him and placed a hand on his shoulder. Sam stood, a hand on the other shoulder, but Ben dropped to enfold him in his arms. "I'm sorry about your father, Jeff," he said through tears. "I loved him too. But he didn't believe in who he was . . . and no one, including me, helped him believe. We just kept telling him to try harder."

Ben looked into Jeff's glistening eyes. "Would you forgive us,

Jeff?"

Jeff nodded.

"And may I stand in for your father and ask forgiveness for him?"

"Can you do that?"

"Jesus does it. He always intercedes for us."

"Okay, then, go for it."

"Jeff, would you forgive me for my insecurity and pride? I taught you to stand alone and that you're not a man unless you can solve your own problems." Ben's voice cracked. "I abandoned you. I didn't believe I was a son of God and you suffered because of it. Will you forgive me?"

"I forgive you . . . Dad."

At this, a load of grief broke loose and Jeff convulsed with emancipating sobs.

Ben wept with him.

Billy and Sam prayed silently, their hands remaining on Jeff's shoulders.

After a while, the tears abated.

Ben rose with Jeff and they all shared an embrace.

With his hand on Jeff's chest, Ben declared, "By the power of the blood of Jesus Christ, I cancel and retract the words spoken against Jeff by his parents, grandparents, or other relatives.

"I break and cast off every bondage of sin, including an independent spirit. Jeff has forgiven his father. He is reconciled to God, his true Father. He has a new family. He's a new creature in Christ. The old is gone, the new has come!"

⊱ ⊱ ⊰ ⊰

It was Friday.

By now Cassie had given up on Jeff contacting her. She had seen him once earlier in the week and he smiled at her, but didn't approach or attempt to speak with her at all. He looked happy, but was evidently in no hurry to talk or spend time with her.

After classes, Cassie walked home, close to tears. "He confuses me. What's wrong? I just don't understand. He apologized! I apologized. I thought things would change . . . He must not like me the way I like him. After last week, he probably thinks I'm an immature little brat."

When she opened the front door to her apartment, Kristy lay on the couch. "Hi, Kris."

Kristy sniffled, grabbed a tissue and turned her face away.

Although roommates since October, she and Kristy had not shared much or drawn very close. Kristy was consumed with a boyfriend that Cassie didn't like and of course she had expressed her opinion. Kristy had pulled away and Cassie gave her space, keeping busy with school.

But something must have happened.

She was obviously in bad shape.

Cassie threw her books down on a chair and hurried to her side. She dropped to her knees. "Are you okay?"

"No," Kristy said. "I just broke up with Bob. I can't take his lies anymore. He doesn't love me, Cassie! He won't talk to me, I mean really communicate. And last night he tried to pressure me to have sex. We've been dating for three months now and I told him at the beginning that's not what I wanted!"

"I'm glad you got rid of the scum. Men! I've about had it with the lot of them." Cassie sank to the carpet, leaned back and stretched out her legs.

Kristy looked at her curiously. "Is there something going on with you too? I noticed you haven't been too happy."

Cassie leaned back and sighed. "It's Jeff. I thought maybe he was going to call me this week."

Giving her a sideways glance, Kristy sniffled. A small smile appeared on her swollen face. "You really like him, don't you? You haven't said much, but I could tell a long time ago. Why don't you call him?"

"I'm thinking about it. But I may be wasting my time. I'm afraid as far as he's concerned, I'm just the pesky little sister of his best friend."

"I doubt that," Kristy said, unable to breathe through her nose.

Cassie leaned forward and crossed her legs. She brightened. "Hey, want to go with me to the Prayer Room tonight? Remember I told you about it a few months ago?"

"The way you've been acting, I figured you'd be eager to get home to your horse."

Cassie smiled. "I am," she said, "but, I need to study this afternoon. And I really need some time with God. I'm confused. But I think you'll like the Prayer Room. It's incredible. You can feel the presence of God as soon as you walk in."

Kristy let out a short laugh. "Sure, why not? I'm a free woman now!"

⋅⋰ ⁂ ⋱⋅

"Kristy, it's time to go. We're late!"

Cassie emerged from the back room to find Kristy with her phone in her ear and a frown on her face.

"I don't think I can see you tonight," she said. "No, it's not that. There's no one else . . . It's just not working, Bob."

"Don't be nice," Cassie whispered in her ear. "Say goodbye!"

Kristy winced. "Bob, you don't understand. It's over."

Rolling her eyes, Cassie mouthed, "SAY NO. HANG UP." She sliced her throat with her finger and repeated silently, "HANG UP."

After a few rounds of trying to be polite, Kristy finally met Cassie's eyes and drew strength from her friend. "Bob, the answer's no. Goodbye." She hung up the phone.

"You did it! I'm proud of you!" Cassie cheered. "God has someone better for you. That whole situation was a trap. He didn't honor you and you didn't respect him. You were just using each other."

"I know." Face downcast, Kristy said. "But it was nice to be wanted, even if it was only for my body."

Cassie took her friend's hand and looked into her eyes. "Kristy, you are wanted! You're God's creation. You're beautiful, intelligent and loving. You just don't know it. You're looking to guys to give you what only God can give you. What you want is close, loving relationship. Bob can't give you that. He doesn't have it. You need the love of Jesus. I know you believe in God and want to please him, but he has much more for you."

Cassie and Kristy arrived at the prayer meeting and quietly hung their coats. After removing their shoes, they entered.

Cassie froze.

Jeff knelt at the far end of the room, eyes closed and head bowed. Billy stood beside him and acknowledged their presence with a soft, welcoming smile. After a deep breath to calm her racing pulse, Cassie led Kristy to a corner and they sat against the wall.

You are God in heaven
And here am I on earth.
So I'll let my words be few
Jesus I am so in love with you . . .[7]

After an hour of worship, Cassie finally relaxed. God's presence was thick and enveloped her like a warm blanket.

"God, you've been good to me," she said. "Why do I get so worked up about Jeff? Forgive me for not trusting you. I want to trust you." She took a peek. He had shifted positions and was now face-down on the floor. Muscular shoulders revealed themselves through the back of his T-shirt and powerful tanned arms with strong, capable hands supported a head of short, dark, shiny hair.

Her heart turned over.

She knew he was strong, both in body and mind. Also, he could be incredibly gentle. Something stirred in the core of her being while she studied his form, lying there totally surrendered to God.

He was beautiful like that.

He looked so peaceful, so serene.

He looked . . . strong . . . yeah . . . strong.

Why didn't he talk to her anymore? Was he still upset about what she said last week? Would he ever consider her or trust her now?

Release him.

"Release him? How can I release someone I never had?"

If you release him, I'll give you a stronger man.

"I don't want a stronger man. I want Jeff. I love him."

Head bowed and resting in her hands, Cassie sat cross-legged on the floor. Tears rolled down her cheeks.

Sniffling and sighing brought her back.

Kristy!

Cassie had totally forgotten about her friend. Shaking herself, she set aside her confusion and embraced Kristy, comforting her.

People soon rose and started praying for each other. Finally, Jeff acknowledged her presence. Nodding, his blue eyes found hers and held.

"Hi, Cassie."

Something passed between them.

It was sweet.

But . . . painful.

Then the moment was gone. He turned back to the rest of the group and started praying for the teenage boy beside him.

What was that all about?

Cassie turned to Billy, who remained by her side. Was that a smile of *sympathy* on his face? He knew what was going on!

She glared at him.

Later, in their apartment, Kristy assured her. "Cassie, I saw Jeff looking at you. I've never seen a big brother look at a 'pesky little sister' that way. He's in love."

Cassie let out a short, protesting groan. "You know," she said, "I'm getting tired of everyone but him telling me he's so interested in me. If he loves me so much, I'd think he would at least say something besides, 'Hi Cassie.' What's his problem, anyway?"

"Sorry I mentioned it," Kristy said, turning away. "Just trying to help."

Saturday morning, Cassie sat at her desk, staring at her phone.

A faith in God she didn't have was required of her. Concerning

Jeff. Its birth was painful.

She couldn't deny the longing she'd seen in his blue eyes the night before or the attraction she felt for him.

His apology had seemed sincere.

He'd always been sincere.

Why wasn't he talking?

"Call him, Cassie," Kristy said.

Her roommate sat curled on the couch across the room with a textbook in her lap. Her eyes studied Cassie's face. "Just pick up your phone and ask him how he is."

"I'm not good at this."

Blue eyes stared at her. "Call him."

Expelling a breath, Cassie gave in. She grabbed the church phone list and punched in his number, steeling herself against a pounding heart.

"Hello."

"Jeff. This is Cassie."

"Oh . . . Hi, Cassie."

"How are you?"

"Fine."

"Could we talk?"

"Uh . . . Sure. What about?"

"Could we meet somewhere?"

"Uh . . ."

"Look, if you don't want to, just say so. I probably shouldn't have called. I just thought—"

"It's okay, Cass. It's not that I don't want to see you. I just can't right now. I need some time—"

"Time? Time for what?"

"To . . . uh . . . Well it's just—"

"I get the message. This was a bad idea. Sorry I called."

She folded her phone.

THE WAIT

*In repentance and rest is your salvation, in quietness
and trust is your strength.*   *Isaiah 30:15*

Gray clouds added to Cassie's gloom as she left for home late
Saturday morning.

He needed time?

What was that about?

He'd taken plenty of time already. And the way he had looked
at her last night, she was sure he had feelings for her.

Was she crazy?

Why wouldn't he talk to her?

When she arrived, she carried her bag through the front door.
"Mom! Are you here?"

No answer came. She lugged her bag upstairs and changed into
old jeans and a sweatshirt. A worn jacket on her arm, she headed
back down the stairs.

"Mom?"

In the kitchen she opened the refrigerator and found fixings to
make a turkey sandwich. Just as she finished, the back door

opened and Billy appeared.

"Hey! How's it going, Sis?"

"Okay, I guess."

At the sight of the sandwich and fixings his brow lifted. "Could you make me one of those?" He grabbed an apple out of the fruit basket and leaned against the counter.

An idea struck and she brightened. "I suppose. Where is everybody?"

"They went into town to run some errands. I stayed to finish working on the tractor." He munched on his apple, studying her. "Are you headed out? You look like you're dressed to ride."

"Yeah. I thought I'd go up to the cabin on the Grazing Association and check it out. I'm sure there are some supplies to replenish. I'll make a list." Piling on extra slices of meat and lots of mustard, she made the sandwich just the way he liked it.

He bit into his apple.

"Billy?"

"Hmm?" He continued crunching, devouring the crisp and juicy fruit.

She cleared her throat, searching for the right tone. "You said you'd like to help." Turning to him, she smiled sweetly, sandwich in hand. "Well, I was wondering . . . What's going on with Jeff?"

Suddenly, Billy choked on the apple and went into a violent coughing spell.

"I can't . . . say," he said, sputtering.

"Billy, I know you know. He's talking to you. I can tell!"

"Yeah, he's talked to me," he said, voice still raspy.

Baiting him with the sandwich, she tilted her head to one side. "Well, what's going on?"

"Have you asked him?"

"Sort of. He said he needed time."

Billy turned on his heel, opened the cupboard and found a glass. "Then, there you have it. Give him time," he said.

"But why? Tell me what's happening."

He coughed again. "Why do you have to know?"

"What do you mean? What's the big deal? I want to know! Why are you being so mysterious about this? Does he like me or not?"

He filled the glass at the faucet and gulped down the water. The coughing finally ceased and his closed expression relaxed into a condescending smile.

He reached for the sandwich, but she pulled it away. "Not until you tell me something."

"Sorry, I can't help you there, Cass. This is between you, him and . . . God." He filled the glass again.

"Billy, you're my brother! Why can't you tell me?"

After gulping down another glass of water, he turned to her, gray eyes intense. "Cass, this whole thing really frustrates you, doesn't it? You want to be in control. Every other guy who's come around here has given in to that. Well, Jeff is different. Besides, you don't have to know what's going on. Why not just wait and see? What part of 'trusting God' don't you understand?"

Cassie glared. "Thanks. You're a lot of help." She threw his custom-made sandwich on the counter. After gathering her own sandwich, jacket and water bottle, she scurried out of the kitchen and slammed the back door.

"Men!"

She yanked open the barn door, leaned against a stall and gulped down the sandwich. Still fuming, grumbling and muttering, she threw a saddle on Ginger. "This is so stupid!"

He needed time? What a lame excuse. If he didn't like her, he could at least be honest with her.

And quit looking at her like that!

And if he did like her—

She closed her eyes and groaned.

At a fast gallop, she left the ranch and headed up the mountain to the 'Grazing Association.' Her father, with other cattle ranchers, had pooled their resources to buy the large, isolated, wooded area for pasture.

An hour later, the horse moseyed through the mountain

meadow, approaching the small cabin. Cassie muttered, "I don't think I can let go. He likes me. I can see it in his eyes. This isn't fair." She looked up. "Why are you asking this of me?"

Outside the cabin, she tied Ginger, lifted a rock under the step, retrieved the key and unlocked the door. Musty odors greeted her and she wrinkled her nose. The one-room cabin, with its small wood stove, rustic kitchen and futon bed was a great get-away in the warmer months, but hadn't been used all winter. After forcing the windows open, fresh spring air swept through the room, liberating it from winter isolation.

The cupboards were close to empty and there was no water. She pulled a piece of paper and pencil from her pocket and took inventory.

"My heart's aching," she said, making her way back down the mountain on her horse. "Father, why did I fall for him? I thought it was your will. Didn't you tell me to *fight* for him?

"It was stupid of me to get myself in this position. I shouldn't have let myself fall in love with him. This is so stupid! . . . I thought you were in it! I just don't get it . . . You know how long I've prayed for someone like him." Tears trickled down her face and she wiped them away with the sleeve of her jacket.

Let go, Cassie.

Ꙭ ❧ ❧ Ꙭ

After church the next day, Cassie and Hannah raced in from the pasture on horseback, laughing as they approached the barn. Several cars lined the driveway and music wafted across the cool, spring breeze. They stopped to listen.

Solid male voices drifted toward them from the living room, accompanied by guitar.

> *Men of faith rise up and sing,*
> *Of our awesome King of Kings,*
> *You are strong when you feel weak,*
> *In your brokenness complete . . .*[8]

The two girls looked at each other and dismounted.

Cassie settled her horse in the barn and entered the back door. The sound of loud praying came from the living room. Ed, a good friend of her father's, had a distinct, deep and hearty voice that rose above the others. Laughing loudly, he prayed. She peeked around the corner.

Men of all ages stood in a circle with arms on each other's shoulders.

A stocky older man, Ed stood in the center with his own hand on his forehead, laughing and praying. "Bless-Ed! . . . Love-Ed . . . Forgive-Ed . . . Enrich-Ed . . ."

The others joined his laughter. Soon each man, one by one, young and old, took their turn in the center as the rest prayed for them. Some confessed sin. Some shed tears. They encouraged each other, laughed together and embraced each other roughly.

"Cassie."

She jumped. The whisper over her shoulder had taken her by surprise.

"Give them some privacy."

She turned to her mother. "Is it okay if I walk through there to go to my room?"

She nodded. "Go ahead."

On her bed, Cassie looked up from her biology book at the digital clock.

Nine o'clock. Time to head back to town.

She paused, remaining on her belly, feet wagging in the air. It was quiet downstairs.

"They must be gone now." She rolled off the bed, stuffed the book in her bag, grabbed her good coat and started down the stairs. A few young men, including Joey, still lingered in pairs, praying. She crept into the kitchen, where her parents conversed at the table.

"Goodbye. I'm leaving." She bent to kiss each one. "It's late."

"Good-night, Pumpkin." Her father rose to embrace her. "Have a good week."

Her mother stood and walked Cassie to the front door. "Drive careful, Sweetie."

At the other end of the lighted porch, Cassie heard Jeff's voice. "You can have peace. Ask Jesus. Believe in him. Surrender control. I've never had so much peace in all my life . . ."

She stopped.

Jeff continued speaking softly to Jacob Wheeler, a sixteen-year-old who was new in church the last few weeks. Seated side by side in lawn chairs, they chatted in the cool of the evening. Jeff's Bible was open in one hand and the other was on Jacob's shoulder. Suddenly aware of her presence, Jeff straightened and stood. His eyes met hers in the dim light.

"Hi Cassie."

Searching her face, his smile faded.

"Hi," Cassie said, dropping her eyes. She descended the steps, strode to her car, slammed the door and sped down the driveway.

☙ ❦ ❧ ☙

Jeff couldn't sleep. Visions of Cassie's large brown eyes visited his thoughts. That look she gave him on the porch just about broke his resolve.

"Father, she looked hurt," he finally said, after tossing in bed without relief. "I'm having a great time with the guys, and I have been at peace, but don't you think I should talk to her? Maybe I could write her a note.

"But what would I say? I'm not ready to tell her everything. And she wouldn't be satisfied until she got it all out of me. I could make it worse. But I've got to say something . . . Don't I?"

Trust me.

"I'm not sure she's going to survive this. She thinks I'm *rejecting* her. I can see it in her eyes."

Don't be afraid.

"Okay Lord. If you say so. I'll leave it to you."

☙ ❦ ❧ ☙

"Not this weekend, Mom. I've got a lot of studying to do."

Linda paused and looked at the telephone. Over the past

month, she had sensed her daughter's distress. It had been two weeks since Cassie had been home for the weekend and that was unusual.

"Are you sure that's the only reason?"

Silence.

"Cassie," Linda said, "it's about time you and I had a talk. Would you like me to come in on Saturday? We could go out for lunch. What do you think?"

"I'd like that," Cassie said.

"I'll pick you up at noon."

The next day, Linda sat with her daughter at Chang's Chinese Dynasty.

"Mom, it isn't fair," Cassie said. "I'm so confused about Jeff! On the one hand I'm still angry with him for the way he snubbed me. But he isn't treating me bad now. And the smile's back on his face, the light's back in his eyes. He talks to everyone. But . . . he won't really talk to me. And I get no explanation! It seems his apology was useless.

"I believe God encouraged me concerning Jeff. He was at the center of our relationship. Jeff helped me get back on track. But the other day I thought I heard God tell me to let go of him. Do you think that sounds like God?"

Linda smiled and reached across the table for her daughter's hand. "I'm not surprised, Cassie."

"Why would he ask that of me?" Cassie said, her dark eyes tearful. "We've been through a lot together. Are my feelings supposed to just go away? I can tell he has feelings for me. But I can't force the issue and make him talk. I already tried that." She sighed. "This is torture! Why is God doing this to me?"

"I'm not sure, but we're all asked to 'release' the ones we love from time to time. It's a test," Linda said.

A fire lit in Cassie's eyes, dispelling the sadness. Her voice rose in frustration. "A test of what? Sanity? I'm not sure what it means to 'release him,' anyway!" The food arrived and she pulled her hand away to pour the tea.

Again Linda grabbed Cassie's hand and bowed her head. "Father, thank you for this food and bless our conversation. Thank you for my beautiful daughter and give her the desires of her heart."

Head rising, she smiled and picked up her fork. Laughing softly, she pointed it at Cassie. "I know for me," she said, "I like to be in control, or at least think I have some control in a relationship."

Cassie groaned. "Billy says I have control issues."

A smile teased Linda's lips. "Don't we all? You just seem to have more success at it than some of us."

"Mom!"

"Cassie, you have a strong personality. That's good, but there are times when you need to give up control. I had to. It seems like I have to do it regularly. Submit all my opinions, expectations and agendas to God."

Linda chewed a mouthful of rice, studying her daughter's thoughtful face. "So, you talked to Billy?"

Cassie sampled her broccoli, rolling her eyes. "Yeah, I tried to squeeze some information out of him."

"Did he tell you anything?"

"Are you kidding? His lips were sealed. Even my attempts to bribe him with a turkey sandwich didn't work."

Linda laughed and pointed her fork again. "Your father won't tell me anything, either."

Cassie's head shot up. "Did you ask?"

"Sure. I tried, but without success. Don't worry, it's probably a guy thing. At least Jeff's talking to them. He looks so much better."

Cassie frowned. "Yeah, that's part of the problem. He looks better," she said. "Mom, I don't know how to let go of him. Before all this happened, I thought maybe I loved him. Now I know I do. How do I let go?"

"It doesn't mean you quit loving," Linda said, reaching for a piece of chicken. "It's a test of your faith in God. Do you believe he wants to bless you? Or do you grasp and strive to bless yourself?

When the time is right, God will bless you. But now's the time to lay down your expectations and wait."

"I hate waiting."

"I had to wait for your father."

"You did?"

"He and I had some real struggles after we were married. But when I released him to God and waited, not only did he become stronger, but my love and respect for him grew stronger as well."

Cassie went quiet. She pushed the food around on her plate.

"But you were married, Mom. Jeff never made any kind of commitment to me. I've never been sure of our relationship. He's only kissed me once and that was under Grandpa's fake mistletoe at Christmas." Her eyes rolled. "That was sure the beginning of the end. All I have are hopes and dreams. Sometimes I think it's all in my head."

"Hopes and dreams die hard, Cassie. But God knows us better than we know ourselves. He knows our heart's desire and wants us to have it. The scripture says, 'he is able to do immeasurably more than all we ask or imagine, according to his power that is at work within us.'"

"I know, but what really burns me is that Jeff is so fine with staying away from me. He's having such a great time with the guys, like everything's just hunky-dory. I heard him say the other night he's never had so much peace. That bugged me. When he looks at me, I know there's something there. How can he just—"

"He's okay because he's let go of you," Linda said.

Cassie raised her eyebrows. "You know this for a fact?"

"Well, he hasn't told me, but I've watched him and I have a feeling there's something powerful going on in Jeff."

"Well, I don't know how much longer I can stand this. Did I tell you that I tried calling him? That just made things worse. It was so humiliating! He said he needed time. Do you know how long I've waited already?"

"Cassie, be patient."

Cassie exhaled. "How can I do that, Mom? I go home and he's

always there. It drives me crazy. He looks at me and I melt. I'm afraid to ask him what I really want to know, especially after what happened a few weeks back. He just worships, prays, laughs, ministers to kids and avoids me. And he looks so . . . good. When I see him smiling at me from across the room with those blue eyes, I—"

Linda laughed. "You do have it bad," she said. "Hey, why don't you come with me to our Women's Advance at the lake next weekend? You need some girl time. Maybe you could invite Kristy."

A smile finally found its way to Cassie's face. She nodded. "That sounds like fun. I do need some time to get away. I'll ask her."

⋅⋆ ⧓ ⧒ ⋆⋅

"Why do they call this an 'advance?'"

Cassie turned to answer her friend. "The women at our church felt they were pressing in and making progress at these get-togethers, so decided to call them 'advances' instead of 'retreats.'"

A clear blue sky and a brilliant sun brightened their long drive to Lake Sayaki. Fresh spring air blew into the partially opened car windows. Tall pines and majestic firs graced the rugged mountains as they drove along the winding river. Sparkling clear water rushed over the rapids, finding its way down the canyon.

"This is so infuriating," Cassie muttered, interrupting the silence. "I guess I'm used to getting my own way."

"Hmm?"

"Oh, I'm just talking to myself."

Kristy smiled knowingly and nodded. "About Jeff."

"You're right." Cassie laughed. "I'm having a hard time just laying the whole thing down. You know how stubborn I am."

"Yeah, I know," Kristy said. "I'm that way too. Life isn't always what we planned, is it?"

"No, but I still believe God wants to bless us. He knows our hearts and he loves us."

Kristy frowned. "I wish I could believe that. My experience has been one disappointment after another."

"You can believe. And I'm trusting you will. You just need to experience his love. That makes all the difference. Then you'll know for sure that God's heart is for you and not against you."

Looking at her curiously, Kristy lifted her brow. "Experience his love?"

"Yeah. Ask for it. God says if we seek him, we'll find him."

Crisp mountain air spilled through the car windows as the two circled Lake Sayaki. Deep blue waters, smooth and tranquil, mirrored the rugged, snow-capped peaks. Ancient trees, stately and proud, honored their presence as they approached the gravel turnoff to the retreat center.

A two-story log home with covered porch, came into view. Nestled against the mountains, it was surrounded by a vast, green, wooded lawn. Smoke billowed from the chimney, welcoming them. After parking the car, they struggled through the front door with their luggage and sleeping bags.

Cindy Harding greeted them both with warm hugs.

"Hi Cassie! Who's your friend?"

"Cindy, this is Kristy."

"Cassie and Kristy! You're here!" Hannah said, running to embrace them. "Anne made her amazing beef stew and Mom and I made cheesecake!"

Women of all ages lounged in the large living room around a wood stove. Several stood to greet Kristy and introduce themselves. Upstairs, Cassie and Kristy found bunks and deposited their bags.

SURRENDER

No one has ever seen God; but if we love one another,
God lives in us and his love is made complete. 1 Jn. 4: 12

Cassie had forgotten what these "advances" were like.

Young and old met in a unique setting of warm intimacy and casual rest. To the uninformed eye, it appeared to be a giant slumber party. But it was far more. Life changing things happened here. The younger ladies often sat at the feet of the middle-aged and silver-haired, leaning against their knees and cuddling against their sides. The older women stroked hair and rubbed backs and shoulders.

Warmth and safety embraced Cassie. She relaxed. This was a place for healing and revelation. In her experience, no other setting offered so much loving touch or such a strong sense of well-being.

Dawn, constrained to a wheelchair, sat to one side, a teenage girl in her lap. The young girl relaxed in her embrace while Dawn whispered in her ear.

Happy noises came from the carpet nearby where another girl sat. With clear skin and large shining eyes, she peered into each face, smiling. Occasionally, she burst forth in expressive, but unintelligible sounds. She was mentally impaired, but no one seemed to mind or notice. The young woman sitting beside her stroked her hair and kissed her forehead.

Cassie took a fresh look at these older ladies in the circle. She had known most of them as long as she could remember. Many had flowers sticking out of their hair at different angles. Smiling and chatting, they enjoyed one another, eyes twinkling and fiery, full of life and love, giving and receiving.

While watching the younger women receive affection from the older ladies, Cassie's heart ached. She'd never considered herself needy. Not like these women. Most had rough backgrounds. Many came out of sexual promiscuity, substance abuse and general brokenness.

They were wounded.

Of course they needed this.

Healthy and whole, she planned on staying that way. She had never taken drugs, or even been drunk, and was certainly not considering sex outside of marriage. Her family was strong and her parents loved her. She planned to marry a godly man and raise strong, believing children.

In the past, while observing these women pour their hearts out with tears of need and grief, she had decided she wasn't going to do the things that had injured them and caused so much grief. She was going to follow God and trust him for a blessed, full life.

But now, recalling her attitude, her conscience pricked her. She'd never considered herself one of them. But obeying God wasn't all that easy when you felt lost and out of control. Now it was she that could only see a long, bleak future ahead. It was she that needed to trust God. Yet she resisted.

Now she understood.

She'd always been above this kind of thing. Quite fine.

But tonight, she wasn't fine.

She was lost. Confused. Out of control.

Blessed are the poor in spirit, for theirs is the kingdom of heaven.

Okay, so she hadn't been poor in spirit. She'd been haughty and stubborn. A know-it-all, who didn't know much. She'd been protected from a lot of pain and had taken it for granted. When Jeff rescued her from that bully, she hadn't immediately recognized or appreciated it.

It still bothered her.

Sometimes she was so proud.

Even though it hurt, she let herself look at it.

In reality, she too, was needy. And something was coming undone.

"God, I'm worse than any of them," she said. "I need love."

Yearning eyes searched the room and found her mother, raking fingers through a young woman's hair and massaging her neck and shoulders. Eyes glowing, the girl smiled.

Feeling very alone, unexpected tears filled Cassie's eyes. She tucked her chin to her chest and prayed, "Father, I need you. Help me."

From where she sat on the carpet, Cassie looked at the plump elderly woman on the couch above her.

Glenda.

Flowers in her white hair and a three-legged cane standing within reach, Glenda was outlandishly dressed in sparkling polyester. She had always been good for a hug. Cassie leaned her head against Glenda's leg and snuggled close. Pushing Cassie's hair behind one ear, Glenda ran warm fingers through it and Cassie's heart opened. Radiant comfort filled her soul. Substance soaked in, flooding her senses. She snuggled closer and drank in love.

Then Dawn changed the music and turned it up.

"Let's praise the Lord!" Gloria shouted, "He is good! His love endures forever! From everlasting to everlasting!"

The whole room erupted in song and praise.

Gloria and Cindy began to dance, pulling others into the middle of the room.

Cassie lifted her hands and the heaviness in her heart

dissipated. Now on her feet, she danced with the others, kicking, swinging and laughing in delight.

Even the older ladies, some who needed a cane or a walker, were not able to resist the dancing and celebration. They clapped their hands, tapped their feet, swayed from side to side and beat the floor with their canes.

"Life is good and God is great!"

The music subsided and peace filled the room. Many lay on the carpet, some giggling with joy, others listening, resting, worshiping and praying.

Cassie stretched out on the floor, soaking in the peace of God. Eyes closed, she rested in a cocoon of love. Thoughts and questions concerning Jeff surfaced in her mind.

Cassie, leave it to me.

Tears gathered at the corners of her closed eyes.

She felt his presence. He was in control and he loved her.

She relaxed.

Conviction tugged and new light gave her clarity. "Father, I surrender," she said softly. "Forgive me for fighting you. I wanted to fix Jeff. I wanted control. But I have no control here. You are in control. I haven't trusted you. I haven't believed you want the best for me. I've been rebellious and prideful. Forgive me. I release Jeff to you and trust you with him."

Suddenly aware of warm hands, her wet lashes lifted. Glenda had settled on the floor beside her with a hand on her shoulder. Anne, a close friend of her mother's, knelt on the other side, her hand on Cassie's foot. Both prayed softly. She hadn't noticed their presence until now. Through her tears, she smiled and sniffled.

"Thank you."

Soon it was time to retire. She and Kristy retreated to their bunks.

"These ladies are wild," Kristy said, climbing into bed.

"Yeah." Cassie laughed. "They're happy and full of life."

They both grew quiet, settling into their warm beds.

"Cass?"

"Yeah."

"This is different. It isn't what I expected. All that touching and hugging . . . It's awkward for me. Makes me uncomfortable."

"Really? You didn't seem all that uncomfortable with Bob touching you."

"Cassie!"

Cassie laughed. "I guess I'm used to it. I forget what it's like for someone new to all of this. But you're doing well. A couple years ago, a lady left in the middle of the first night. She couldn't handle it. But by the next advance, she was here and soaking it all up.

"Trust me. Their love is genuine. Try to relax. You'll find out how good and healing it is. Get comfortable with love, and you'll be comfortable with God. God is love."

કા ૐ ⁇ કા

After breakfast the next morning, they gathered in the living room, many still in pajamas. Anne, a vivacious gray-haired lady, sat beside the wood stove, smiling and laughing softly as she watched the others interact.

Suddenly, she stood. "I have something to say!" her voice rang out. "I love Daddy God so much!"

All eyes turned to her and the room quieted.

"We invited Holy Spirit to come and he came! The love and peace you feel here are signs of his presence. This isn't the result of being up here on the mountain. And it isn't just our magnanimous personalities."

A wave of giggles swept through the room.

"The sense of well-being you feel is Holy Spirit. We are experiencing his presence and his love. What he's doing here is wonderful. It doesn't come from us. I know from experience, it's not of us. When I tried it on my own, I was a real 'Frankenstein.'"

"That's for sure. I knew her back in those dark ages," Glenda piped in, a broad smile lighting her weathered face.

Cassie had heard this story before, but she laughed with the others.

Anne smiled and continued. "I read the Bible and was taught that we're to love one another, so I set out to do just that. I tried with all my might to love all those weird and crazy people who rubbed me the wrong way. But when it came right down to it, everybody irritated me. As far as I was concerned, the entire human race interrupted my life. I was as clueless and clumsy as Frankenstein and just as effective at scaring people off."

Laughter rippled through the room, but Cassie abstained.

Maybe that was it.

Maybe she had scared Jeff off.

The laughter subsided and Anne continued, "But our Daddy's so merciful. He knows what I need. I need just what you're giving and receiving right here with such grace. It's the gift of love. Daddy God's love."

Cassie straightened. No matter what, that was what she needed. It had always been so.

"When he first began to change my heart and make room for his love, it was very painful. I was full of fear, rejection and pride. These things kept me from receiving love. But in his mercy, he removed them to make room for this precious gift. Daddy is always faithful and I was desperate. I had to receive his love for myself alone. I used to think I only needed love so I could serve God and help others. But I need it for me . . . I need to know and rely on the love Daddy has for me. His love displaced the fear and rejection."

Cassie's eyes fixed on Anne's.

Have I been relying on God's love?

". . . Receiving Daddy's love for yourself can be difficult. But it's essential. You can't really live without it."

Cassie exhaled.

"You must be utterly selfish about this, just like a new baby. It's not wrong. Infants die without the basics of food, clothing and shelter, but they'll also die for lack of affection or love. What makes you think you need it any less? It's the way our Daddy made you. You were made for intimate relationship with him and others."

Shifting on the floor, Cassie folded her legs.

I know this, don't I?

". . . When I received this revelation, my vision was transformed. I look at you now and see Daddy's glory in your smiling faces and loving affection for each other. I see the beauty of his holiness in your beauty. For you too, are holy."

Cassie glanced at Kristy, who sat quiet, looking confused.

Kristy was a gentle and tender soul. She had no idea of her beauty. Cassie scooted closer and placed an arm around her shoulders.

"As his love flows between us, it's what the Bible calls the unity of the Spirit in the bond of peace. We have it with him and with each other. We're not afraid, striving, or jealous, because each of us is loved more than we ever dreamed possible. Out of the overflow of Daddy's love, we love each other.

"So, does anyone want more? Let the redeemed of the Lord say so!"

"Yes!" A chorus of voices erupted in the room.

Cassie rose to her feet with the others, but Kristy remained seated, like a deer in the headlights.

"Well, let's go for it then! Express Daddy's love any way his Spirit leads!"

"Tanti Baci! Tanti Baci!" Dora bounced around the room. "Many kisses! Many kisses! Who wants a kiss?" A middle-aged Italian woman, Dora was affectionately known as "Tigger." With wild hair and a huge, animated smile, she lived up to her nickname. Grabbing Cassie's head between her palms, she planted one firmly on each cheek.

Cassie laughed and yanked Kristy to her feet, hugging her tightly. "I love you," she whispered in her ear.

Kristy seemed to relax. But just then Dora returned, pulled her away and kissed her enthusiastically.

Cassie laughed at her friend's surprise.

Finally, Kristy laughed along.

Kissing everyone in a similar manner, Dora didn't miss a soul.

The other women followed Dora's lead, embracing and kissing

each other warmly. Laughter broke out. Holy chaos filled the room.

Cindy emerged from the kitchen with a basin of warm water, a towel over her shoulder, a bottle of lotion and a container of soap. She knelt before Glenda and asked to wash and rub her feet. Gloria disappeared, only to return with another basin, starting at the other end of the room. Making their way around the room, they washed feet and massaged them with lotion. Most received it wholeheartedly, but a few hesitated.

⁂

"I just don't feel comfortable with all the dancing, laughing, crying and stuff. It's emotionalism," Kristy said on the drive home. "My home church warned us against emotionalism."

"Have you ever read C.S. Lewis's Screwtape Letters?" Cassie asked.

"No."

"It helped me to understand the importance of outward expression of emotion. In the book, the demon, Screwtape advises Wormwood, a lower devil, to discourage his assigned human from physical expressions of any sort. He says we humans do not understand that the position of the body affects the position of the soul. Our body, soul and spirit are intertwined.

"Freedom of expression is encouraged in our church, especially in worship. Of course it can get weird if people are trying to gain validation or prove something by it. But freedom is worth the risk. How else can we know what's in our hearts? Suppressing emotion smothers love, along with everything else. It smothers the soul."

Kristy crinkled her nose. "I'm not sure I can make the transition. It doesn't seem safe to be so vulnerable."

After negotiating a bend in the road, Cassie turned to her friend. "Well, how's it working out for you? The fact is, you are vulnerable. Who are you going to receive from? Jesus and his slightly strange people or the *guys* you've been looking to for comfort?"

Kristy groaned and looked out her window. "Thanks. You don't have to be so subtle about it."

"Look, Kristy, I know at times you were uncomfortable, especially when we started kissing, hugging and washing each other's feet. It was pretty intimate. It bothered you, didn't it?"

"Yes, it did. I don't know why, but I just couldn't let Cindy touch my feet. I was glad she respected my space and didn't make a big deal out of it."

"I haven't always appreciated the foot washing either. But Jesus did it for his disciples, so from time to time we do it for each other. My pride often gets in the way and makes it difficult. You'd think after growing up with this, I wouldn't have any trouble, but sometimes it just rubs me wrong. I guess it's hard for me to be vulnerable too. I have to make a conscious decision to receive love. And you know what? Every time I do, I'm blessed.

"I remember the old days when everyone was so stiff and isolated. They didn't trust each other. I was young, but I sensed it. Insecurity ran rampant and Mom says there was always division and backbiting. Now the women truly love each other. Tremendous healing has happened in each one of their lives. I'd say this way is much safer than the old way."

For several miles, Kristy remained quiet. Then, releasing a pent up breath, she turned. "Okay. How do you suggest a person start?"

"First you admit you need love. Women now-a-days are taught to be tough. We try hard and work hard, then end up worn out, burnt out and starved emotionally. The truth is, we don't have to prove anything. God loves us as we are."

"So, okay, I admit I need love . . . Now what?"

"Go to Jesus and tell him you need him. Turn from your pride, doubt and anything else that keeps you away from him. See yourself as a little child, willing and ready to receive love. Surrender your whole life to Jesus and return to the Father of your soul. Ask him to meet your needs and change you. He'll do it, Kris."

Kristy looked at her curiously. "Is that what you did?"

"I do it all the time."

"Then why are you so stressed about Jeff?"

Cassie paused. "You got me there. I've been resisting God. But

I made a decision this weekend. I repented from pride and grasping for control. I love Jeff, but I gave him to God. I let go."

Kristy's eyebrows rose. "Really? How did you do that?"

"God touched me." Cassie laughed. "He gave me peace. No man can do that. He asked me to let Jeff go. So I did."

Near the ranch, Cassie turned off the highway. "Let's grab a cup of tea and take a break." She drove up the driveway and parked.

"Is your brother having a party or something?" Kristy asked, squinting in the sun. "It looks like a bunch of guys are here playing basketball."

"They've been getting together every Sunday afternoon. They have a prayer meeting after the game."

"Wow! I seem to remember you *complaining* about this. All these guys come to your house every weekend?"

"It's not what you think, Kristy. They're not here for me."

"I suppose you're right," Kristy said, smiling shyly. "Still, if I had an older brother like yours bringing friends over, I certainly wouldn't complain!"

꙳ ❧ ❦ ꙳

Jeff stopped dribbling the basketball. "Hey, I'm going in for a minute." Dripping with sweat, his mouth was dry and he needed to use the bathroom. "I'll be right back." He threw the ball to Billy. Jogging toward the house, he hurried through the back door.

On his way out, he stopped in the kitchen, reached into the cupboard for a glass and filled it with water.

"Hi, Jeff."

Startled, he turned to see Cassie standing in the kitchen doorway, watching him. He didn't know she was home.

He flashed her a grin. "Hi, Cassie." Still breathing heavily from exertion, he gulped down the glass of water.

"Jeff, I need to tell you something." Her chocolate eyes pierced his. "I release you. You're free."

Jeff sputtered on his water, watching her turn to leave.

What did she mean by that?

Confusion, then panic surged through him.

He wasn't sure he wanted her to "release him."

Mouth gaping, he stared at the empty doorway.

At last he laid down the glass, scratched his head and turned to make his way back to the others.

"God, what am I supposed to think of that?"

Trust me.

"I don't have much choice, do I?"

DARK CLOUDS

My grace is all you need. My power works best in
weakness.   *2 Corinthians 12:9 (NLT)*

Cassie hugged Kristy close. "I'm going to miss you!"

Outside their apartment, they said their goodbyes for the summer.

"It's been so good these last few weeks," Kristy said. "I don't want to go home."

"Yeah, it has been fun," Cassie said, smiling.

Kristy twirled a strand of long brown hair. "Maybe we don't need men after all."

Cassie lifted an eyebrow. "I wouldn't say that."

"Of course you wouldn't. You're in love with Jeff." Kristy placed one hand on her hip and squinted in the sunshine. "I can't believe you two. The looks he gives you across the room are loaded. There's a roaring fire behind those blue eyes. How can you be so calm?"

"I gave it to God," Cassie said. "I told you, we're fine. He's doing well, so why not just enjoy myself? I'm intrigued, but not frustrated. For all I know, he looks at everyone like that."

Kristy shoved her. "Trust me, Cassie. He does not look at everyone like that!"

Cassie laughed. "I really don't know what's going on, but it's okay."

"I guess I have a lot to learn." Kristy folded her arms. "But I don't think I could stand it."

"You might surprise yourself. All you need is peace with God. And you have it. You've grown. You're stronger than you think."

A smile lit Kristy's face, her blue eyes shining. "I *have* grown. I never thought it would feel so good to walk with Jesus. I feel so happy and clean! And I'm going to miss our church, especially the worship. You know how I love to sing."

"Keep singing. You don't have to be in church to sing, but I'm sure you can find a good one in Seattle."

Kristy frowned, suddenly troubled. "I'll try. But pray for me. I don't get along too well with my mother. I'm worried about spending the whole summer there. Even though she goes to church, she doesn't understand this Jesus thing."

"I will, Kristy. Keep in touch, okay?"

"Sure," she said. "I'll bet you can't wait to get home to your horse."

Cassie smiled longingly. "You're right. I think I'll take Ginger up to the cabin this afternoon."

"The cabin? The one you and I drove to last month?"

"Yeah."

"Ooo," she said. "I'm jealous. It's so beautiful and quiet up there. I'll never forget it."

Cassie recalled her failed attempt to get Kristy to ride Blackfoot. Finally giving up, she borrowed Billy's pickup and drove to the cabin.

"It's one of my favorite places," Cassie said. "Well, I'd better get going." She embraced Kristy again. "Maybe you could come back a little early this fall and spend some time with me at the ranch." She winked. "We'll get you past that fear of horses."

Kristy crinkled her nose. "I'd like to, but I don't know about the horse thing."

Cassie giggled. She strode toward her car while Kristy followed. Before opening the door, she turned and gave Kristy one last hug. "Have a great summer! And call me!"

She climbed into the car. "Bye!"

"Goodbye!" Kristy said.

On the highway towards Fishtrap, she cranked the radio up and began to sing. Mid-June sun glared off the road, the air hot and humid.

School was out. She was going home for the summer!

Later, pulling into the ranch, Cassie searched the lot near the barn. Where was the stock truck? Oh yeah, the guys went camping. Now she'd have to wait to ride Ginger. Disappointed, she grabbed the last of her things from the back seat and entered the house.

"Mom! I'm home!"

Her mother emerged from the back room. "Cassie! How did your chemistry final go?"

"I think I did okay." Cassie put down her bags and kissed her mother. "When are Daddy and the boys getting back from camping?"

"I expect them this evening," her mother said.

Bags in hand, Cassie headed for the stairs, her mother following. "That's disappointing. I was looking forward to a ride this afternoon."

Her mother smiled. "You're in luck. They didn't take the horses. The truck broke down and it's in the shop."

Cassie halted. "They didn't take the horses? That's great!"

While unpacking her bag and arranging clothing on the shelves, Cassie continued the conversation from her bedroom closet. "Where's Hannah?"

"She's babysitting for the Johnson's this afternoon."

"Oh," Cassie said. "I was thinking about riding up to the cabin. I was hoping she'd go with me."

Her mother frowned. "It looks like it might rain. Are you sure you want to go today? It's a ways up there."

"Oh, I'll be fine. If it rains, I'll stay in the cabin until it lets up. It's been so hot today, it'll feel good. And I doubt it'll last long. It's been a long week and I've been looking forward to this. I'm gonna do it."

"Okay," her mother said, "but be back before dark."

Cassie emerged from the closet, smiling. "I will."

※ ❧ ❦ ※

Dark clouds rolled over the mountains and the wind picked up. It was still warm, but cooling. Thunder rumbled in the distance when Cassie left the barn lot on Ginger.

"Come on, girl! Let's stretch your legs!" Ginger's hooves thudded on the soft pasture road. After running the horse, Cassie reined her in at the north gate and dismounted. She opened the gate, led the horse through, shut it behind her and started up the mountain.

An hour later, they approached the meadow. Rain fell in soft, misty sheets and the mountain air smelled fresh and sweet. Cassie zipped up her jacket against the gusty wind and steady drizzle.

Out of the trees, Ginger hesitated.

"What's wrong, girl? Is there something out there?" Cassie strained to see, but the misty rain clouded her vision.

Ginger shifted nervously.

"Let's circle around the meadow on the other side and check it out," she said in the horse's ear. Leaving the road, they went around the meadow, but Ginger shied, still nervous.

Cassie leaned out in the saddle for a better view. "What's wrong?" Through the fog of rain, the middle of the meadow was barely visible. She strained to see.

There it was. A black bear hunched over a carcass of—

A blinding flash lit up the sky.

Boom! Crack!

Ginger jumped sideways and Cassie flew through the air. Hard ground rushed to meet her flailing body.

Thud!

Compacted sod jarred her frame and rattled her teeth. Ginger bolted away.

Stunned, Cassie rolled to her back on the wet grass.

After gathering her senses, she rose to her elbows and checked herself for injuries. Her right hip hurt, but moved easy enough. Each arm, each leg, everything seemed fine. But when she tried to roll to her knees, her muscles seized in protest.

Cautiously, she pushed herself upright to a sitting position. "That feels okay," she said.

Bending one knee and putting one foot under her, she attempted to stand. Hip and thigh muscles cramped and seized. Excruciating pain radiated throughout her lower body.

Groaning, she fell back and rolled over. The pain was intense.

"Oh God! Something's wrong! My legs won't hold me!"

A calmed Ginger returned and nuzzled Cassie's shoulder, urging her to stand.

"Sorry, girl. I can't get up."

Pushing the horse away, she said, "It's okay. It's not your fault."

On the wet ground, Cassie sat with her knees pulled to her chest. Taking a deep breath, she forced back the mounting fear.

Now what?

"Father, help me!" Shivering, she pulled her jacket tight and tried to shield herself from the intensifying rain. Ginger gave up and wandered out further in the meadow, grazing.

The bear was gone.

⁂

Jeff parked in front of his apartment. "What a day." He slammed the door and reached back into the cab to retrieve his groceries. Work the day before had kept him from joining the guys on the camping trip. The day had been busy and hectic, wrapping things up for the school year. His eyes lifted with longing to the clouded gray hills in the distance.

"I hope I get another chance to go to the mountains this summer."

A cold shiver of fear swept through him.

Cassie.

He shook himself. "Yeah. She's sweet."

In his apartment, he removed his shoes. After plopping the groceries on the counter, he opened the refrigerator and put the milk, eggs and butter away.

"I'm always thinking about her. It's torture. She's 'released me,' whatever that means and I guess we're both fine."

He flopped on the couch, put up his feet and checked out the newspaper.

The cold fear returned.

Cassie.

He laid the paper on his lap and looked up. "Father, I've already dealt with this. I've given Cassie to you. I have no fear."

Raising the paper, he tried to read. But something sat on his chest. It was heavy, cold . . . A pain throbbed in his right hip. He shifted. "What the heck?"

Cassie.

He sat up. "Is this you, Lord? What about Cassie?"

Go to her.

"Now? Is this my imagination?"

Go to her. Go to the ranch.

"But now? It'll be almost five o'clock before I can get there."

Go to her.

"Why now? Ben and the boys won't be home. It'll be awkward. I could talk to her after church tomorrow. What's the hurry?"

She needs you.

He could've sworn the voice was audible. "She needs me?"

Springing from the couch, in three long strides he was at the door, pulling on boots and a leather coat. He grabbed his hat, dashed out to his truck and left the parking lot, heading for the highway in the driving rain.

"God, be with Cassie right now. Protect her and keep her safe!"

Was he going crazy?

The rain had subsided and a cool wind blew over the wet

landscape when Jeff pulled into the ranch driveway thirty minutes later. He parked the pickup, jogged to the door and opened it.

"Hey! Anybody home?"

Linda called from the back room, "I'm back here! I'll be out in a minute!" She emerged shortly, hair wrapped in a towel.

"Jeff! What brings you out this afternoon?"

"Uh . . . Is Cassie around?"

"No. She took Ginger up to the cabin a couple of hours ago. She said she would be back before dark."

"Do you know it's raining out there?"

"I thought it looked like rain, but you know Cassie. She had her heart set on going today." Linda motioned toward the couch. "Have a seat. Have you eaten?"

"No." Jeff ran his fingers through his hair and paced the entryway. "I thought they took the horses camping."

"They were planning on it, but the clutch went out on the stock truck and they decided to road camp this time."

"Oh."

"What's on your mind?" she asked, taking a seat on the couch.

He continued pacing. "I need to find Cassie."

"Why don't you just make yourself comfortable and wait until she gets home? She should be back before too long."

"I don't think so. I felt like I was supposed to come out here. I need to find her right away."

"Oh?"

"Yeah," he said, "Could I take Blackfoot and ride out to meet her?"

Linda rose to her feet. "Sure."

In a flash, Jeff was out the front door and headed for the barn. After saddling Blackfoot in record time, he mounted and galloped north.

From the kitchen window, Linda watched him ride away. "That's strange," she said, smiling. "But it's about time."

HERE HE COMES!

Listen! My lover! Look! Here he comes, leaping across the mountains, bounding over the hills.   *S.S. 2:8*

Spasms of pain wracked Cassie's hips and thighs. She stopped scooting. Breathing heavily, she grimaced and gathered her wits. Cool rainwater mingled with caustic tears, streamed down her cheeks and dripped from her chin. With the sleeve of her dirty nylon jacket, she wiped them away. Determination renewed, she continued dragging herself backwards until, finally, she reached a large fir and leaned against it. At least there she had a little protection from the driving rain.

Knees bent to her chest, she shifted, only to be arrested again by pain. Wincing, she pulled her knees slowly back to her chest, the only position she could tolerate on the cold, wet ground.

"I should have worn my rain coat," she said through chattering teeth.

Soaking wet and shivering, she huddled in a ball. "Father, please help me. I don't know what to do. My hip really hurts. I'm freezing."

It was raining hard when Jeff reached the meadow. Scanning the field, he saw Ginger standing near the trees on the other side. His heart quickened.

Why didn't she tie her at the cabin?

Heels digging into Blackfoot's sides, he galloped to the cabin and leapt off the horse.

The door was locked. Ominous silence greeted him with no sign of Cassie.

Turning, he yelled, "Cassie!"

A hammering heart beat against his ribs. Where was she?

Her horse! Maybe she was with Ginger.

He jumped back on Blackfoot and galloped across the meadow to where he had last seen Ginger and approached the grazing horse.

"Cassie!"

Stopping short, he went silent, listening through the rain.

"I'm over here!"

Turning, he glimpsed a curled form huddled under a large fir on the north side of the meadow.

He raced toward her. Then stopped.

Drenched and shivering, her smiling face was lightly smeared with mud. Dark hair hung in wet strands, dripping on her wet and muddy jacket.

"Jeff! It's you!" she said, her voice raspy. "You came! I can't believe you came!"

Jeff leapt off his horse and fell to his knees beside her. "What happened?"

"My horse spooked. Lightning struck nearby and uh . . . she threw me. I was watching a bear and it took me by surprise."

"Are you all right?"

"I'm fine. Except I can't walk."

"That doesn't sound fine to me! Can you stand at all?"

"No. When I turn to my side, my muscles seize up. My legs won't support my weight."

"You've got to be freezing!" Jeff tied up his horse. "We'd better get you out of this rain. Do you think you can stand with my help?"

After a few unsuccessful attempts to support her, Jeff leaned over. "Here," he said. "Put your hands around my neck. I'll carry you to the cabin."

"Are you sure?" she said.

His eyes lit with teasing. "I've carried you before, remember?" Grinning, he reached his arm around her back. "I was a little rough last time, but then, you weren't very cooperative." He winked.

Cassie blushed. "Don't remind me."

"Don't worry. This time I'll be more gentle."

She locked her hands around his neck while he scooped her up under the knees and stood. Adjusting her against his wet jacket, he took a firm hold and walked toward the cabin, tilting his large felt hat to keep the rain out of their faces.

"What about the horses?" Cassie asked.

"I'll come back for them. Right now we've got to get you dry. You're freezing."

"You feel warm," Cassie said, teeth chattering.

Jeff looked briefly into her eyes and squeezed her against him.

Shifting in his arms, Cassie said, "Are you sure you don't need a rest? It's a long way to carry me."

"I'm fine," he said, "just fine."

"Jeff?"

"Hmm?"

"How'd you know to come out here looking for me?"

"God told me to come."

"Really?"

"Yeah." He smiled, a drop of rain lingering on his chin. "I'll tell you about it later."

At the cabin, Jeff set Cassie on the step. He found the key, opened the door and carried her in, shutting it with his foot.

"How about setting you on one of these chairs for now?"

"You can try."

Gingerly, he settled her on a hard, wooden chair near the bed.

"Are you going to be able to sit there?"

Cassie shivered. "For just a minute, maybe."

Kneeling, he removed her wet boots and socks. "Are there any blankets in here?"

Cassie pointed her finger. "Over in that cupboard by the kitchen."

"Ah-hah!" Jeff said, after rummaging through the cupboard. He produced a set of tattered gray warm-ups and a wool blanket. Then he covered her in the blanket and laid the sweatshirt and pants on the futon bed.

Jeff arranged cut wood from the wood-box in the small stove. With matches from the kitchen, a fire soon snapped and crackled, warming the cabin.

"Listen," he said, turning to Cassie, "You think you can get out of those wet clothes and put on these old warm-ups while I go back to get the horses?"

"I think so."

"Okay. Can I do anything more to help before I leave?"

Cassie blushed. "I don't think so."

"Wait." Back in the kitchen area, he found a teapot and filled it with water from a plastic jug. Placing it on the stove, he turned to Cassie and caught a glimpse of her pale face. She swayed slightly. He hurried to her side.

"Are you okay?"

"I can't sit here long." Grimacing, she gripped the sides of the chair.

"I'll be right back." He strode to the door. "Get the dry clothes on, okay?"

"I'll try," she said.

The door closed and he left.

Cassie shifted on the hard chair, quivering inside and out. "I hope I can do this without his help. This is so embarrassing!"

Panting, she peeled off her wet jacket, shirt and bra, pulled the sweatshirt over her head, then unzipped her wet jeans with trembling fingers. Hip throbbing, the room spun.

"I can do this," she said, shaking herself. She struggled out of her wet jeans on the hard, wooden chair, twisting, pulling and breathing hard. Then reaching for the sweat-pants, she bent over and forced her cold, wet legs into them. She tugged at them, and twisting and turning, finally pulled them on.

Now to get to the bed.

Determined, she braced herself with her hands on the chair and breathing hard, she rose, but her pelvic muscles would have none of it.

Was she going to break in half?

"Oh!"

Legs giving way, she collapsed on the floor and found herself in an awkward, twisted position. She tried to turn, but spasms of pain arrested her. She couldn't move. Tears rolled down her cheeks.

"Oh God," she said, "it hurts!"

Finally, she called out, "Jeff!"

Bursting through the door, his eyes widened when he saw her crumpled on the floor and he hurried to her side. "What happened?"

"I fell," she said, breath coming rapidly. "I just couldn't get to the bed. I'm sorry. My muscles seized up."

"Here," he said as he bent over and placed his arm around her back. After she'd locked her fingers around his neck, he rose and scooped her up, laying her gently on the bed and covering her with the blanket.

Cassie stifled a cry and shifted position.

He leaned over her. "Is there anything I can do?"

"I think I'm okay now." A brave smile on her face, she gathered herself, chin quivering. She shifted again.

Sure, she was "okay." Her bladder was full and she was really going to embarrass herself if she ignored it much longer. But what could she do? Ask him to help her use the *bathroom*?

His hand touched her shoulder. "Father," he said, "help us. Come, touch Cassie and heal her."

A wave of shock and trauma swept over her at his gentle prayer. She fought it, hiding persistent tears.

Jeff turned to arrange her wet and muddy clothes on a chair in front of the stove.

Reality struck as she watched him hang her clothes. A choked sound escaped and she pulled the blanket over her head. Curled in a ball, her whole body shook.

He sat next to her and placed a hand on her back. "Cassie, you're going to be all right. I think you must've broken your pelvis or something."

"I can't move," she said from under the blanket, "and . . . I have to . . . to use the bathroom! This is so awful. And my hip really hurts!"

"I'm sorry, " he said. "Do you want me to carry you to the outhouse?"

Cassie remained under the blanket. "No. But what else can I do? . . . This . . . is so . . . embarrassing!"

She heard him bolt to his feet.

"Listen," he said, standing over her. "We do what we have to do. If you have to go, you have to go. We can take care of it. The rain has let up. Now's the time. Are you ready?"

The blanket came off her head. Cassie sniffled and wiped her face with her sleeve. "I guess so."

He removed the blanket from her knees and held it behind her shoulders. "Here. Wrap up."

Cassie took hold of the thick wool blanket and pulled it around herself. Still shivering, she raised her head and put her hands around his neck.

It wasn't as difficult as she had imagined. He carried her outside and placed her on the seat of the outhouse.

"I'll be right outside the door if you need me." Winking, he smiled. "Think you can handle this?"

"Yes!" she said, shoving him out the door.

She finished and he carried her back, placing her gently on the bed.

"Well, at least we know that system's a go."

Casually, he leaned over her, smiling and bracing himself with the palms of his hands. A teasing light shone in his blue eyes and his warm breath fanned her cheek. "I've heard that can be a problem with this kind of injury."

Blushing, she shoved him away. "How would you know?"

He continued to smile, folding his arms and standing by the bed. "A kid broke his pelvis at one of our basketball games in Seattle. He acted a lot like you do. There was no one else available, so I went with him to the hospital. They were concerned about his ability to pee. They wanted to check his urine for blood. Of course there's no way we can do that now." He paused. "Did it hurt you to . . . you know—"

"No."

"Good. I thought not. It sounded like you were okay in there."

The blanket went tighter around her shoulders. "What? You were listening?"

He chuckled, patting her arm. "Relax, okay?"

On the chair beside the bed, Jeff leaned back and crossed his legs. Silence prevailed, each drifting into their own thoughts, while the crackling fire warmed the room.

Jeff removed his jacket. "Are you getting warm?"

"Yes."

Something sat on her chest and tears leaked from the corners of her eyes. She fought them.

What was wrong with her?

"I'm sorry," she said, inhaling a jagged breath. "I don't know why, but it all seems to be . . . catching up to me . . . I was doing okay, but I can't help it."

Against her will, her body surrendered to shock and trauma, stomach quivering and limbs trembling. She repressed a sob.

"You've been through a lot today, Cass." Tenderness laced his voice. "Go ahead and cry."

Cry she did, releasing uncontrolled, convulsive sobs. Jeff watched in silence. Then, crossing over to the bed, he sat beside her and placed a hand on her shoulder.

"Is there anything I can do, Cass?"

Her breath came in ragged gasps. "Could you . . . hold me?"

Gently, he took her in his arms, lifted her on his lap and held her close. Clinging to him, she cried into his shirt, shaking with pent-up shock, pain and frustration.

Suddenly she stopped, straightened and wiped her face on the blanket.

"How am I going to get home?"

"Don't worry," Jeff said, "I'm not leaving. Your mother will send your dad or Billy up to check on us when they get home. She knows where we are."

"I suppose you're right."

Staring at the wet spot on the front of his shirt, Cassie frowned and let out a nervous laugh. "I'm sorry for getting snot all over you."

She wrinkled her nose, settling back against his shoulder. "I guess I'm just the 'pesky little sister,' more trouble than I'm worth. Like Billy used to say—"

"Pesky little sister?" Head bent, he studied her. "Why would you say that?"

Cassie cleared her throat. "Well," she said, "I have been a pesky little sister. Haven't I? I've caused you a lot of trouble. I've made you really mad and I—"

A low hiss escaped his lips. He jumped from the bed, dropping Cassie on the mattress. She gasped at the sharp pain.

He turned back. "Oh, I'm sorry. Did I hurt you?"

Making a face, she shifted to a more comfortable position. "It's okay now, but I am sore," she said, "and a little fragile."

He walked briskly across the room and expelled a long breath, staring out the window.

"Is there something wrong?"

He turned to face her. "Is that what I am to you? A big *brother*?"

She looked down.

"Cassie?"

She didn't answer.

"It's about time you know my feelings toward you are certainly not those of a brother toward a sister." Pacing the room, he ran his hand through his hair. "Cassie, I've probably been in love with you since you were twelve years old. And lately I've had it real bad."

Her swollen eyes went wide. "You . . . you *love* me?"

"Of course I love you." He turned to face the wall.

"If you love me, why haven't you said anything?"

He turned back, blue eyes intense. "I denied it at first. But then, the more I admitted to myself how much I loved you, the more afraid I became."

"Afraid? Afraid of what?"

"Rejection, I guess. I didn't think your parents would approve, especially your dad and Billy. They know me too well. And my family—"

"Whoa! Wait a minute! What about *me*?" Cassie pointed at her chest with an indignant forefinger. "Did you ever stop to consider telling me? Why were you all worried about my family, when you hadn't even talked to me? Don't you think that I might want to know this, apart from my family?"

"You're not apart from your family," he said. "I couldn't pursue you without your parent's blessing. It wouldn't be fair to you."

"Maybe," she said. "But Jeff, my family loves you. They always have."

"I know that now. But I didn't trust your dad and Billy enough to accept me in that way."

"This just doesn't sound right. Even if you were afraid, you're one of the bravest men I know. You would've overcome it. It had to be more than that. What else was wrong?" She searched his face.

He turned away. "You're right. There is more," he said, stopping at the stove, his back to her. "And it's the hardest part to confess."

Arms folding across her chest, she pressed her lips together. "I'm listening."

He turned back and came to the side of the bed. "Cass," he said, "when I was a teenager, I was addicted to pornography. Your brother and your father knew. They helped me through it and I was free for six years.

"When I realized I loved you, old insecurities and fears resurfaced and I withdrew. I didn't think your family would consider me good enough for you. I was too proud to tell anyone what was wrong and I was afraid, especially of your dad and Billy's opinion. Your dad says it happened because I doubted my identity in Christ. Nothing seemed to help. I was miserable.

"One evening at the grocery store, I saw a picture on a magazine cover. It seemed to suck me into a vortex. That night I visited a porn site on my computer—"

She lifted her hand. "Uh . . . that's enough information. I don't want to know anymore. You can tell the guys."

He smiled. "I have told the guys."

"That's good."

Both fell silent.

"But why pornography? I've never thought of you as a lusty sort of guy."

"I was sinking into hopelessness. There was short-term comfort there. At the time, even desperate prayers to God didn't seem to help. After six years of freedom, I was back in it and I felt terrible. But the more miserable I felt, the greater the compulsion grew. It was like I was in a dungeon of shame and satan chained me to the wall with pornography. I was trapped and frustrated." He smiled ruefully. "When you rattled the bars of that cell, I'm afraid you got the brunt of my anger."

Blue eyes met hers. "Cass," he said, "that whole scene between the two of us at the rock ledge was a wake-up call. It was then I realized I was in real trouble. I'd never hit a woman before. My anger scared me. I knew I had to give it to God or I was toast."

"I made you that mad?"

"I was already angry," he said. "You just exposed it."

"What were you so angry about?"

"My whole life I've been angry. The root was fear. I didn't want to admit I was afraid, so I'd get mad. A lot of anger left when I got saved, but not all of it. I used to think I was afraid of being locked in, but now I think I was more afraid of being locked out, shut out from the blessings and joy that others have. It seemed unavailable to me. I felt cursed. I wanted to be blessed. To live! But lies kept me from it, lies about who I am. About my identity.

"I believed the curses spoken by my father. He used to call me a wimp. A mama's boy. I was afraid I couldn't make it, couldn't be blessed, couldn't rise up, couldn't overcome, couldn't be strong. I was afraid I was like him. Weak."

Tears pooled in her eyes.

Weak? Jeff?

He thought he was *weak*?

"Oh, Jeff. But you're not—"

"Yeah, but believing all this stuff made me weak and pretty soon I was seeking comfort in pornography."

It all started to make sense.

His depression and withdrawal.

The long wait.

God's instructions to release him.

She sniffled. "So, this is why you had so much trouble last winter? This is why you wouldn't talk to me?"

He nodded.

WONDERFULLY, GLORIOUSLY REAL

See! The winter is past; the rains are over and gone. Flowers appear on the earth; the season of singing has come.   S.S. *2:11-12*

Jeff studied Cassie's sober face while she stared at the stove.

Knowing the ugly truth might be more than she could take.

He hadn't been in a hurry to tell her. He didn't want to disappoint her. Or himself. He wanted to be the hero she fantasized about.

Some hero he was.

Well, now she knew the truth. And it was about time.

He searched the side of her face. She didn't seem devastated. Just sad. He knew what she would have said when she was younger. Did he have a chance?

He crossed over to the chair and sat near the bed. "Pretty bad, huh?"

She turned to him. "You know," she said, "I can hardly see your face. It's getting dark. There's an oil lamp in the kitchen. Would you light it and bring it over here?"

While he put more wood on the fire and lit the lamp, she said nothing. He placed it on the counter, then busied himself by the sink, preparing tea. After setting the lamp beside the bed he returned to with two full mugs, handed her a cup and sat.

She quietly sipped her tea.

"So, what do you think?"

"I don't know what to think," she said, wrinkling her nose. "It's hard to imagine you, the guy who's scolded me since I was young for improprieties, one who always had such high standards, gawking at nasty pictures of naked girls."

He winced. "I know Cassie. And I'm sorry."

"But I do know I can't compete with those girls. I've seen a few." She blushed and turned the hot cup with her fingers, studying its contents.

A mix of question and hurt in her dark eyes, she looked directly at him. "What exactly do you want from me?"

"I'm asking you to forgive me and give me a chance."

"Do you still look at that stuff?"

"No," he said. "After that blow up we had during Spring Break, your father came to visit. I confessed it all. He prayed for me and talked me through it. I haven't gone back since. Also, your dad suggested I start getting closer to the guys, so that's what I've been doing."

"Are you okay now? Do you have desires to go there?"

"No, Cassie. Jesus set me free. Why would I want to give up the real peace and joy I have now for that garbage? I have peace with God and more of a grip on who I am. I know he's forgiven me, I'm in fellowship with others and I know how to fight the temptation if it should arise." He paused, sipping his tea.

Twirling the hot cup in her fingers, she blew at its contents.

"Are these the kind of girls you dated when you were in college?"

"Girls in college?" He sputtered. "I really only dated one girl.

And it didn't last long."

"What happened?"

"I wasn't good enough for her."

"Was that *her* conclusion? Or yours?"

"Hers. But I just found out she's pregnant. Without benefit of husband." Jeff shook his head. "And she was the church's most adamant crusader against sexual immorality."

Cassie twisted her lips, eyes still fixed on her cup. "That's too bad. It seems some of the most legalistic people screw up the worst."

Sad brown eyes came to lock with his. "It's too bad you didn't go to someone right at the beginning of this ordeal. It could have saved us both a lot of suffering."

"I know," he said, holding her gaze. "Will you forgive me?"

"What exactly are you asking me to forgive?"

Jeff let out a long breath, rose to his feet and set his mug of tea on the counter. He paced at the side of the bed. "Look, Cassie, I didn't trust you or your family to receive me. Then I withdrew from relationship and allowed this perversion to come between us. I betrayed your trust before I even had it."

She studied him. "Thank you for clearing that up. I forgive you. But there's one thing I want to know."

"What's that?"

"Do you think *I'm* sexy? Do you fantasize about me?"

Surprised, Jeff gave a short laugh. "What?"

Was she serious?

He studied her. Propped against the wall, she sat with her knees bent in overlarge, tattered and stained warm-ups. Rumpled hair hung in damp strands around a dirt-smudged face. Her eyes and nose were swollen and red.

"Uh . . ." He cleared his throat. "It's not the same."

Cassie bristled. "So, you don't think I'm sexy?"

"I didn't say that. You're the most beautiful woman I know."

"I asked if I was sexy! I want to know if you'll have to return to porn sites to be satisfied. I've heard that happens to some men when they start doing that sort of thing. Don't evade the question!" Eyes flashing, she set her mug of tea on the floor and folded her arms across her chest.

Agitated, he turned and continued pacing.

"Cassie, pornography is *fantasy*. It's safe. There's no risk. With you, you're real. I fight with you. I make mistakes. You fight back. You get mad. I get mad. You get hurt. I get hurt. I have to forgive and seek forgiveness. There are life decisions to make and I have to deal with them. There's always the possibility of rejection. If not from you, then from any of those who are important to both of us. With that fantasy garbage, I could always be in control. But now I realize life isn't about control. It's about trust."

He came close and faced her squarely. "You're real, Cassie. Wonderfully, gloriously real. Beyond my control, risky and yes, very sexy." He smiled, raising his eyebrows.

"Pornography is idolatry," he said. "It's man made and it's dead." He turned and paced the floor again. "It doesn't require relationship. I could pretend I was in control."

Returning to the chair, he leaned forward, elbows on his knees. His eyes pierced hers. "I took the coward's way out with that garbage, pursuing a cheap imitation of the real thing. What I really wanted was intimacy and comfort. What I got was sick with shame, guilt and loneliness.

"After talking to the guys, I found I not only had to forgive my father, but also my mother. Close as I am to her, I had to forgive her for coddling me and protecting me from my father. I was so busy trying to prove myself a man, I couldn't receive the comfort she had to give. When I forgave her, I found I was able to connect to Holy Spirit. He's the Comforter. In the last few months, I've been learning to receive more comfort and security from him.

"I understand now the verse that says, 'Those who cling to worthless idols forfeit the grace that could be theirs.' Now that I'm secure in him, I don't fear relationship. Life's all about relationship, Cassie. We were created for relationship. With him and each other. The essence of sin is broken relationship. Sin always damages relationship."

Eyes holding hers, he rose from the chair and sat on the bed. He turned, braced his arms on either side of her and brought his face close.

"So yes, Cassie, you're very sexy. I fantasize about you. But in a wonderful, scary sort of way, that's filled with possibilities for the future."

A wide, joyous smile lit Cassie's face. Dark curls tousled and face streaked, he had never seen her more beautiful.

He wanted to protect her.

Love her.

Comfort her.

Know her.

He leaned closer and brushed a strand of hair from her cheek. His fingertips found their way to her chin and tilted it.

"I want to kiss you . . . Is that okay?"

Eyes shining, she nodded.

His mouth brushed over her soft lips.

Pulling her to him, he kissed her again.

Forehead leaning against hers and nose resting on hers, he lingered. Eyes closed, her long, dark lashes fanned against smooth cheeks. Pink lips turned up at the corners.

"I've wanted to do that for a long time now," he said.

Her smile broadened and she opened her eyes. "Me too."

"I love you more than you know, Cassie," he said into her ear.

Her arms came around him and she pressed against him.

"Oh, Jeff," she whispered, "I love you." Her warm breath tickled his neck.

Legs straightening under the blanket, she sank down in the bed with a contented sigh, pulling him with her.

His arms went around her and his lips found hers again, kissing her soundly. A soft moan escaped and his head lifted. His lips found her eyelids, the tip of her nose, each cheek.

She nestled into his shoulder and he held her close.

Suddenly coming to his senses, he sat up. "Uh . . ." He cleared his throat. "I'm sorry, Cassie. We'd better stop. We're alone in here."

She giggled.

Pulling herself upright, her back propped against the wall once more. "You're right. We're quite alone. And I'm in bed."

Jeff huffed, rising to his feet. "Don't remind me."

He turned away to the kitchen, taking the oil lamp with him.

"Is there anything to eat around here?" he said, rummaging through the cupboards. "I don't know about you, but I'm hungry."

"You might find a can or two of pork and beans."

"That sounds perfect. Ah-hah, here's what I was looking for. And a can-opener too!"

⁂

It was almost dark when Ben, Billy and Joey arrived home from their camping trip, tired and dirty. While they unloaded the supplies, Linda and Hannah appeared to greet them.

"Daddy!" Hannah said, "You're home!" She ran to embrace him, jumping into his arms.

Linda followed. "How was your trip?"

"It was great!" Ben said. "The fishing was better than ever. But we're all bushed. Billy and Joey had to conquer a few mountains and I couldn't let them outdo me."

After setting Hannah on her feet, he embraced Linda, swinging her around. With one arm around her and the other around his daughter, he kissed them happily.

"Of course I missed my favorite gals! Where's Cass? Did she make it home from school?"

"Cassie got home all right," Linda said, "but isn't back from the cabin. She went for a ride about three this afternoon."

"Three? And she's not home yet?"

"No. But she's with Jeff. He showed up here about five, looking for her. He rode up there on Blackfoot."

Ben smiled. "I saw his truck. It's about time they talk."

"Billy, take the cooler to the kitchen. Joey, put those sleeping bags and tents back into the shed." After checking on Joey's progress, he closed the shed door and started toward the house after Billy. "We're hungry. Did you save us some dinner?"

Linda came alongside, reaching around his waist. "There's food on the table."

"What time is it?" Ben said.

"I'd guess about nine." Linda frowned. "Jeff's been gone four hours, Ben. And Cassie's been gone for six. Don't you think someone should check on them? Maybe something happened."

"Ah, they're probably alright," He chuckled. "They probably just got to talking and the time got away from them."

"That's what I figured. Jeff looked like he had a load on his mind and I'm sure they had a lot to discuss, but the more I think about it, Jeff looked worried. There's no cell phone coverage up there, wedged between the mountains. Ben, I told her to be back before dark and it's dark," she said thoughtfully. "I'm worried. If you won't check on them, I will."

"Okay, then. If you put it that way, I'll go." He entered the back door and started rummaging through the coats. "But could you pack me a little something to eat?"

Linda hurried toward the kitchen. "Sure. I'll be quick about it."

Ben chose a clean, light jacket, put his arm in a sleeve and called after her, "Just enough to tide me over. I can eat when I get back. Go ahead and feed Joey and Billy, they're hungry."

He zipped his jacket and reached for a clean cap just as Billy emerged from the bathroom.

"Where are you going?"

"Up to the cabin. Cassie and Jeff are up there. They should be back by now. Your mother is worried."

"What? Cassie and Jeff? Together?" He looked at his watch and grabbed a jacket. "I'm going too."

Sliced bread and meat in hand, Linda followed them out the door. She stuffed the food in a bag and handed it to them as they got in the small pickup.

They took off toward the pasture to find the dirt road up the mountain.

ꙮ ꙮ ꙮ

An overcast sky made the night dark, but the pick-up headlights flashed on two horses, tied to the hitching post in front of the cabin. A dim light glowed in the window.

"They're in there, all right," Ben said.

They approached the cabin, but before they reached the threshold, the front door opened and a smiling Jeff greeted them.

"Hey! We're sure glad to see you guys!" He stopped. "Uh . . . Cassie's over there on the bed. I found her out in the rain. She can't walk."

"Can't walk?" Ben said. "What happened?"

"She fell off her horse. I think maybe she broke her pelvis or something."

Ben crossed over to where Cassie lay snuggled in a blanket. "Hey, Pumpkin. Are you okay?"

"I'm okay, Daddy. Don't worry."

A white undergarment caught his eye. It was draped with wet clothing over a chair by the stove. The place was warm and cozy.

Maybe a bit *too* cozy.

"Are you dressed?"

Cassie pulled back the blanket to reveal old gray warm-ups. "Jeff found these in the cupboard. I was soaked to the skin."

Ben sat on the bed. "So, where are you hurt?"

"Jeff thinks it's my pelvis. I can't put any weight on my legs. I fell directly on my right hip, so it's pretty sore. Other than that, I feel okay. As long as I don't move." She smiled up at Jeff, adoration shining from her dark eyes.

Pure joy radiated from Jeff's face. He grinned down at her.

"For two people who've been through such a traumatic experience, you sure look happy." Ben studied their faces. "What's up?"

Smiling, Jeff reached for Cassie's hand. "I'd like permission to date your daughter."

She returned his smile. Then her questioning gaze flew to Ben.

244

Billy whooped. "I knew it! You finally spilled the beans. It's been a long time coming!"

"Permission granted," Ben said. He smiled and stood to his feet. "Let's get Cassie home."

22

CAN TWO WALK TOGETHER?

Can two people walk together without agreeing on the direction?   Amos 3:3 (NLT)

Ben carried Cassie to the pick-up where Jeff sat waiting in the cab. He gently handed her over to Jeff and settled her into his lap. They started down the mountain with Billy following on Blackfoot and leading Ginger.

The pickup bounced and jarred on the rough and muddy road while Jeff held Cassie close, trying to soften the jolts. In spite of the pain, Cassie seemed to enjoy her position on his lap. Ben noted the contentment on his daughter's face. With an arm around his neck, she leaned against Jeff's ear.

They were in a world of their own. Obviously, they'd settled a few things on the mountain. Jeff was confidently laying claim to her and she was not objecting at all. Ben pulled up to the house and stopped.

"Shouldn't we take her to the hospital?" Jeff asked.

Cassie yawned and reached for the door handle. "I'm tired. I want to eat a little and go to bed. We can go in the morning."

Jeff didn't budge. "Cass, you need to get checked out. Sometimes there's complications with this kind of injury."

"Oh, pooh! If there were complications, I'd know by now. It's been over six hours since it happened."

"It doesn't matter. It would be best to get you checked as soon as possible. You can't walk! You can't even go to the bathroom without help."

"I'll be fine!" Cassie said. "I'm sure there's someone here who can help me."

Ben chuckled. "All right you two, let's not go back at it quite yet. Why don't you carry her into the house and get a bite to eat, Jeff? Then, we can call the Emergency Room and see what they say. Okay, Cassie?"

She nodded sheepishly.

Jeff opened the door and gently scooted Cassie off his lap. While bending over to lift her, Linda appeared.

"What happened?"

"Cassie fell off her horse and can't walk. I think it might be a broken pelvis," Jeff said, adjusting her in his arms.

"I wondered if something happened," Linda said, placing a hand on her arm. "How bad is it? Are you in pain?"

Smiling up at Jeff, she clung to his neck. "I'm fine. Just as long as I don't try to move." Cassie jabbed Jeff's arm playfully. "And I didn't *fall* off my horse. I was *thrown*."

"Bring her in through the back door, Jeff," Linda said, hurrying to open it. "I kept dinner warm. You've all got to be starving."

"I'm actually not that hungry and I really don't want to sit," Cassie said, wearily. "I just want my bed."

Linda looked at Jeff. "Can you carry her upstairs?"

"Sure," he said, holding her close.

After consulting the Emergency Room and satisfying Jeff's concerns, they agreed it would be okay to take Cassie to the hospital in the morning.

Refreshed with food and showers, everyone settled in bed and the house grew quiet. Propped with pillows, Linda lay in bed waiting for Ben. He approached and pulled off his T-shirt, expelling a long breath.

Linda smiled. "It's been a full day, hasn't it?"

He sat on the bed. "Yeah. I'm beat."

"It seems two people in this house are very happy tonight."

"You noticed, huh?" He chuckled. "The way they're acting, I don't think this 'dating' thing's going to last long. How long do you give them before they're engaged?"

"I have a feeling it'll be soon," she said, laughing softly. "I'm sure Jeff has that in mind."

Her blue eyes shone. "Remember when we were at that place in our lives?"

"Are you kidding? I remember quite well. And it's even better now." He crawled into bed and reached for her. "It gets better every day."

⠻ ⠻ ⠻ ⠻

"Hey, Bro. Now's the time for some of that expertise you offered me a few months ago."

"Oh?" Billy said. "What's the trouble?"

Jeff smiled. "No trouble," he said as the two drove home from church. "But what do you think about me marrying your sister?"

Billy laughed. "Do you need my approval?"

"No. But I'd like to have it anyway. Do you think I'm ready to get married?"

"How would I know? I'm not sure anybody's ever ready to get married. But you have a good head on your shoulders and a good heart. You also seem to be able to put up a good fight," he said. "Most important, you trust Jesus, love my sister and she loves you. You'll be happy together. And you'll have a great brother-in-law!"

They shared a hearty laugh.

Jeff sobered. "As soon as I'm ready, I plan to ask her."

Billy smiled. "The way the two of you were acting last night, I'd say you'd better get ready fast. You already can't seem to keep your hands off each other."

Jeff looked at Billy, a smile playing at the corners of his lips. "It's been a long year. We both waited a long time for the talk we had yesterday."

"The way I see it, you did more than *talk* up there in that cabin," Billy said, his eyes glinting in amusement.

Jeff grinned. "Maybe. But only what was necessary to express some very important sentiments."

They laughed again.

Jeff stopped. "All this excitement about Cassie has distracted me from something else I've been meaning to ask."

"Fire away," Billy said, eyes straight ahead.

"How about you? I haven't noticed you looking for a girlfriend, or even dating anyone. Do you have any desire to get married?"

Billy smiled. "I can't say I haven't thought about it. I believe God has someone for me, but he'll probably have to give me a word. I don't seem to have the grace to go shopping. I'm too analytical and have too many opinions."

"That's true," Jeff said. "Where do you think I learned it?"

Chuckling, Billy slowed to turn off the highway. "You can't blame me for that, Carson."

"I suppose you're right. You just make me more aware that I have them."

Jeff changed the subject. "I hope everything's all right with Cassie. I just about had a heart attack when I saw her horse standing alone in the meadow without her."

"She'll be all right. If they think there's any reason to keep her in the hospital, I guarantee they'll have a fight on their hands. She's determined she's going to recuperate at home. They won't find anything seriously wrong. She'll be home when we get there."

They soon reached the long driveway that led to the ranch. Passing by the front porch to park the pickup, they noticed the family's Suburban parked beside it.

"They're home," Billy said.

Jeff burst through the front door and stopped when he saw Cassie. She lay stretched out on the living room couch, back propped against the arm, crutches beside her.

"There you are." He crossed over to sit on the edge of the couch where she reclined. "So, what did they say?"

"I have a broken pelvis like you said. Everything else checked out fine. They weren't sure about letting me go home, but I proved to them that I could get out of bed and use a bedside commode." Voice triumphant, she continued, "I can stand on one leg and will be able to get around better with these crutches in a few days. They say the muscle spasms should be gone by then."

Jeff scooted over and put her feet in his lap. "How long will you be on crutches?"

"A month or so," Cassie said.

"Six to eight weeks," Linda said, emerging from the kitchen. "Would you guys like a glass of iced tea?"

"Sure," Jeff said, looking at Cassie. He rubbed her foot and whispered, "I'm sure glad you're okay, Cass."

"You're my hero," she whispered.

Rolling his eyes and shaking his head, Billy disappeared into the kitchen.

⁊ ❧ ❦ ⁊

"What do you mean, you don't believe in spanking? Come on, Jeff. We both know what you can do if you're really angry. I don't think you know what you believe."

Doors and windows open, Ben and Linda listened from the front porch, two weeks after the accident. The conversation carried through the screen door on the soft, warm breeze. Inside, Cassie lay propped against pillows on the arm of the couch, feet resting in Jeff's lap. They were having one of their probing discussions.

"I don't want to hurt my children."

"Hurt them? You think you're going to hurt them by spanking? You could hurt them if you don't. You might teach them to disrespect authority. That's the worst thing you can do for their self-esteem. I want to raise children I can enjoy. Read what the Bible says about it."

"I'd rather not get that physical," Jeff said. "I'm just not comfortable with it."

"Get over it. If you don't spank them, you'll probably say or do things you'll regret. Words can cut deeper and do more lasting damage than a few slaps on the rear end."

He paused. "You might be right about that."

"If you're so set against spanking, why did you spank *me*?"

"You were pushing me."

"You don't think kids will push you?" Cassie said.

"Yeah, but I don't think that was the right way to handle it. I was really mad—"

"You're right. Anything done in anger is not the best. But I was lucky, wasn't I? It could've been a lot worse. You could've really hurt me."

"I wouldn't hurt you. I was really mad, but I restrained myself—"

"Aha! My point exactly. You *restrained* yourself. You can do that, can't you?" She giggled, then shrieked.

Ben strained his neck to see the two wrestling on the couch. Jeff tried to hold Cassie down while swatting at her playfully.

"Jeff! Don't! Remember, I'm wounded!"

"You're right," he said. "You'd better take advantage of that while you have the chance!"

"I knew it! You do believe in spanking!"

Laughter rang throughout the living room. "You're incorrigible," Jeff said, righting himself and plopping her feet back in his lap.

Ben grinned. "I wondered when that subject would come up."

"How many children do you want?" Cassie asked.

Jeff rubbed her feet. "Sixteen."

Giggling, she threw a pillow at his head, which he caught before tickling her in the ribs.

"Jeff!" she said, "That's enough! Sixteen's crazy, but I do want a big family. Well-behaved children that respect me."

Jeff sobered. "I want happy children."

"Well-behaved children are usually happy children. I was

spanked and I was happy. My parents loved me and I knew it."
Curious, she looked at him sidelong. "How were you disciplined?"

"It wasn't good, Cass. I still cringe at certain memories. Dad
would be so angry and out of control and Mom would cry and try
to protect me.

"But the words my father spoke and the names he called me,
they were the worst. They still hurt."

Cassie winced. "I'm sorry. I can't imagine . . . I always knew
Mom and Dad loved me and believed in me, even when I was
disciplined. And there were a few times they got really angry." She
smiled ruefully. "I suppose I wasn't the easiest child to raise."

She straightened. "You can decide right now what you're going
to do instead of losing your temper. If you don't, you'll probably
fall into the same trap as your father. You don't have to pass that
pain on to your children."

"Spanking, especially a young child, defines boundaries in
seconds. Relationship and honor are restored quickly. Children get
the message that they're not in control and need to adjust and
submit. It's not the solution to every problem and many times it's
not the way to go. But, like any form of discipline, if it's done right,
it won't bring shame or condemnation. The goal is to improve
relationship."

"After being spanked, I would inevitably end up in my father's
lap. He would always remind me that he disciplined me because he
loved me. I couldn't resist his love."

"Wow!" Jeff let out a laugh. "You've thought this out, haven't
you? . . . So did mine work?"

"Your what?"

"The spanking I gave you. Did it establish boundaries, restore
honor and give you the message that you're not in con— Ouch!"

"Jeff! I'm being serious here! I'm not a child!"

He laughed. "No, you're not a child. But if I remember right, it
was pretty tough when you were. And spankings were not all that
effective."

Her feet put aside, he stood and leaned over her, blue eyes

alight with teasing. "But come to think of it, if I had a child like you, I'd want to have that option open."

Cassie slapped his arm. "You're not exactly the compliant type yourself. Just remember, I don't want to marry someone who's going to be a weak father to my children. You might need to forgive your father."

Jeff took her up in his arms, adjusting her against his chest. He laughed. "Don't worry, I've forgiven my father. I'm a new man and I'm different. God has made me strong."

"You are strong," she said. "And you're not cruel. I thank God for the discipline you did receive, even if it wasn't perfect."

Their voices trailed off.

Out on the porch, Ben turned from the window and smiled at Linda. "Jeff's carrying her up the stairs again. Her crutches don't seem to work as well when he's here." He smirked. "Those two are still working a few things out, aren't they?"

"Yeah, I think so," Linda said, suppressing a laugh. "It's intriguing to hear Cassie talk like this. A few years ago I'd never have guessed that she would be so adamant about such things."

Ben laughed softly. "Me neither. There were times I wondered if she'd ever speak to me again."

⁓ ⸱⸱ ⁓

"From now on, I'm driving!"

Jeff held the screen door open for Cassie as she hobbled through on her crutches. Returning from an outing on a rainy Saturday afternoon, they stormed into the living room.

Across the room, Ben sat in his recliner, hiding behind the newspaper. He took a quick peek over the top.

"No, you're not!" Cassie said. "I'll drive whenever I want to!"

She hobbled to the middle of the room.

"You were going too fast!" Jeff said, following behind. "You almost hit her!"

She turned to face him, chin lifting. "I wasn't that close. And it was just a cow."

Jeff snorted. "Just a cow?" He rolled his eyes. "That's crazy and

253

you know it. I told you to slow down! Why are you always pushing the edge?"

"Why are you always yelling at me?" she said. "I can't concentrate when you're yelling."

They squared off, uninhibited by Ben's listening ears. Eyebrows raised, he suppressed a laugh. Maybe Jeff could get through to her. The newspaper was now in his lap.

Jeff stood over her, scowling, hands on his hips and eyes boring into hers. "You don't listen to me!"

"You're too critical and bossy. Maybe if you changed your tone, I would listen."

She hobbled toward the stairs and he followed. "I'm right and you know it, Cassie. But you're too proud to admit it!"

She started up the stairs. "At least I've never gotten a ticket. Unlike some people I know."

Jeff stood at the bottom of the stairs, addressing her retreating back. "But you've had close calls," he said. "And what about all those warnings? Did you get those for good behavior? Some of us can't look so cute and innocent. I was with you last time, remember? It would've taken a pretty tough cop to give you a ticket after the way you schmoozed him."

"Leave me alone." Cassie said over her shoulder. "I don't want to talk about it." She continued gimping up the stairs.

"I'm trying to warn you and you won't listen! You need to be more careful, Cassie. The fact that you're on crutches with a broken bone should give you a clue. You're not invincible!"

She reached the top and glared. "Are you saying it was my fault I got hurt?"

"No, I didn't say that. But it could encourage you to be more cautious." Jeff craned his neck, looking up at her from the bottom of the staircase.

"This discussion is over." Cassie escaped down the hall and shut her bedroom door. Firmly. Jeff crossed over, sank to the couch and exhaled. "Sometimes she scares me. Have you noticed how she drives?"

Ben chuckled. "Yup . . . That I have."

"What should I do?"

Smiling, Ben lifted the newspaper. "You're doing fine, Son. Just fine."

Two weeks later, Linda emerged from the bathroom and heard the screen door slam. Her daughter and Jeff entered the living room. She was headed to bed, but paused to listen.

"That's not what submission means!" Cassie said. "The Bible says to submit to *one another*. And love has to come first!"

"That's true, but someone has to take the lead! That's part of loving!" Jeff said. "Someone has to make the final decision and take responsibility. Are you saying you won't follow?"

Cassie's voice rose. "I'm not saying I won't follow, but a good leader listens to opposing opinions!"

"I'm not sure I could listen to all opposing opinions," he said. "Sometimes that's just an excuse, so you can bulldoze people and run things yourself!"

"It sounds like you're *threatened* by someone who has opinions!"

"There are times when a man knows what's right and has to do it, regardless of what anyone thinks."

"That's the stupidest thing I've ever heard!" she said. "You're just insecure. I'm not going to be your doormat. Goodnight!" Footsteps thumped up the staircase and the bedroom door slammed.

Cassie had completely shed the crutches that day and evidently didn't need help up the stairs. The front door closed.

Linda entered the bedroom, removed her robe and climbed into bed. "It doesn't sound like that went well."

"I guess not!" Ben said. "Sometimes I wonder about that girl. She has her own ideas on that subject." He flipped off the light. "I wonder where she got them. Certainly not from me!"

Linda smiled into the darkness, laughing softly. "They'll be all right, Ben. Remember what happened two weeks ago? What was it they were arguing about? Oh, yeah. It was her driving. They made up the next day. Cassie actually apologized."

"Yeah. I remember," he said, chuckling. "They do seem to be able to make up."

⠑⠁ ❧ ❦ ⠑⠁

"Jeff!" Joey said, opening the front door the next evening. "I'm sure glad to see you. It's about time you showed up."

The family relaxed around the fire, but Cassie wasn't in sight.

"Is she here?"

"She's up in her room," Ben said over his magazine.

"Should I go up there? I need to talk to her."

"Please," Billy said, smiling and strumming his guitar. "Deliver us from our suffering."

"Billy!" Linda said. "Don't be rude."

She turned to Jeff. "Cassie hasn't been too happy today."

"That makes two of us," he said. "Do you think she'll talk to me?"

"Give it a try, Son." Ben turned the page of his magazine. "Good luck."

⠑⠁ ❧ ❦ ⠑⠁

Cassie sat leaning against pillows on her bed, fully dressed and futilely trying to read. She frowned.

Jeff hadn't called and she didn't care. He had no respect for her anyway. A tear betrayed her, escaping and rolling down her cheek. She brushed it away, sniffled and grabbed a tissue.

A hesitant knock on the door interrupted her thoughts.

"Who is it?"

"Cassie, it's me. Jeff."

Jeff?

She froze.

"Can I come in?"

"I guess so."

Jeff entered the bedroom and stood next to the bed.

"Hi."

Cassie's swollen eyes fixed on the book.

256

"Hi."

"Are you still mad at me?"

"Of course. Why wouldn't I be?" She didn't look up. "I know you're nervous, but unless you want the whole house to hear what I have to say, you'd better shut the door." Jeff kicked backwards and the door slammed. Cassie jumped, but still pretended to read.

Thick, awkward silence engulfed them, neither willing to break it. Finally, she looked over the edge of her book into his sober face.

"I'm sorry, but I can't be the *submissive* wife you fantasize about, so we might as well end it right here." She dropped the book to her lap. "I'm never going to be the type who lets you win every argument. I won't let you have your own way just because I'm supposed to be submissive. If I have an opinion, I'm going to express it, *especially* if I know you wouldn't agree. I can't be any less than who I am. And I feel it would be a disservice to you as a friend and partner if I didn't express myself."

Jeff stared at her. He raised his palms. "Whoa, Cassie! Whatever gave you the idea I wanted someone like that? How could I be attracted to *you* if I did?"

"Humph! Well, it's the way you sounded last night. You don't seem to appreciate my opinions. I think you would be happier with a passive little wife who lets you walk all over her!"

He grimaced and turned away. Running a hand through his hair, he paced.

"Your opinions aren't always convenient. And it's true I don't always properly appreciate them. But for the most part, I do. And I appreciate your strength of character and courage."

He paused. "You told me you didn't want a weak father for your children. Do you think I want a weak mother for mine? Or a weak wife? The point I was trying to make is that I believe in leadership and you may not always appreciate it. I didn't mean I can't or won't listen to you. I do listen. I value your opinions. You have good opinions."

She huffed. "For a woman."

His eyes widened. "I didn't say that!"

"But it's how you feel! Admit it!" She sat up, threw the book on the night stand and glared at him.

"So you think I'm a chauvinist."

"Somewhat," she said. "Well, yes!" Her arms folded across her chest. "I do!"

He groaned, crossed over to the chair in the corner and sat. Leaning back, he crossed his legs and heaved a sigh.

"Cassie," he said, "tell me, when have I not taken you seriously?"

She folded her legs and sat up. "I don't know. I just feel like sometimes you don't respect me. Take for instance up on the rock ledge—"

"Oh, that," Jeff said, wincing. "I thought you forgave me. Is it still bothering you?"

"Well, it wasn't exactly respectful!"

He released a long breath.

Tense silence hung in the room.

"I can see how you would feel that way," he said. "I feel the same way about you."

"You do?"

"I do. Why do you think I resorted to such barbaric tactics? You weren't showing me any respect that whole week!"

Cassie went silent. She lay staring at him, eyes wide and lips pursed.

He did have a point.

Lips twitching, she felt herself relax.

"You're right. I wasn't. I had other priorities. I was trying to get you to fight." She looked down, a smile quenching her indignation. "And I succeeded."

Tension ebbed from the room.

"Cassie," he said, "you don't always show me the respect I imagine I deserve, but I love you. I've forgiven you for what you said that day. Even though it seemed disrespectful, it was the truth and probably needed to be said."

He paused. "So, do you respect *me*? Or would you rather I was more like the other guys you've dated? I thought you said you didn't appreciate them tip-toeing around you, desperate for your approval."

Her eyes lifted to meet his and she smiled sheepishly. "If I hadn't respected you I wouldn't have bothered to confront you. Yes, I respect you. And I love you."

"Cassie, will you forgive me again for what I did? It was stupid. And disrespectful. I got carried away in the heat of battle, but I do respect you."

She lowered her eyes. "I forgive you."

"Do you believe me when I say I value your opinions?"

"I believe you."

He rose from the chair and approached her. "Are we okay then?"

"Yeah. We're okay."

He held out his arms. "Can you get up and give me a kiss?"

She smiled ruefully. "I suppose."

Cassie rose from the bed and went to him.

He pulled her close, lowered his lips to hers and buried his face in her curls. "I love you, Cass," he said into her ear. "And I need you. I'm sorry for accusing you of trying to bulldoze people. I appreciate your boldness, even though it sometimes scares me."

She let out a tearful giggle. "I forgive you." Eyes brimming with tears, she pulled back to look at him. "You're not insecure. Would you forgive me for saying that yesterday? It was disrespectful."

His eyes twinkled with teasing. "You're forgiven, but only if you give me another kiss."

She smiled and lifted her arms to encircle his neck.

The door opened and her father stepped into the room. "Just checking," he said.

She caught a glimpse of his wide grin, but didn't break the embrace.

He cleared his throat. "Looks like progress."

⁂

It was the end of a long, hot day. Ben was driving the grain truck home. From the seat beside him, Jeff said, "I love Cassie and I want to marry her."

"Has she agreed to this?"

The light was dim, obscuring Jeff's dusty face, but a hard swallow betrayed jittery nerves.

"No. I haven't officially asked."

"Do you think she'll say yes?"

"I hope so," Jeff said. "Do you think she'll say yes?"

Ben chuckled and shook his head. "I know she loves you, but she's pretty opinionated about some things. I'm not sure I can help you. She hasn't told me what she'd say."

He turned to Jeff, smiling. "I've overheard some of your discussions. How's it going?"

"She's right most of the time," Jeff said. "I'm going to have to eat a lot of humble pie if she agrees to marry me. But I need her. I'm a better person when I'm with her. She refuses to let me be wounded."

Ben smiled. "You do need her. I can see that. But she needs you too. You have a humility about you and a steadiness that she needs. You're a strong man, Jeff, and you're becoming more comfortable with that strength."

Jeff looked up nervously. "Thanks." His eyes sought Ben's. "So, do I have your blessing?"

Surprised, Ben's brow lifted. "Jeff, there's no one else I know that I would choose to marry my daughter. You're a good son. You'll be a great son-in-law."

Jeff beamed. "I am a good son."

A wide smile spread across Ben's dusty face. "I'm glad to hear you say that." He turned back to the road. "So, when are you planning to ask her?"

"Next Sunday. I should have the ring by then." He smiled mischievously. "I have an idea."

Ben laughed. "Good luck!"

❧ ❦ ❧

Jeff opened the door to his mother's apartment.

"Mom? Are you home?"

His mother appeared at the top of the stairs. "Jeff! Come in! Where have you been lately? I've been trying to call you." She descended the stairs.

After an embrace, she stood back and examined him, noting his wide grin. "You sure look happy today. What happened?"

"I was helping at the Watsons again."

"So, what's new with that?" she said. "You're there every weekend."

"I had a talk with Ben, Mom. He gave me his blessing. Next week I'm going to ask Cassie to marry me. I thought you should know."

Her eyes brightened with tears, a hand covering her gaping mouth. "Oh, Jeff!" she said. "That's wonderful!"

She embraced him tightly, laughing for joy. "I'm so happy for you!"

Jeff smiled, took hold of his mother and held her at arm's length, his intense gaze meeting hers.

"Mom," he said, "I haven't realized how blessed I've been all along. You've loved me, prayed for me and stood by me. Thank you."

Tears streamed down her face. "You're wonderful, Jeff. I'm so proud of you."

"And your father would be proud of you too," she said. "He wasn't all bad, you know. There was a reason I stayed with him all those years. I'm sorry it was so rough on you. Especially when he drank. He loved you, Jeff, but couldn't get past his own pain and fear to express it. Sometimes I wonder if it was the right decision to stay with him. But it was the best I could do at the time. I kept clinging to the hope that things would change."

She gave him a watery smile. "I guess they did, but not the way I'd hoped."

Jeff pulled her to him. "I love you, Mom."

23

TOKEN, TROTH & TRIUMPH

How beautiful you are, my darling! Oh, how beautiful!
Your eyes are doves.   *S.S. 1:15*

A soft breeze caressed Cassie's face as she and Ginger ambled in from the pasture. Crickets chirped in the dry grass. Bullfrogs croaked in the stock pond. Breathing deep, she stopped and closed her eyes, drinking in the rich evening air.

"Jesus, thank you for life. And for beautiful summer evenings."

The triumphant sun hung over the mountains to the west and Hannah's melodious giggle drifted toward her. Orange autumn light radiated dusty beams through the backyard trees where Joey pushed her on the tire swing. Though now young teens, they hadn't tired of that swing.

Grain harvest fully upon them, Cassie and her mother had been helping drive trucks. Thanks to Jeff and Grandpa, today they were able to stay home. After preparing dinner, Cassie had escaped for a short ride, waiting for the crew to arrive.

The horse's rhythmic walk soothed her. She smiled. Tomorrow was her twenty-first birthday. And something was up. Since it was

Sunday, the whole family was taking the day off and she suspected some sort of surprise celebration was in the works.

Cassie dismounted Ginger and led her into the barn. She wrinkled her brow.

Jeff was acting strange. He hadn't paid much attention to her in the last few days. He hadn't called at all. When she called him, he was always busy and when he was around, he seemed preoccupied. She was a little rough on him last week, but hadn't they worked through it?

"I guess I'm pretty stubborn and do get carried away with my opinions," she said. "I have apologized a few times. Does that count?"

"He's so amazing. I never knew it would be this wonderful to love a man. I'm so happy with him! He loves you, Father, and listens to you. He's not perfect, but I trust him. Everything's going to be okay. Right?" She sighed.

Loud grain trucks rumbled into the driveway.

Cassie continued combing Ginger methodically, the familiar repetition calming her puzzled thoughts.

Hannah hurried into the barn. "Cassie! Daddy's home and Mom says dinner will be ready in ten minutes." She turned and left.

"I'll be right there."

Minutes later, a familiar voice startled her.

"Cassie?"

Jeff!

She hurried to him, leaned over the stall door and smiled up in his dirty face. "Hey, handsome! You're back! I'd give you a kiss, but I'm afraid I'd itch all night."

He grinned, white teeth gleaming through the dark dirt on his face. "Cass, I'd like to take you on a date."

"A date? When?"

"Tomorrow evening."

"Tomorrow's my birthday."

His smile broadened. "I know. That's why I want a date."

"I think the family's planning something."

"Maybe, but that would be tomorrow afternoon. I'm reserving the evening."

"What do you have planned?"

"Be ready at seven o'clock. And dress up. It's a surprise."

"You want me to wear a dress?"

"Yeah. Something nice," he said over his shoulder, while exiting the barn. "And it's a dinner date."

Cassie raised her eyebrows. A dinner date? She giggled.

This was unusual, especially at this busy time of year.

ᶳᵃ ᶳ ᶘ ᵃᶳ

Ben glanced at his watch. Seven o'clock. Time for Jeff to arrive. He and Billy had left Cassie's birthday party early, making an excuse for their departure.

The screen door opened and Jeff appeared, decked out in a black suit, royal blue shirt and black tie. His blue eyes sparkled with anticipation.

Ben raised his eyebrows. "Wow!" he said, "Not bad! You look great!"

Flashing a grin, Jeff strode to the foot of the staircase. "Thanks," he said. "Is Cassie ready?"

At the top of the stairs, she appeared.

Jeff halted, jaw hanging.

A satin dress glowed in the dimly lit stairwell, clinging to her slim curves. It tapered down from a fitted, strapless bodice and billowed in a long flowing skirt. The shimmering forest green accentuated her silky smooth skin.

A mesmerized Jeff stood tall and straight beside Ben. His gaze traveled from Cassie's lower legs to her face, where dark curls framed flushed cheeks.

She floated down the stairs. Shining brown eyes met Jeff's riveted gaze and her face lit in a dazzling smile, dimples winking on smooth cheeks.

Jeff swallowed hard. "Whoa! You're beautiful!"

"Of course she's beautiful," Ben said, placing an arm around his shoulders and smiling at his daughter. "What did you expect?"

"I just haven't . . . uh . . . seen her dressed like this before."

Ben chuckled, watching Cassie glow in Jeff's adoration. Her dark eyes danced with delight.

Joey appeared beside his father. "Wow! Cassie, you look hot!"

Laughing, Ben nudged him with his elbow. "That's enough, Buster."

Linda appeared at the top of the stairs, comb in hand. Hannah followed.

"You forgot something," Hannah said. She ran down the stairs and handed her sister a soft, cream-colored cape.

Cassie's arm in his, Jeff escorted her out the front door. Everyone followed.

Cassie squealed.

"A buggy!" she said. "Where did you get it?"

Jeff smiled mysteriously. "A friend."

Sure enough, he'd done it. A black buggy with a flat leather top stood near the porch. The red cushioned seat was perched on springs suspended over wooden spoked wheels. A black and white pinto, harnessed to the buggy, was tied to the back of Jeff's pickup. The horse waited patiently, oblivious to the excitement he had caused.

Hands around her waist, Jeff lifted her to the seat, then untied the horse, went around and climbed in beside her. Reins in hand, he waved to the family on the front steps and turned the horse toward the pasture gate.

Linda took Ben's hand and snuggled into his shoulder. His arm went around her, pulling her close.

"I wonder if it was something like this when Adam first saw Eve," he said. "Wo! Man!"

Linda giggled.

He smiled at her. "That's the way it was for me when I first really saw you."

Blue eyes shining, she returned his smile.

⁂

Cassie shifted on the seat. "So, where are we going?"

"You'll see."

"Can you drive one of these things?"

Jeff laughed. "What do you think I'm doing? Just relax." He took her hand and placed it in the crook of his arm.

At the pasture gate, he pulled up the reins.

Joey appeared and stood at attention, Scruffy at his side. Jeff saluted him soberly. Joey returned the salute with a grin before opening the gate and closing it behind them.

They turned to go up the mountain.

"Jeff, this is so romantic!" Cassie said. "You're taking me up to the cabin!"

Jeff smiled, wiggling his eyebrows.

"So are we going to eat dinner up there?"

"You'll see. Let me surprise you, okay?"

She smiled knowingly. "So that's why you've been making yourself scarce lately. Were Mom and Daddy in on this?"

"Maybe." He turned twinkling eyes back to the road.

She held tightly to his arm, resting her head on his shoulder. Lifting her nose, she sniffed the pine-scented air. "I love that smell, don't you?"

Easy silence settled on them as they made their way up the dirt road. Together they listened to the serenading of the mountain on a summer's eve, soft wind swaying the tree tops. Drumming hooves and chirping crickets accompanied their singing hearts.

Cassie cuddled close.

At a clearing, he pulled the horse up and stopped to enjoy a picturesque view of the valley.

The sun hung low over the mountains, lighting wispy clouds in oranges, reds and pinks. An ethereal glow reflected from vast golden fields.

"Valley of Peace," Jeff said, "It's true. I have found peace here. And it came in a package with love and joy." Arm around her shoulders, he pulled her close.

Her gaze stretched out over the valley and she cleared her

throat. "There was a time not long ago I would've taken that wrong."

Jeff looked at her curiously. "Really?"

"Yeah. I was offended you could have so much peace without me."

Jeff smiled. "I remember." He kissed the top of her head.

"Cassie," he said, "staying away from you last spring was one of the hardest things I've ever done. But I'm glad I did it. My lack of peace had nothing to do with you, so I had to find it apart from you. I needed to be at peace with God and myself, otherwise I wouldn't have had much to offer."

"You're right," Cassie said. "It was good for me too. I had my own battles to fight."

Jeff nodded, eyes returning to the view.

"God says I'm a good son. I'm finally convinced I'm not the son of a drunk. I'm a son of God and my Father loves me."

Soon both hands returned to the reins. He snapped them and urged the horse forward. The clip-clop of hooves and the creak of wagon wheels lulled them into rapturous silence. Twilight lingered on the tall trees and cool mountain air whistled easily through evergreens guarding the road before them.

Cassie shivered. "It's chilly up here."

Jeff covered her bare shoulders with the cape.

At the cabin, he hopped down, snapped the lead rope to the horse's halter and tied it to the post. He took her by the waist and gallantly lifted her to the ground. Hand in hand, they strolled toward the front door.

"It seemed fitting to bring you here tonight," he said.

"Why's that?"

Smiling, he opened the door and stood aside.

She squealed.

"Oh, Jeff! It's beautiful! How did you do all of this?"

Ablaze with candlelight, the small cabin was transformed. A dozen red roses graced a table covered in white linen and set with her mother's best china. Shining wood gleamed from floor to ceiling. The futon bed, on which she laid helpless and hurting just a few months before, was made into a couch and covered with a brightly colored quilt.

Billy stood next to the table dressed in a dark suit, white shirt and black bow tie. A towel draped over an arm, he bowed and presented the table.

"At your service, my lady." He motioned with his hand toward the food on the counter and the rest of the warm, cozy cabin.

Jeff crossed over to the table, pulled out a chair for Cassie and seated himself beside her. "Happy birthday, Sweetheart," he said.

It was the first time he'd called her that.

She smiled into his eyes. "Thank you."

He pulled an envelope from his pocket and handed it to her.

The card sweetly declared his love for her and wished her a happy birthday. Puzzled, she studied the cryptic message at the bottom, then read it aloud.

"I promise to listen to you and discipline the kids . . . If they need it."

Heart pounding, she lifted her eyes to search his.

"The kids?"

A mysterious smile was his only reply.

Billy approached with bowls of colorful green salad. "Dinner is served."

He poured them each a glass of sparkling cider and brought out freshly baked bread on a small platter. Baked potatoes and slices of tender roast beef came next, served with whole, seasoned green beans.

Silence punctuated the charged atmosphere while they ate.

Cassie searched Jeff's sky blue eyes. They sparkled with mischief. Even with that knowing smirk on his face, he made an attractive picture. Thick, dark hair was closely trimmed to a clean-shaven face. The shirt collar fit tight around his tanned and muscled neck and his well-fitted suit outlined a lean athletic body.

After dinner, Jeff reached for Cassie's hand. He held it while Billy crooned, strumming his guitar.

You are so beautiful to me . . .
You're everything I've longed for,
You're everything I need
You are so beautiful to me . . . [9]

"Oh, Jeff!"

His eyes held her captive. She was unable, unwilling to escape.

From his pocket, he produced a small black velvet box. She held her breath. He opened it dramatically. A simple diamond, set on a smooth gold band, sparkled in the candlelight. He dropped to one knee and took her hand.

"Cassie, I want to spend the rest of my life with you. Will you honor me by becoming my wife?"

"Oh, Jeff. Yes. I will!" Throwing her arms around his neck, she fell into his embrace, laughing.

They rose to their feet.

He took her hand and placed the ring on her finger.

"It's beautiful," she said, holding it before her.

"It's bold and beautiful. Like you."

Intense blue eyes held hers and his hands gently cradled her face. His head lowered. Both arms went around his neck and she clung to him, returning his kiss.

Suddenly, Jeff broke away. One arm encircled her waist and the other went under her knees, lifting her off the floor. He swung her around and whooped.

Placing her back on her feet, he looked into her eyes and moaned dramatically.

She giggled.

Enfolding her in his arms, he kissed her again. Passionately.

Billy cleared his throat. "Uh," he said. "Hello! Don't forget you're not alone here."

Called back, Cassie and Jeff lifted their eyes to see Billy's wide smile. Laughter filled the cabin.

༺ ❦ ༻

"Here they come," Ben said from the front porch. He and

Linda, with an excited Joey and Hannah, sat waiting for the party's return.

A round, bright moon lit the landscape. Headlights bobbed their way through the pasture, followed by the dim outline of a horse and buggy. A contented giggle and low chuckle floated through the summer night air.

Joey and Hannah ran to greet them. After hitching the horse near the barn, the happy group entered the house, talking excitedly and laughing with joy.

"Oh, Cassie, it's beautiful!" Hannah stood grasping her sister's left hand, gazing in awe at the sparkling ring.

"So, what's the news?" Linda asked.

Jeff stood behind Cassie, holding her possessively and beaming.

Billy and Joey stood by, smiling triumphantly.

"Are congratulations in order?" Ben asked.

Cassie flew into her father's arms. "Daddy," she said. "I'm engaged to the most wonderful man on earth!"

Ben hugged her close and kissed her hair. He reached over and included Jeff in his embrace, hugging them both.

"Congratulations, Son!"

Epilogue

Five years later . . .

"Grandpa! I got one!"

Ben Watson took hold of the pole and tugged, careful not to take it out of the small boy's hands.

"Hey, Champ, you're right," he said, "Take it easy, now. Let's see if we can bring him in."

Soon a good sized trout wriggled on the bank and the small boy beside him jumped up and down, squealing in delight.

"Daddy! Mommy! Come quick! Look what I got!"

The two came running. A curly-haired tot in a bold pink dress rode on Jeff's shoulders, hands gripping his hair and chubby legs wrapped around his neck. He gripped her feet and squatted to admire the fish.

"Wow! That's a great catch, Son!" He grinned broadly, lowering his precious cargo to the ground.

Cassie stood beside him and took her daughter's small hand.

Jeff turned. "Molly, do you want to touch it?"

The little girl wrinkled her nose and recoiled.

"No!"

"I've seen that look before," Ben said. "Good luck!"

They all shared a laugh.

Jeff stood. "Josh, go show it to Grandma!"

Giggling floated across the waters of the lake and they turned to see a rubber raft coming close, Billy at the oars. A young woman sat at the other end of the raft. Round with child, she lay back against the inflated side, long brown hair gleaming in the sunshine and hanging over the edge. A plump toddler sat in her lap, snugly wrapped in a life jacket. Billy's low voice drifted across the quiet waters and the giggle evolved into a hearty laugh.

"Hey, you lovebirds!" Cassie said. "It's time to eat! The food's ready!"

Ben gathered the tackle and watched as the little boy ran toward the picnic table, fish in tow. Jeff and Cassie followed, Molly perched on Cassie's hip. Jeff reached around her shoulders and pulled her close.

A warm feeling of gratitude filled Ben and he smiled. Raising his eyes, he looked up to the surrounding mountains and inhaled the fresh air.

"Father, you're so good to me."

He laughed.

"I'm rich!"

How joyful are those who fear the Lord
and delight in obeying his commands.
Their children will be successful everywhere;
an entire generation of
godly people will be blessed.
They themselves will be wealthy, . . .
Ps.112:1-4 (NLT)

. . . They will be my people,
and I will be their God,
for they will
return to me
with all their heart.
Jer. 24:7

And His name shall be called,
Wonderful,
Counselor,
The Mighty God,
The Everlasting Father,
The Prince of Peace.
Of the increase of
His government and
His peace,
there will be no end.
Isaiah 9:6b-7a

Bonus Scene

---

*The people walking in darkness have seen a great light;
on those living in the land of the shadow of death a
light has dawned.*   Isaiah 9:2

Jeff's first visit to Fishtrap Family Fellowship:

> "You were created to have relationship with God.
> He created you in his image, because he wants to
> love you and be loved by you. God is love. Love
> has a need to give and to receive. You were made
> with that same need.
>
> "Because of sin's power, you have been
> separated from God. Without him you are subject
> to doubt, fear and pride, which bring death and
> destruction. God longs to totally restore you to
> himself. He is your true father . . ."

A *father?* Why would he want one? He shifted in his seat,
avoiding the pastor's gaze.

> "For some this is a problem. Your experience with

your natural father has not been good. You assume
God is like your father, so you can't trust him.
However, God is the perfect father. He's the
father you've always longed for."

Long for a father? Not him. He couldn't trust his father. And
for good reason. His head dropped in his hands and bloodshot eyes
stared at him from a hospital bed. Begging forgiveness.

Pain, anger and confusion assaulted him.

The pastor's voice pulled him back.

"You have suffered because of sin. Because of sin
you have not believed God loves you, nor can you
trust him. Sin darkens your mind and gives you
false ideas about God and his heart for you.

"Starved for his love and relationship, you
grope around in that darkness. Without God, you're
empty, frustrated and dissatisfied. This causes you
to do things that hurt yourself and others.

"You need help. You need to be forgiven and
to forgive. You need the true light to shine in the
darkness."

Light? To shine in *darkness?* It sounded like Billy's dream about
him in the dungeon.

The pastor continued,

"How can you know the God who loves you and
wants to forgive you?

"Jesus said, 'He who has seen me has seen the
Father.' In Jesus, you can know the Father's
goodness, faithfulness and love.

"Jesus demonstrates that God's heart is *for* you.
He proves this great love by his kindness, miracles
and death on a cross. Jesus did this with forgiveness
and love, in the face of our betrayal and hatred.

"When you believe in Jesus and receive him,
you are no longer a slave, but a son; and since you
are a son, God has made you also an heir."

A son? He didn't even know what it meant to be a son—
"Being a son is not dependent upon your
performance. It's about your position. Slaves have
to perform 'duties' for their masters.

"But sons have relationship and privilege
because of who they are. They belong to the family.
God is offering you this relationship today. He
wants to restore you to relationship like Adam and
Eve enjoyed in the Garden of Eden. Yes, he wants
to walk and talk with you."

Jeff stared. Would God want to talk to *him*? Listen to him? Be
with him? He used to talk to God when he was little.

The pastor's eyes met his.

"Jesus died for you so that you can have what he has.
He rose from the dead and he's alive! He broke the
power of sin and death by his resurrection. You can
have the same intimacy with God that he has.

"You can be born again as his son or daughter,
reunited to the Father of your soul. As his child, you
can go to him whenever you want. With confidence.

"This is why Jesus says, 'I am not saying that I
will ask the Father on your behalf.' No, the Father
himself loves you . . ."

God *loved* him? On the edge of his seat, his eyes remained
locked with the pastor's. Something shifted. Could this be true?
He remembered as a child praying for his mother and father. And
himself. Specific instances came back when he was in danger and
wasn't hurt. Had God been listening to his prayers all along?

"If you don't know God as your Father, today is
your day. Right here, right now he's waiting for you
to return to him.

"If you want to leave here today as part of
God's family, return to your Father God. I invite
you to stand, open your heart and receive Jesus.
He will restore you to the Father."

Jeff found himself rising to his feet. Billy stood beside him. Others gathered around and he fell to his knees, pouring out his heart.

"God, I'm sorry for not believing in you. For running from you," he said. "Forgive me. I need you. I don't know where else to turn."

Following Billy's lead, Jeff repeated a prayer.

"Father God, I believe in Jesus. . . .

"I believe he's alive. . . .

"I believe he's God. . . .

"He's the revelation of you. . . .

"Because of him I believe you love me. . . .

"I believe you forgive me. . . .

"I receive your love and forgiveness. . . .

"Jesus, I receive you as my Lord and my Savior. . . .

"I want to follow you and have what you have. . . .

"Holy Spirit I receive you. And your help and comfort. . . ."

Those around prayed with him and for him. They embraced him and gave many words of encouragement. Peace flooded his soul like never before.

He felt brand new. Something had changed.

Author's note:

This is Jeff's story. He was saved from a life of hopelessness, false identity and destruction. A life of abundance in union with his father God awaited him. He struggled to believe he was a true and loved son and walk in that identity with confidence, but you have the advantage of reading this book!

You can return to your true father just like Jeff did. Jesus said, *I am returning to my Father and your Father, to my God and your God (John 20:17).* The same relationship Jesus has with God, is available for you. He came not only to show us the Father's heart, but also how to live as a beloved child of God.

Father God created you and loves you. He desires your friendship. Your love. Your commitment.

Love, joy and peace await you though Jesus Christ.

Let your heart return.

Look for Book Two in the "Valley of Peace" Series.

Hearts Restored

It takes a child

Circumstances cause Kirsten Turner's return to Haywacah Valley to help on the Watson Ranch. She drives a truck for Billy, who is initially gruff, blunt and distant. Eventually he wants to get closer, but she pulls back, unsure it's safe to reveal her pain and failure. Possibilities of rejection keep her from risking deeper friendship.

Hurt as a child by her wounded, religious parents, Kristy resists God's request that she become a child again. Why would he ask this of her?

She finds her answer through relational resolve in another *relational adventure.*

Cheryl Hug and her husband of thirty-six years live in Eastern Oregon. They have seven children and eight grandchildren. Experiencing God's love is changing her life, marriage and family. Her passion is for others to know the One who restores all things

1. Charlie Hall, "Give Us Clean Hands" (worshiptogether.com songs sixsteps Music, 2000)
2. Belfast Metro Tabernacle Choir
3. Chris Tomlin, Jesse Reeves, Louie Giglio, "Kindness," (worshiptogether.com songs sixsteps Music, 2000)
4. Marie Barnett, "Breathe," (Mercy / Vineyard Publishing, 1995)
5. Kelly Carpenter, "Draw Me Close," (Mercy / Vineyard Publishing, 1994)
6. Brian Doerksen, Paul Janz, "Father Me," (Vineyard Songs Canada, ION Publishing, 1995)
7. Beth Redman, Matt Redman, "You Are God in Heaven," (Thankyou Music, 2000)
8. Martin Smith, "Shout To The North," (Curious? Music UK, 1995)
9. Billy Preston, Bruce Fischer, "You Are So Beautiful," (Universal Music)